Glad You Exist

KAYE ROCKWELL

Glad You Exist

Copyright © 2021 by Kaye Rockwell

This is for you.
I miss you, Mama.

Liz

The familiar blaring of my phone alarm goes off at exactly 5:30 AM, but just like every morning since school started back up, I was awake way before it had a chance to do its job. I swiftly turn it off and throw it in my backpack. I do a quick once over and make sure I have everything. Pausing to check my reflection, I notice that the bags under my eyes are looking like they need to start paying rent with how much space they are taking up on my face.

I sigh, smoothing the skirt of my yellow midi dress, and head downstairs to start breakfast for Mom and go over the week's grocery list. I heave a sigh at the sight of the mess Mom has left in the kitchen from what looks like another late night spent writing.

I quickly get to work cleaning up before starting on breakfast—and prepping for lunch, while I'm at it. If I don't make something for her, I'm sure she will just skip it altogether. Again.

An hour later, I run up the stairs and let myself in to Mom's room, flipping the light switch on as I tentatively sit beside her sleeping figure.

"Mom," I whisper.

Nothing.

"MOM," I repeat, a little louder this time, nudging her.

She grunts as she burrows deeper under the covers and I

chuckle, knowing I have her attention now. I bend over to pull the blanket off her face, uncovering her down to the waist.

"Mama. I made breakfast."

She rolls towards me and opens her eyes, adjusting to the light. She offers me a slight smile and a whisper. "Good morning baby. You did my job for me again."

I shrug noncommittally.

She tilts her head at me as she scoots up to sit, brushing tendrils of hair off to the side of my face. "You could always wake me up earlier, you know? You don't have to do this every day on top of having to get ready for school."

I purse my lips and bite back the retort on the tip of my tongue. She could wake herself up and set an alarm, but she never does. It's a routine that I'm used to. I do what I have to do.

A familiar ache pierces me in the chest. Moments like this make me miss the time when Daniel and Dad still lived with us, pre-divorce.

God, I miss my brother so much.

"I don't mind, Mom." I force a smile.

Lying to my mom is something I try never to do, but what else am I supposed to say to that? "Can we eat? I don't want to be late for school," I add gently, hoping she will drop it.

She pats my cheek and kisses me on my forehead as she pulls me off the bed with her.

"What's for breakfast?"

Pulling on her robe, she leads the way out of her room and down the stairs.

"Tocino, eggs and fried rice." Her favorite.

She claps giddily as she sits down at the little round table we have in our kitchen and helps herself to the Filipino-style breakfast I made for us.

I brace myself for what's to come.

"Do you want me to take you to school today, or are you okay to drive?"

Yup, there it is.

Like clockwork she asks me the same thing, like she's done every day since freshman year.

I resist the urge to sigh as I feed myself a spoonful of fried egg to delay answering her.

I can never put anything past my mom, even when her mind was still half asleep, she always sees past my airs. It's always better to keep my answers simple.

"I'm good enough to drive." I lift a shoulder.

There's a crease between her eyebrows. Telltale sign, she's not buying my attempts.

She scoots her chair closer to me and wraps a protective arm around me, coaxing me to lean on her. "Do I need to call Dr. T?"

I shake my head, carefully extracting myself from her grip to finish my breakfast.

"He'll just offer an extra session, like he always does. It's just stress from school. It'll pass."

She is quiet for a few moments while she studies my face before turning her attention back to her plate. "It's been a few weeks, and you're still not sleeping any better than you did in the summer. Let's make the call, okay? Do it for me. And no more cooking breakfast this week."

She eyes the grilled chicken salad I have left covered on the island. "Or lunch."

"Mom..."

I start to protest but stop when she raises an eyebrow at me as if challenging me to defy her.

She leans over to kiss the top of my head, "I appreciate all that you do to help me out, Liz, but I sent my final draft to

3

Mary last night. I've got time. I can take care of everything from now on."

Casually reading my mind, she holds her hand out to me. I hand her the grocery list, knowing I will still have to text her to remind her about it later.

"How's school?" She tucks a hand under her chin, studying me again.

I grin, thrilled that she finally asked. "Principal Gardner says if I keep my GPA the way it's been, I'll be a shoo-in for valedictorian."

She squeals and takes my hand in hers, "I'm so proud of you, baby, I know how hard you've worked and what you've given up, especially after what you went through."

I look at her, and unable to do or say anything in response, I force a smile and make a move to get up to start cleaning, but she puts a hand up, gesturing at me to stop.

"Time for school." She grabs my backpack from the island and walks me out the front door, pausing by the hall closet to grab my sweater then follows me to my car. The car, that once belonged to my brother, is a Ford EcoSport that our parents gifted him for his sixteenth birthday, so luckily, it's only a few years old and never gives me any problems.

I kiss her cheek as I grab my things from her. "Don't forget to pick up Danny's stuff, okay?"

She cups my cheeks, kissing the top of my head, "How about I wait for you, and we'll go together so you don't worry, okay?"

"Deal. See you tonight, Mom."

I start my car and wait until she's safely inside the house before I drive off, feeling a tiny weight lift off my chest, relieving a bit the resounding guilt that I can never completely shake.

. . .

As I PARK my car at school, the nerves settle back in, and I have to work on my breathing like Dr. T. taught me. Anxiety is a bitch, and it has been raging every morning lately.

I check the time on my dash, grateful that I have twenty minutes before homeroom.

I look around the parking lot before getting out and then walk briskly on the cobbled lot to the stairs going up to the school. I am so busy focusing on not looking like I am gasping for air, clenching and unclenching my fingers to try and gain control of the impending panic attack, that I completely miss seeing a person approaching in my periphery and almost twist my ankle as I stumble back clumsily. Just when I think I will fall on my ass, I feel strong, calloused hands grasp my arms to hold me upright.

"Lizzy?" I would recognize that voice anywhere. "You good?"

My eyes go up of their own volition, meeting those chocolate brown eyes I know so well. *Knew*. I remind myself.

I struggle to keep my voice steady as I take a step back, then another, and force a small smile.

"Good. I'm good."

Brad

G*ood*? Who is she kidding?

Lizzy legit looks like she is on the verge of a nervous breakdown.

"You sure?" I crouch down to pick up the tablet I dropped when I instinctively reached out to steady her as she bumped into me.

"Yeah, never mind me. Is your iPad, okay?" I look back down at her and find her biting her lip as she looks worriedly up at me. I have to force myself not to stare at her mouth as I flip the iPad over to show her it is fine. The Otter-Box did its job.

She trembles a little as she sighs in relief. I've known this girl her whole life.

She. Is. *Not*. Okay.

"Do you need to sit down?" I cock my head towards the empty classroom behind me, trying to appear nonchalant when I desperately want her to keep talking to me and tell me what the hell is wrong because although I don't want to be, I *am* worried.

It doesn't escape me that this is the longest we've spoken since the day she broke my heart.

She shakes her head, looking over her shoulder, and makes as if she was going to just turn around and walk away. I reach out to touch her shoulder, but she jerks so fast that she almost tips over, and I have to reach out and hold on to her to keep her from falling over. Again.

As soon as she steadies herself, I step back and put my palms up.

"Sorry, I was just going to tell you that your locker is this way."

I casually point in the direction I came from, behind me, where she had so obviously been headed to before our collision.

She doesn't say anything for a beat, and I worry I might have embarrassed her, but when she finally looks at me, that impassive look on her face that she wears like armor is back on.

Damn it.

"Thanks, and sorry about not looking."

Then she walks away from me in the exact same way she did when we were freshman, and I just stand there like a starved idiot, knowing full well the girl I know better than I know myself won't look back at me. Still, I stare and wait until she is no longer in my line of sight.

I fight back the urge to call out to her. It still pisses me off that our friendship has been reduced to nothing. Our moms have been best friends since high school, even had Lamaze class together, gave birth to us at the same hospital, just months apart.

As far as I know, they still have brunch at least twice a month, yet I can't even have a freaking conversation with my oldest friend.

I sigh, then turn back and start walking towards the student council office.

Out of the corner of my eye, I see the familiar sight of another old friend. I find Kim looking back and forth between me and Liz's retreating back with a questioning eye.

I almost stop walking to acknowledge her, but as soon as her eyes meet mine, she shuts her locker and walks away too.

Damn, that was cold, even for her.

I shake my head, trying not to laugh at how absurd this all is. Out of the four of us, Kim seems like she holds the biggest grudge. Even though it was Liz who said the words, it was Kim who acted the part. We have exchanged a few words here and there in the last few years but only because we are both active members of the student council and have to plan events together. As far as I know, she and Kyle are the only ones who maintain any sort of friendship since our big fight, largely due to the fact that they run in the same circle, but it doesn't seem anything like it used to be.

I notice a few people vying for my attention, but I'm so lost in thoughts of old friends that I know if I stopped to talk to anyone right now, my brain wouldn't be able to process a coherent response. I simply nod, smile and keep walking.

I finally enter the office and plop down at the small makeshift desk reserved for the Student Council President. My reasons for coming in here are abandoned because right now, all I can think of is Liz and that damned look on her face.

I'll just have it to wing it third period and hope I can pull a B on my Spanish test.

I rub my temples, dropping my head into my hands.

Thinking about her is, as always, agonizing torture.

I'm done. I don't want to be friends anymore.

I can still hear her voice in my head, uttering those nine words in disparagement.

Almost three years later, I still don't know why.

Liz

I blink rapidly, trying to extract myself from the fog of thoughts clouding my mind and back to the conversation my mother is trying to have with me.

She nudges me with her shoulder, "Liz, did you hear what I said?"

I bend down to grab a pack of razors and a tin of shaving cream and shrug as I toss them in the corner of the cart where I have been keeping track of all the things my brother will need for his visit. "Yeah, mom. I'm sure Dan will go with you; he won't mind."

She has been talking my ear off for the last twenty minutes while we scrounge the aisles of Target about a writer's panel, she has next year that includes a contest where a fan and a plus-one will win a dinner with her. She doesn't want to go solo if her dinner date technically will have their own date. But it is starting to feel like she wants an excuse to go with Dan.

She tugs on an earlobe, a far-off look on her face, the one she has reserved for whenever she thinks about my brother. "I mean, I guess I could always just take you."

"Whoaaaa. Don't sound so excited," I tease; I know she didn't say it to minimize me. Their relationship has become strained over the years since she and Dad started having problems, largely due to the fact that Danny started distancing himself from our parents during high school when their bickering became near constant.

Who could really blame him?

She laughs, but it sounds strained, and she pats my hand to keep pushing the cart as we walk around the toiletry aisles to grab what we need.

"Mom, seriously though. I don't know why you have it in your head that Danny hates you or something. He loves you; he'll go with you if you want him to," I say.

She stays quiet for the next few aisles. Just as we enter the bread aisle, our last stop, she nudges me with her shoulder again, takes hold of the cart, and pushes it off to the side while she gazes down at me with a thoughtful look on her face. "What about you?"

"What about me?" I grab a bag of bagels, sighing.

This will have to do for now. At least until I can make a trip downtown to the bakery at the Filipino store for some pandesal and pastries.

"If I asked you to do something for me, would you do it?"

I shoot her an incredulous look. "Just lay it on me, mom."

"Put that back, Liz. I'll grab some from *Valerio's* when I head downtown tomorrow."

I raise an eyebrow as I trade the bagels for some powdered donuts. The kind Dan likes. "*Mom*?"

"Come to brunch with me this weekend."

I tilt my head at her. "AND?" There has to be more to it than that. There always is.

She makes a point of dragging out her answer as she pushes the cart out of the aisle, forcing me to hurry after her as she leads the way to the checkout aisles.

Then she looks sideways at me, a mischievous look on her face, as we fall in line.

"Say yes first."

Unconvinced, I just shake my head as I start unloading the cart.

"You're being vague on purpose. What is it?"

She leaves the question hanging in the air while she pays, and I bag our groceries. After thanking the cashier, we make our way out to her car, and I have to swallow a groan at her audacity to look innocently at me as we put our stuff away and get in the car.

She deliberately takes her sweet time to answer me as she presses the button to start the car then shifts in her seat, so she is facing me.

"Have brunch with your Aunt Rose and me this Sunday."

I eye her warily, "What's the catch?"

"At her house."

I have an inkling there is more to it than that, but I want her to completely spell it out for me. I stay silent until she senses my trepidation and continues.

"She invited the Andersons and Thompsons. *Everyone* is expected to come."

"For brunch?" I look away feeling a churning in my stomach that is a mixture of dread, fear, and guilt about what I was being asked to do.

"It's her and your Uncle Dave's twenty fifth wedding anniversary. She wants to celebrate with family."

My head snaps back at her, "We're not—"

She cuts me off, raising a hand and leveling me with a unyielding look on her face, her frustration evident with the lines etched on her forehead.

"*We are family.* I know it's hard for you to remember that after falling out of touch with your best friends—"

"Ex-friends," I mutter under my breath.

"—but you need to understand that the adults are tired of

entertaining this insane notion that since you guys aren't friends anymore, we all have to stop too."

I hug my knees to my chest as I fight against the urge to cry. You could hear a pin drop with how quiet it suddenly gets between us. There it was. I have always felt like, in some way, my mom, along with everyone else, blames me for changing the whole dynamic. That because of me, there aren't any more get togethers or vacations with our—her—closest friends.

"Mom..."

My voice catches on a sob, and I have to swallow the lump that has formed in my throat.

She reaches out, cradling my chin in her hand, and forces me to look at her.

"I'm not blaming you. I would never blame you for what happened, nor will I question your decision to become this version of yourself who cuts off the whole world. It's what you had to do to get better. To survive what happened."

The dam breaks and tears stream down my face in silent waves.

She clucks her tongue as she wipes my tears away with her thumbs. "I also know you, Elizabeth. More than you think I do. I think it's time to stop hiding. You do not have to tell them what happened, and you have my word that it will not be brought up at the party."

She cups my face between her palms and kisses the tip of my nose, "Whatever transpired between the four of you, find a way to address it before you go your separate ways after graduation. It doesn't have to be on Sunday, but at least it's a start. You do not want to live your life regretting that you didn't at least approach the possibility of reconciliation."

She pauses and forces me to meet her gaze.

"Or at the very least, forgiveness."

Brad

"Kyle Anderson."
"Elizabeth Jenkins."
"Bradley Stevens."
"Kimberly Thompson."

I shake my head in disbelief as Mr. Santos moves on to recite the next batch of students, calling them out one at a time. A loud sputtering breaks through my shock as I notice Kim shooting up to her feet, her cheerleader uniform swinging around her as she raises her hand.

"MISTER. SANTOS."

Our Social Studies teacher lets out an exasperated sigh as he looks up from his desk, pausing his announcement of the next group to look at her.

"Miss Thompson. I am not entertaining any questions until after I have called all the groups."

Kim visibly bristles with annoyance at being told to wait, but she sits back down in a slump.

Clearly nothing has changed—Kim is still as impatient as ever. I almost laugh at that but manage to stop myself. I do not want to be on the receiving end of her temper. Apparently, I would be spending the next few months working closely with my old friends for this class.

Mister Santos is friends with my mom. I have a feeling she

has something to do with this "coincidence" that we are all suddenly grouped together after three years of limited to no contact with each other. But I know better than to even ask my mom, she'll deny it, tell me I'm overreacting.

I peer over my shoulder at Kyle to gauge his reaction. Kyle is leaning back on his chair, ankles crossed, looking unfazed. He looks over at me and shrugs, nodding Liz' way.

Dude doesn't care. Noted. One less thing to worry about.

I hazard a look at Liz. Her hair is down today, and it hides the expression on her face. I adjust my position to get a better view. It doesn't take long for her to feel my gaze on her. She looks right at me, rewarding me with a small, awkward smile.

My eyebrows shoot up in surprise, and her smile grows. I might have allowed myself to feel special about that, but she turns that same smile at the others. Her shoulders stiffen, and the smile fades away as quickly as it came when she shifts her gaze to Kim, who is still obviously seething and ignoring us. Liz pulls her purple sweater tighter around her, and I fume.

I am about to do something about that, like throw my pen at Kim, when I'm interrupted by Mr. Santos shutting his planner loudly.

I sit back as he stands up from his desk to address the room.

"All right. I know this is unconventional, but last year, my class had a spike in failing grades." He leans on his desk and peruses the room.

"So, this year, with permission from Principal Gardner, I've decided to change it up. I want to give everyone the best chance to bring your GPA up. You will be doing all your projects and exams with this same group for the rest of the school year. Your group grade will also serve as your final grade."

He raises an eyebrow as if expecting us to either applaud or challenge him. "I'm sure some of you could use the extra help," he says. But no one says anything in response. Not even Kim, whom Mr. Santos looks at pointedly. "Miss Thompson? You had your hand raised? Care to share anything?"

"No, sir," Kim grumbles as she unfolds her arms.

Mr. Santos tries to cover a smile as he coughs into his fist.

"All right. So put four chairs together in a circle with your group, and I will be passing out instructions for the first group project, which will be due at the end of this month."

I grab my stuff. I'm about to stand when I feel a heavy hand grip my shoulder. I turn to find Kyle offering his fist. I grin and return his fist bump, grateful for at least one friendly face in this group. He motions for me to stay seated as he pulls two other chairs around us.

"Yo, Lizzy. Kimmy, get over here." Kyle all but hollers at the girls.

I chuckle. "You have a death wish. We were told to stop calling her that in the sixth grade."

Kyle folds his arms as he leans back on his chair. He's smirking as he watches Kim stalk over in a huff. She smacks the back of his head. "I told you not to call me that."

"What are you gonna do about it, *Kimberly?* Not be my *friend?*" He challenges.

I sit up and shoot Kyle a warning look. Liz is right behind Kim and hears that last part. Her gaze turns downwards, as she quietly sits beside me.

Kim apparently notices this. She looks right at Liz, her ponytail swinging, when she says, "Nah. That's *Elizabeth's* trademark move, remember?"

"Well, shit," Kyle mutters under his breath, rolling his eyes.

Liz's head shoots up, and I start when I see that her eyes eerily hold the same blazing intensity, they did three years ago. Before I have time to dwell on that, Kyle gets up and plants himself between them as a buffer. He grabs Kim's hand, gently tugging her down to take his chair.

Kyle then looks Kim up and down. Frowning, he jerks off his varsity jacket, leaving him in just a jersey, and he tosses it on Kim's lap. "Here. You look cold."

Kim tries to get back up, but Kyle once again reaches for her hand. He squeezes it, holding her gaze until her shoulders slump and she gives in, draping Kyle's jacket over her knees.

I would have asked what that was about, but I'm too preoccupied with the way Kim is glaring at Liz, making her shift uncomfortably in her seat.

I sigh and lean forward, my elbows on the desk. "Kim."

She raises an eyebrow. "What?"

I shrug. "Let's not attack each other."

Out of the corner of my eye, Liz is gripping her thumbs as if she is willing herself to calm down, and I feel her panic setting in.

Before I can drive the point further, Mr. Santos hovers over us, handing each of us an individual packet.

I look down at the packet. It's entitled *"The Role of the Arts in the Fight for Social Justice and Racial Equity."*

I feel Liz stiffen beside me. She looks up and glances at Kyle. He's rubbing his forehead in thought, a deep frown marring his face.

"Mr. Santos? Is the whole class assigned the same topic? Or is it specific to the group?"

Mr. Santos takes a moment to sweep his gaze around at the rest of the class before looking back at us. "Each group will be working on a different topic within the same subject matter. But before you jump to any conclusions, the reason I chose this topic for your group is because you all participate in the arts." He gestures to Kyle and Kim. "Mr. Anderson and Miss Thompson are both musically inclined, while Miss Jenkins you are quite the writer just like your mother. And Mr. Stevens here is adept in digital media and app creation."

App creation? I cringe inwardly at our teacher's lame attempt at saying I build apps, which I guess I did if you count the ones, I created for the school last year. One made online fundraisers easily accessible for students and their families, and the other, a rideshare app, that helps students who attend our school coordinate rides.

Neither would have been possible without my dad and his software company's sponsorship.

Liz, seemingly satisfied with that explanation, wastes no time, and starts scanning the packet. She takes out highlighters and colored pens from her panda pouch that she no doubt bought at *Daiso*, her favorite store.

Mr. Santos shakes his head in amusement as he moves on to the next group.

I understand what made her question the validity of this assignment there for a moment. With what's been going on in the world lately, it's a touchy subject. One I know she often struggles with being half Asian. Growing up, she used to confide in me how out of place she always felt like. Not knowing where she belonged. Whether to classify herself as White or Asian. Her deep-seated insecurities whenever there wasn't even a box, she could check for herself, when asked what she was. I can't begin to understand her struggle or Kyle's, but I do acknowledge my privilege of not knowing what that is like. The best I can do is use this project to educate myself better and learn how to be a better ally.

I lean towards Liz, nudging her arm. She barely spares me a glance before going back to highlighting and writing notes on the packet. "I think we should all talk, don't you?"

I can almost hear the way Kim's eyes roll next to me. I ignore her and wait for Liz to acknowledge the elephant in the room.

Liz lets out a soft sigh, putting her pen down. She's still avoiding looking at any of us.

At this point, I am only half-aware of the rest of the class, which is seemingly oblivious to the tension that exists among the four of us, so thick it will take *Mjolnir* to cut through it.

Before I address it, Liz takes a deep breath and looks straight at Kim.

"I didn't tell you guys to stop being friends with each other...you know?"

She says it so low that I have to strain to hear it, but the effect of those words cuts through like Thor's hammer itself.

I drop my forehead on my open palm. I start rubbing circles on my temples as I absorb her words. Suddenly all the repressed disappointment and hurt comes rushing back. I have to grit my teeth to keep them from spilling out. We were in class, for *fuck's* sake. I can't exactly grill the girl who used to be my everything in front of everyone. Especially since I never told her about liking her in the first place. Between the four of us, only Kyle was privy to that piece of information.

"Are you kidding me, Lizzy?" Kim's voice gets caught on a whisper, which catches my attention. I'm surprised to find her eyes shining with unshed tears.

"I..."Liz stammers at Kim, looking dumbstruck as if not quite understanding what she just dug up with that statement.

"After all these years? That. *That* is what you choose to say?" Kim's voice is filled with conviction now. I can tell she is amped to go off.

I know Kyle and I should say something, but I am at a loss. Out of all the times I imagined finally sitting down with them, this scenario never even crossed my mind.

Now Liz has to go and insinuate that we stopped being friends because she said so.

"I have an idea," Kyle says.

Kim's head snaps towards him. She is vibrating with repressed anger now. She makes a move towards Kyle, presumably to hit him again or shut him up, when he raises his hand to grab hers. Again. *Interesting.*

I shelve that away for future questioning.

"We're in class. I really don't feel like going to detention for disrupting because that's what's going to fucking happen if we keep shittin' on each other like this. So, calm down."

I sit back. Unable to do anything but ball my hands into fists, I place them on my knees, trying to calm my rising frustration.

Kim and Kyle are too busy engaging in a silent stare down. Liz is now refusing to look up at any of us or acknowledge what her words have just set off.

After a few moments that pass like eons, the bell rings. It feels like a cold bucket of water over my head. I work on calming down as everyone else starts rising and rushing out of the room in a stampede that only happens when it's the last class of the week.

I realize how this really isn't the time or place to hash it all out. Knowing Liz, she is most likely feeling defensive over Kim's verbal jabs. I may not be friends with seventeen-year-old Liz anymore, but I've known her my whole life. I know deep down she wouldn't say anything with the intent to hurt. I need to convince them to talk, but not here.

Just as I am about to suggest continuing this conversation somewhere else, Liz starts shoving her things in her bag and stands. She slings her backpack over one shoulder.

"I'm sorry for saying that and for what I did before." Her voice breaks as her face scrunches up like she's holding back tears. "I hope you guys can forgive me enough that we can at least work on these projects together, but if not, I'd be willing to do all the work."

As she turns to walk away, Kim reaches out and catches her arm.

"No."

Liz turns back in surprise. From behind her, I can make out Mr. Santos raising an eyebrow, clearly wondering what is going on but smart enough not to ask questions. He nods to me, further adding proof to my earlier thought that Mom asked him to group us together like this. He gathers his things and walks out of the room, leaving the four of us alone.

Kim stomps her feet in irritation bringing my focus back to our confrontation.

"Look, I'm still pissed, and I don't have a filter. I'm bound to say some pretty crappy things without thinking them through, but you need to stop walking away and own up to your shit."

Liz tilts her head and levels her with a stare. "I thought I just did?"

"Throwing a vague apology three years too late and saying you'll do our homework for us is not owning your shit, *Elizabeth*."

"What do you want from me, *Kimberly*?"

Liz

"The truth."

This time, it comes from Kyle. In the middle of our exchange, he has gotten up and is now leaning on the windows. His arms are folded over his Seahawks jersey, his legs crossed over his dark jeans.

My head snaps back towards Brad involuntarily. I wait to see if he's going to add another knife to my gut, but he doesn't. Instead, he looks at me like I am a stranger with his stupid soulful brown eyes. I guess at this point, that's what I am.

I glance back at Kim and Kyle, who are both looking at me expectantly.

Even with all of them staring at me, somehow, I'm not feeling seen in all of this.

Hell, I barely recognize myself. Why do I expect them to? I hardly even know them either.

I guess despite everything, I expect Brad to at least recognize that I'm still here, hidden behind all the self-preservation walls I've erected. I let my gaze trail back to him. There is something else entirely simmering deep behind his eyes. Something that feels like more than just frustration or anger. I want to break that silent stare, but he remains hunched over his seat. I give up on getting him to back me up here.

I expel a breath; I am not prepared for their anger. Maybe my mom is right—it is time for me to tell them everything. I search for an opening. Something I can say to start the conversation about what caused me to walk away from them. In the back of my mind, the nagging voice that says it wasn't all my fault, that they severed ties, is getting louder. Self-preservation is winning over logic because, damn it, they distanced themselves just as much as I did. My mind starts conjuring up memories of middle school and freshman year.

Kim and Kyle got popular. Kim started hanging out with other girls. Kyle was busy playing football, dating, and then came his music. Brad started playing basketball while working on his app ideas and learning his dad's business. All while I was struggling at home and nearly died.

Looking back now, it was like dominoes falling one by one. The incident was simply the catalyst to the end of our already crumbling friendship, so why are they all throwing the blame on me?

I stand up straighter now, angling back so Kim's hand falls off of my shoulder.

"Listen. As much as I appreciate you all ganging up on me, maybe it's time you all took a good hard look at yourselves."

That gets to Brad, and he shoots up to his feet. "What do you mean by that?"

Oh? So you can *talk?*

I have to tilt my head up to look him in the eye, but I manage to huff it out. "I mean that you need to stop saying this was all my doing. We all had a hand in destroying this friendship. It was over way before I said it was."

I mentally pat myself in the back for that winning retort.

Brad blinks, opening his mouth as if to argue, before closing it and turning to look down at Kim beside him, then at Kyle, then back at me.

"You're gonna have to walk me through this, Liz."

"Why?"

"Because I don't know what in the hell you're talking about!" Brad growls.

My mouth drops open in shock. In the almost 18 years I have known Brad, he has never once raised his voice at me or spoken to me in such a careless manner. It prompts Kyle to push himself off the windows and stand next to Brad, with a hand gripping his shoulder.

I take a step back, trying not to show them just how anxious I am becoming because I needed to stand my ground. This is not going to be all on me. *Not anymore.*

"I'm tired of being the bad guy in all of this. Yes, I walked away after I said I was done. Yes, I regret that. I AM sorry, I mean that, but I am not about to stand here and be subjected to the blame game, like you guys didn't stop being my friend *first.* I want to point out that I walked away. I never made demands or said you guys couldn't be friends. You guys are so fixated on the idea that I was a bad friend. But did any of you even act like my friend before that? Or did you keep blowing me off? Did any of you even bother to ask if I was okay?"

I manage a look at Kim, who has stayed uncharacteristically silent, and find her deep in thought, like she is recalling all the events that took place before that day. A deep crease forms between her eyebrows, her teeth clamping down on her bottom lip.

When she finally glances at me, I see a rush of emotions in her eyes. Before I can decipher their meaning, she suddenly turns to Kyle. It makes me flash back to ten minutes ago when they held hands. To that moment Kyle looked like he was uncomfortable with her skirt pulling up when she sat down. Yeah, I noticed that. It was hard not to. There is also something there in the look they share now. I shelve it for future dissection before finally turning to Brad, whose face is hard with the rush of realization creeping up as he figures it all out in real time.

This time I direct my words at him knowing it will strike a nerve, because why not?

He hurt me too. He just conveniently forgot, apparently.

"Where were you when I needed you? Or do you not remember at all?"

Before any of them can find an answer to that, I do what I do best and walk away from my problems.

AN HOUR LATER, I dry my hair with a towel and replay that whole painful conversation for the tenth time in my head, each time berating myself about all the other things I could have said instead of laying myself bare like I had. I opened myself up to a whole lot of resentment and disappointment again. Nothing good will come out of me telling them that.

They are still too hurt, and even though a big part of me is more than pissed that they mutually decided I was somehow to blame for the end of our friendship, a rational side of me knows there is some truth to that, and I deserve their anger. They were supposed to my best friends, but I had hidden the most important parts of myself. I hadn't allowed them to be there for me after what happened. They still have no clue about what I did.

I shake those intrusive thoughts before it gets too dark and try to focus. Today is supposed to be a great day. Danny is coming home for a few weeks for a visit. That is all that matters. I needed to focus on that, or my brother will worry. Or worse, my mother will. She can always sense when something is wrong with me, and I'm really not ready to have that conversation.

As if on cue, I hear the garage door open and her car pulling in.

I throw the towel hastily on my bed and run downstairs to meet them.

Just as I reach the bottom step, his booming voice makes me grin from ear to ear as he rounds the corner from the family room.

"Elizabeth!" He drops his bag and scoops me up in a tight hug. With my face smushed on his shoulder and my feet dangling at least a foot off the ground, he spins me.

Laughter comes from behind us as Mom affectionately smacks Dan's shoulder.

"Put her down, Daniel, then you kids go upstairs to catch up while I make dinner."

She takes a minute to take us in, a radiant smile blossoming on her face before she rushes to the kitchen. With how happy she just looked, I can almost taste the sinigang and adobo she's sure to make for dinner, knowing it's each of our favorites.

After he sets me down, I squeeze his shoulder. "I missed you, Danny."

He grins down at me, picking up his bag. "I missed you too, Liz."

I make a show of looking him up and down, pretending to give him a once over as I nonchalantly climb a step then a second one, starting a game we played since we were kids. Flashing an obnoxious smirk on his face, he silently raises an eyebrow as he pointedly looks at my feet before proceeding to skip two steps. Within seconds, we both break into a jog up the stairs, trying to outrun the other.

I collapse on his bed a minute later and throw my arms up in giddy celebration.

"You owe me a movie!"

Chuckling, he tosses his bag on the floor and lays down next to me.

We start catching up as he fills me in on what's new at school and with his friends.

I laugh as he once again gushes about how amazing the weather is in California. Not even being discreet about it anymore. I know he's just throwing it in every other sentence because he's hoping he can get me to choose a college near him.

"It's not working, is it?"

I shake my head, lightly punching him on the shoulder.

"I miss you, Liz. It would be nice to be in the same zip-code again. Tired of being worried about my baby sis from so far away."

I tuck my head under his arm, starting to feel overwhelmed with emotion. I didn't realize just how lonely I am until today. I have spent years counting down the months leading up to my brother's visits, being so incredibly happy during those weeks only to hide in my bedroom in his absence until he came again. I have a feeling that the hour I spent in class with my old friends set me off. Now I'm realizing just how alone and isolated I have let myself become.

"You know you can always come home."

I feel the tension seep through the arm my forehead is resting on as he eases me off of him, pulling me to sit on the edge of the bed.

"Do you need me to?"

I shrug, not wanting him to remind me that it was my idea to split ourselves up between our parents. How he had wanted to change course and stay here with us, but I had worried about him changing his plans for me. UCLA is his dream school, and he deserves to have the future of his choosing and not be tied down at home because his sister needs him.

"I want to come home, if you're asking me to."

I give him my best neutral face, but he folds his arms and

26

peers down at me. I roll my eyes at him, using his height to his advantage, but I sense the interrogation coming.

Dan takes after our dad. Side by side, no one would be able to guess we were siblings. He's tall, I'm short. He's white-passing and I take after our Filipino mother. I can't count how many times strangers have walked up to me to speak to me in a different language or ask me where I am "really" from. Meanwhile, Dan has never been on the receiving end of any of the outward scrutiny, judgment or micro-aggressions that come with being biracial, even though he is. Sometimes I envy that about him. Then I remember he has his own internal struggles. Other people completely disregard the other half of who he is, simply because he doesn't look the part. All of it just comes with the territory of being racially confused.

I look down at my feet, unable to deal with the scrutiny. My brother and I didn't use to be this close. The last few years have made us really bond, and although he is four years older than me, he has never once made me feel like I am not on equal footing with him.

"What's going on, Liz? I can tell something happened."

I grip my thumbs in between my fingers to keep my breathing even as I fill him in on what happened in Social Studies and our sudden weekend plans.

"So..." He sits next to me, propping his elbows on his knees, rubbing his jaw in thought.

Suddenly a thought crosses my mind. "That means Summer might be there too."

He grins at that, lifting his shoulder arrogantly.

"Good. Then maybe she'll realize what she's been missing."

Summer is Kyle's older sister, whom Daniel used to have a huge crush on back when they were in high school. They'd never seemed to be anything more than friendly. There is something in his tone that hints at something more, and I turn to ask him.

He waggles a finger at me. "Don't change the subject."

"Dan, I'm not ready."

"So, you just want to graduate without talking to anyone about it?"

"I talk to Dr T, to you, and to Mom. I had to sit in therapy once a week for two years, and Mom still makes me go once a month. I am all talked out." I lift my hands in exasperation, then ball my hands into fists as I run my knuckles up and down my legs.

He sighs as he leans over and grasps my hands, rubbing a thumb over my knuckles like he has had to do countless of times, whenever I've started having a panic attack.

"Being alone is not the solution. In fact, it's made it worse."

"I—I know that. I'm just…"

"Scared?"

"Yeah…" *and ashamed*. I bite back that last part, not wanting to admit even to my brother that shame is a shade I wear quite often. I can admit to myself that that was the real reason I choose to be alone. I would never have to wonder if they would have kicked me out of their lives if I walked away first. At least with that, it's my choice.

My *only* choice, I remind myself.

He frowns like he knows what I'm thinking, "I don't think you have anything to be scared of. Listen to me, your brother is the most judgmental dipshit on the planet, and I don't judge you one bit."

"That's because you're my brother. You have no choice but to love me no matter what."

"Liz. Tell me one thing. If it were Brad, would you stop being his friend over it? Or would you want to be there for him and be his friend? What if it were Kim? Or Kyle?"

I bite my lip, feeling the tears I have been fighting all day spill down my cheeks.

Deep down, the same thought has crossed my mind at least a hundred times before.

"I thought so." He hugs me now, wrapping his arm around my shoulder.

"I think it's time to stop hiding and start over. Maybe you guys won't be as close as you were before, but at least you can stop pretending you're strangers."

I rub a hand over my face, wiping away my tears as I struggle to compose myself before Mom walks in, sees me in this state, and makes me go to weekend therapy. I nudge him with my shoulder, offering him a small smile to indicate I am okay now—because I really am. Talking to Danny always helps me see things clearly. The only good thing to come out of any of this is this new friendship I have with my brother. We used to bicker a lot growing up and play stupid pranks on each other, but ever since that night, he has been my best friend. I would not trade that for anything. Not even a do-over. Thanks to my brother, one thing has become abundantly clear. I may not be ready to give them all the details, but I am ready to hear them out and let them in. All I can do is hope for the same.

Come Sunday, I will do what I should have done three years ago.

Talk. And not walk away.

Brad

I comb my fingers through my still-damp hair and jog down the three flights of stairs. Today is one of those days when I once again become acutely aware of just how much of a privilege it is to have the third-floor loft to myself. It is quiet and I can focus on my app development. But that is also the reason I woke up late, and Mom is pissed.

I grimace, remembering the way I woke up this morning with my mother smacking my ass with a pillow. Mom mentioned last weekend that she and Dad had decided to cancel the trip they had planned for Aspen, realizing a party is way overdue. That twenty-five years of marriage needs to be celebrated. It was all last minute, so she needs help setting up. I had completely forgotten about it and pulled an all-nighter, working on my new venture.

I reach for my phone from the back pocket of my dark jeans. Mom woke me up at noon and now the clock reads 01:06 PM.

"Shit." The party is supposed to start at three.

I smooth the collar of my grey oxford shirt and look around our front entryway. I grin at what Mom has been able to pull off in just a few days. She has set up the wooden doors with a silver and white balloon arch. I walk past the sitting area into the kitchen. A whole array of appetizers and finger sandwiches have been lined up artfully on the island facing the big bay windows.

I stifle a groan, knowing I was supposed to help do all of this. By the looks of it, there isn't even anything left for me to do. Mom is all about teaching responsibility, so even though she hires people to set up, serve, and make the food, she still expects us to pull our own weight and pitch in.

I sneeze. From the smell of it, she has gone a little overboard with the flowers. She has placed vases full of peonies and tulips everywhere, including the dining area and main living room, which was only slightly bigger than the sitting room. It also boasts its own food displays.

Just how many people did she actually invite?

I squint, feeling the start of a migraine. I barely slept and skipped meals, so the smell of the food and the flowers mixed in the air is getting to me.

I am about to walk past the library when I notice that the door is slightly open. I make a move to close it when I hear books falling to the floor.

"Dad?"

I stop when I find Lizzy crouching down on the floor, her arms filled with books. She startles at the sound of my voice and hits her shoulder on the bookshelves, dropping the rest on the floor. She shuts her eyes, flinching.

Hurrying over to her, I grasp her by the elbow to steady her.

"Sorry, I didn't mean to scare you. Are you okay?"

Liz nods, smiling sheepishly up at me.

"Yeah, your mom just left me unsupervised in here again."

I laugh at that. I'm amazed she even remembers how she used to spend hours in this room when we were growing up. I would be upstairs in the family room playing video games with Kyle and she would be in here reading one book after another. Often getting lost in rearranging the books in a system only she

31

understood, which was what she appeared to be doing now. One shelf is empty, its contents now dumped on the floor.

Without a word, I crouch down beside her, handing her the books. She arranges them back on the shelf. We work silently like that until all the books have been put away. I sneak a look at her as she organizes the last few books in her arms. Her hair is in twin braids, and she is wearing a pink dress that hits her just above the knee. Her forehead scrunches up in concentration, her mouth pursed as she gets lost in her own little world.

I have forgotten how cute she is. The urge to tug on her braids, like when we were eight, is strong. I stick my hands in my pockets to keep from reaching out.

Then I remember my predicament.

"Is my mom mad at me?"

Lizzy's eyes light up in amusement. She giggles. Prompting what feels like an ear-splitting grin on my face. I can't help it. I have missed this.

I've missed *her*.

Seeing her in my house, especially in this room, makes it feel like no time has passed.

"I don't think so. She seems to be in a great mood today. She even brought me here after I helped put the balloon arch up. I think it was more so she and my mom could start on mimosas than to reward me."

Another smile is thrown my way as she looks over her shoulder.

How fuckin' pretty.

I am about to tell her about the ass-smacking I got when what she has just said registers.

"Wait—how long have you been here?"

"We got here around ten." She turns to face me, and I can tell she's starting to feel uncomfortable as she shifts her feet and looks everywhere but up at me.

I sit on the armrest of the couch so she can meet my eyes, "Shit, is everything done? Why didn't anyone wake me up?"

She folds an arm across her chest, gripping her elbow with a hand, resting a hip on the shelf across from me.

"Yes, and she mentioned you could use a few extra hours of sleep."

"She seemed pissed enough to hit me with a pillow, though."

That got her. Liz lets out another laugh, her eyes shutting from the joy of it, but then, seemingly, she catches herself and shrugs.

I should make that sound my alarm; I'd wake up every single time.

"Probably wanted to make sure you were awake."

I rub a hand across my face and nod towards the door.

"You think it's safe to go find her?"

She shakes her head at me, and I balk.

"No, no, I don't mean no like that. I mean, I really doubt she's mad. Mom and I came early to help. She hired plenty of people, so I am in here instead."

She opens her palms and shrugs.

The uncomfortable look in her eyes doesn't ease. The urge to pull her into my arms and out of her head is stronger than wanting to tug her braids.

"Anyone else here?"

"Just—just us. Danny was out late last night so Mom let him sleep in. He'll be here…later."

Something is happening with Liz.

She is twisting her fingers, pinching the skin in between. She starts incessantly tapping her foot. Before she completely yanks her digits off, I lean over and untangle them.

"What's going on in that head of yours? We were doing good there just now."

She sighs, gently removing her fingers from my grasp.

"I guess I remembered how we left things on Friday, and I got all…."

"Got all?' I sit on the floor this time, inviting her to sit across from me. She does.

Then I remember she's wearing a short dress. I give myself a mental slap on the head. I reach behind me and hand her a pillow from the couch.

She hugs it to her chest and finally looks at me.

"I have anxiety."

I nod, not the least bit surprised. She was always fidgety when we were kids, but it wasn't quite like this. I started to notice it escalating sometime in middle school. Then she started getting distant and quiet around me going into high school.

Then we all had that stupid fight.

Once again, I'm reminded of just how much I have royally fucked up. I should have been there for her instead of making excuses and staying busy to avoid my growing feelings for my best friend. I knew her mom had suffered from it, and I should have made the connection back then. Instead, I was too into what I was feeling for her to notice hers.

"So, you're feeling anxious around me?"

She rests her chin on the pillow and shrugs.

"Yes and no. It's more than just feeling it. I overthink and worry a lot. About everything and basically everyone. I get panic attacks often. I have trouble sleeping and forget to eat a lot, but it's definitely gotten easier to manage now, for the most part."

I have so many questions, but I can tell it is already a lot for her to even open up to me like this. I just nod, silently hoping she continue.

"It's like my brain is always on overdrive, I guess… speaking in Brad terms."

I give her a reassuring smile. "How long have you been feeling like this?"

She starts to do the fidgeting thing again with her fingers and I offer her my palms.

To my surprise, she accepts, and I squeeze her fingers reassuringly.

"I guess I've always been sort of like this, but it really started getting bad right before high school. Now, here I am, an anxious overachiever."

She scoffs, gently removing herself from my grasp and hugging the pillow tighter.

The timing sounds about right so I venture, "Right around your parents' divorce?"

She frowns, tilting her head at me. "Your mom told you?"

I nod. "I really wanted to come and find you. To talk to you and make sure you were okay. I thought about reaching out. But then you were gone. My mom said you had taken that vacation with your dad after our fight, and when you came back...well, nothing was ever the same anymore."

She leans back, resting her temple on the side of the couch, and gives me a sad smile.

"I wish you had."

"Me too."

"I'm sorry I let stuff ruin our friendship."

"Me too."

She chuckles, smacking me with the pillow.

"I'm being real, Liz." I shrug in an attempt to hide the rage of emotions starting to build inside me. "When we were kids, it always felt like it was you and me against the world. Until it didn't anymore—"

"I'm sorry I—"

I shake my head, holding my hand up.

Borrowing Kim's words, I need to own up to my shit.

I need to accept that I have served an active role in the destruction of our friendship.

"Because we got busy. Started having responsibilities. Met other friends. It felt like every year, things became slowly different. We stopped having all this time together like we used to, to just be us and hang out. I know I fucked up. I get that now. At the time, I didn't realize I was blowing you off. If I had known that it would lead to us not being in each other's lives anymore? I would have kicked my own ass. I'm sorry I made you feel like I turned my back on you."

Liz takes a moment to study me before she reaches out and pats my knee.

"I didn't want you to stop doing what you wanted to do or demand time together. I just wanted to be a part of your life for more than the occasional facetimes and random text messages. I needed my *best friend*."

I can't do anything but nod at that. If I say anything more than I already have, I will end up confessing the biggest reason I was avoiding her then. "I was an ass."

She sniffs and pulls back. I groan inwardly, realizing there are tears in her eyes.

"There were other things too, Brad. I wasn't all that innocent in it either. I never told you guys about my parents' divorce or what was going on with me or at home. I just expected you guys to read my mind, my mood, and never checked in with you either. That was selfish."

"You had shit going on. I get it now. Have you seen anyone for it?"

"I go to therapy."

I wait for her to elaborate more, but when she picks at the hem of her dress, I realize just how much this is affecting her. I refuse to force her to tell me more than she's ready for.

I rest my head on the couch and go over what I should say

or do next. But she beats me to it. Liz moves to sit next to me and nudges my shoulder playfully, in the same way she used to when were kids, making up after an argument. Just like that, the three years of separation start to crumble.

"I'm still a little mad at you, though."

"I know. I'm sorry we made you feel like we blamed you for our falling-out." I nudge her back, earning a teary smile from her. "I just want you to know I never did. I was just upset because I missed you. I was projecting my frustrations a little. I should have backed you up."

I nudge her again. "I'm here now. This time I promise I got you."

"For infinity?"

Warmth blossoms in my chest as I remember how we used to always say that to each other certain that this time around, there is no way in hell I am letting her down again.

"And forever."

We spend the next hour catching up on little things and I fill her in on the conversation I had with Kyle last night. I watch as Liz' face lights up with a smile and a flash of hope crosses her face. It may not be exactly the way it was before, but it's a start.

I'm reading Mom's text to come meet her and Aunt Cat in the kitchen when Liz pulls on the sleeve of my shirt. I place my phone on my lap, letting her know she has my full attention.

"I may get weird later when everyone is around…"

"What do you mean?"

I frown at that. It is an odd thing to just randomly throw into the conversation.

"I have anxiety."

Liz just told me this, so I nod, but I'm still not getting it.

She sighs like I really should be getting it.

"One of the types I was diagnosed with is called social anxiety. I get weird when I'm around a lot of people."

I nod again, not knowing what I am supposed to say as encouragement. I have a lot of questions, but I can't exactly school her for answers. But this time, I sort of understood what she is getting at. I have a cousin who suffers from social anxiety. It started when we were kids, and I remember my mom explaining to me why Sam acted the way she did whenever we had a big family gathering. So, whenever that side of the family gets together, we always try to do something that she is comfortable with. But lately, she has been going to therapy and is getting better at handling her triggers.

"You don't have to minimize it, Liz. My cousin Sam has it. I get it."

She expels a breath, then hesitantly offers me a small smile. "I didn't know that."

I return her smile, "What do you need from me to help make you more at ease?"

Her smile grows as she tilts her head with a curious look on her face.

"Do you mind if I go up to the family room if it gets to be too much?"

This time, I give in to the urge to tug on her braids. "You never have to ask. Or…you could also go up to your old room if you want. That's an option too."

She looks surprised at that. "I still have a room?"

I tug on her other braid. "Of course, you do."

"**Y**ou look great. Don't worry."

I blink and look up at Brad. I have abruptly stopped just outside the kitchen and am hesitating to go in. Surprised he knows I'm worried about the state of my face before I can even tell him that I am. Which I hope is a sign that things will soon return to normal between us if he can read me so easily like that again. We had a good talk in the library and although there is still so much left to be said, it feels like a giant weight has finally been lifted off of my chest. I can almost feel the walls I've been walking around in start to crack, letting the sun back in.

I just hope that Kim is as open to a reconciliation as Brad and Kyle are. Just before Aunt Rose called for us to meet them in here, Brad mentioned that he and Kyle got together after the game on Friday and talked. He even laughed at how Kyle is just really cool with everything and doesn't hold any grudges. They want to get together with Kim before working on our project to just hash things out. Maybe even today, if she decides to come.

"My mom just worries a lot. Are you sure it doesn't look like I cried?"

He squints, tipping my chin up to scan my face. I suck in a breath.

I don't know if it's because we haven't been in each other's company for this long or the talk we just had. Suddenly, my mouth goes dry at his touch. I don't realize that I've been holding my breath until he lets go.

He smiles and shakes his head at me.

"You're perfect."

Woooshh. There it was again. That oxygen-sucking vortex. *What the hell?*

I must look like I'm panicking because he takes a step back. He stands behind me and grips my shoulders gently, "I mean you look perfect...ly fine."

He urges me to go inside.

"Are you using me as a shield from Aunt Rose?"

Chuckling, he nods. "You caught me. Please protect me from my mother."

I FEEL it the second the glass doors swing open, and we step in. There's weird tension in the air, made even more obvious by the way our moms both suddenly fall silent. They shift in their barstools turning to us as they paste identical casual smiles on their faces.

Earlier when Mom and I arrived, the kitchen was over-flowing with servers and cooks. Now that the party staff have cleared out, probably outside to where the guests will mostly be, I can openly gawk and stare in awe at this kitchen. I notice that quite a bit has changed since the last time I was here. When I was younger, this kitchen was all tan and red-wine wood finishing. Now the entire kitchen still has that rustic vibe to it, but the cabinets have been painted a distressed matte black. All except for the white marble top that tops every surface, including the island, where our moms are perched.

Aunt Rose is a retired lawyer. She now moonlights as an interior designer, mostly catering to her friends and family. The kitchen, along with rest of the house, literally looks like it came straight from the pages of one of the *Architectural Digest* magazines she has laying around their house.

"Hey!" Aunt Rose's eyes dart back and forth between Brad and me. She lifts an eyebrow, and I realize he still has his hands on my shoulders. I step casually off to the side, letting his hands fall, and I turn my gaze towards my mom, who is shoving something in her purse.

"Mom, you okay?"

"Whatdoyoumean?" You can almost hear the air whish in the hurried way she says that as her head pops up and she feigns confusion. "I'm good, Lizzy."

I narrow my gaze at her, about to call her out, when Aunt Rose gets up and claps her hands.

"All right, now that my son has decided to join us, should we all head to the lanai and see what my lovely husband is up to before everyone else arrives?"

She rounds the island and opens one (they have three) of their refrigerators. She shoves a banana and a water bottle at Brad's chest, rolling her eyes. "Here, at least eat that."

Brad hugs them to his heart as he shoots his mom a wink.

"I knew you couldn't stay mad at me, Mom."

Aunt Rose playfully swats his arm as she puts herself in between us then hooks her arms through each of our elbows, beaming at the both of us. "So now that were all friends again…"

Brad nudges his mom, "Mom!" Clearly a warning to not ruin the moment. *Too Soon.*

I resist the urge to groan as my mom joins in and hooks her arm on my other elbow. They sandwich me in. A laugh shoots out from her mouth as her eyes twinkle conspiratorially.

"Rose, come on, let's not embarrass the kids when, judging by my daughter's puffy eyes, they clearly just finished a heart-to-heart."

She pats my cheeks, and my eyes jump to Brad, who is shaking his head in assurance.

Aunt Rose peeks up at Brad now, a mischievous tilt to her grin. "Come to think of it…"

Brad rolls his eyes as he escapes from his mom's grasp to down the water and finish off his banana. Once he drops them in their respective waste bins, he opens the door leading to the backyard. "Let's go before your own guests beat you to your party."

Brad

I push open the door into the house and check the library. *No Lizzy.*

For the last two hours, I have been caught up entertaining relatives, catching up with cousins who live out of state, so I have completely missed the part where Lizzy left her brother's side. Which is another thing I apparently need to be caught up on. Last I remembered, those two couldn't be in the same room without constantly bickering. Now they look closer than ever.

Lizzy lit up the second Dan walked in, and when he came over, I half expected some insults thrown back and forth but was surprised when they hugged like they hadn't just seen each other hours ago. Even more so when Summer followed him in. I will have to ask Liz what that's about. I got pulled by dad just as I am about to ask Summer where Kyle is.

As I pass by the other rooms, I see that their parents are also there.

Aunt Simone, Uncle Nico, Uncle John, and Aunt Jen are hanging out in the foyer talking to each other. The only people missing are Kyle and Kim.

I frown at that; Kyle and I had a chat over burgers Friday night. He said he was coming and even promised that he would talk to Kim. Get her to come with him. I didn't question it when he said that. Something about the way he spoke gave me the impression that something was happening—or already had—

between those two. He would have told me about it if he'd wanted to share that, and I couldn't push the issue either. I know all too well what it is like to have feelings for your best friend—feelings that are hard to explain.

I pull my phone from my back pocket to shoot him a quick text, and that's when I remember what Liz asked me in the library earlier.

I WALK BACK to the sitting area and use the other entry way through the sunroom to get to the other staircase. That will bring me up to the family room faster. I have a feeling Liz might feel more comfortable there given the time she's spent away from this house.

I'm about to shove the door open when I hear what sounds like my mom talking to someone from inside the sunroom.

Her tone stops me in my tracks, "Are you going to tell the kids?"

Another voice cuts in, and this one I recognize as Aunt Cat, Liz's mom. "You know I can't do that."

I hear them sniffing and realize they both sound like they are crying.

I could respect my mother's privacy and back away. Thanks to the hallway in between the sunroom and the sitting room, I am well hidden from them. They would never know I had been here. Something stops me. Judging from the tone of the conversation and my mother's use of the word "kids," I realize that Liz is involved and the urge to find out and protect her pins me to my spot.

"Cat…" My mom's voice wobbles now, sounding like she is about to break. I have to ball my fist into my mouth to keep myself from calling out to make sure she is okay.

What the hell is going on?

44

"Rose… I can't. I want to, but I can't hurt my children again. You weren't there when Will and I sat them down to tell them we were getting a divorce. How they reacted?"

She takes a deep, shuddering breath. "What that did to them? I barely recognize either one of them now."

My mom is sobbing now, and I recognize the sound. It was the same sound she made when my grandpa died. *But no one died. Why is she crying like someone died?*

Then I hear it. What sounds like a wail comes out of Aunt Cat, and that's when I know I've crossed the line. I back away slowly to not alert them to my eavesdropping and hurry out towards the sitting room.

Once I get there, I go up the main stairs and allow myself a few minutes to contemplate whether I should share this information with Liz. I have nothing concrete besides knowing that Liz's mom needed to tell her kids something urgent. That it sounds like my mom is the only one who knows about it. Which might explain how weird they got when we met up in the kitchen earlier. But still, I have nothing. I am still trying to mend my friendship with Liz. What if I tell her this and it turns out to be nothing? Or what if I made things worse by telling her something that needs to come from her mom? I need to trust that if Liz really needs to know whatever it is, that Aunt Cat will tell her—herself. This is none of my business.

Just as I reach the landing that leads to the flight of stairs up to the second floor, I hear my name being called out.

"Yo, B!" I turn to see Kyle bounding up the stairs in a navy-blue sweat suit.

"Hey! You made it." I offer my arm to do a fist bump but stop when I see Kim trudging slowly behind him in a jean jacket and yellow dress, looking like she wants to be anywhere but here.

"Yeah, sorry man. That's on me. I partied a little too hard

last night, woke up hungover. I was late picking up Kim. But we made it. And we're happy to be here, right Kimmy?"

He reaches over to grab Kim's hand and pull her up the stairs faster.

Yup, definitely something there.

Kim sighs as they both come to a stop on the landing beside me. "Where's Liz?"

I chuckle. "Hi to you too, Oscar."

I toss out the nickname I used for her when we were kids whenever she got in one of her moods just to test the waters. And because I can't resist teasing her further, I toss a pointed look at her hand, still holding Kyle's, before raising an eyebrow back at her.

She rolls her eyes at me then pulls her hand back from Kyle to smack me on the arm.

"Okay, I guess someone woke up and chose violence today. Should I be afraid for Liz or are you going to play nice?"

Kyle starts to laugh at the dig then stops when Kim shoots him a glare. *Interesting.*

"Have you guys eaten?" Maybe I should feed her first. Hangry Kim is not a nice person.

Sensing the direction, I'm going; Kyle lets out a booming laugh.

Yup, my friend laughs like a fucking cannon going off.

He nudges Kim's shoulder. "Come on now. You really think I would bring a Hangry Kim here? You saw what happened on Friday. That's what we get when she starves herself to fit in that tiny uniform. Even though she looks perfect just the way she is."

I frown at that. "Wait, you do that? You look fine Kimberly."

Kim taps her foot impatiently, but a smile is tugging at her lips. "Thanks Bradley, now where is Liz?"

I narrow my eyes at her. "I was just on my way up to find her but please be nice."

She makes a *hmmph* sound and tosses her head back, "I am capable of that."

Stifling a laugh, I nod for them to follow me up. "Never said you weren't."

WE GET to the second floor, and I push open the two wooden doors just across the top of the stairs. Our family room takes up one side of the second floor. On the other side are three guests' rooms and, down at the very end of the hall, my parents' room. I check to see if anyone else is around before completely walking in.

Our family room is divided into three different areas. The first area, a home theatre, equipped with a projector setup and screen, reclining seats for twelve people, and surround sound, is completely soundproof and sectioned off from the rest of the room. The second area, in the middle, has a few arcade games, like pinball and Pacman, plus a dartboard, a pool table, and a 70-inch tv mounted on the wall with every gaming console you can think of, an L-shaped leather couch positioned in front of it. The third area is a lounge, furnished with a love seat and a plush sectional. A large cooler filled with drinks sits in between the game room and the lounge area. Next to it are three shelves: one filled with board games, another with blankets, and a smaller one holding books. I suspect those are Lizzy's favorite books. She helped mom set this all up back when we were in middle school, and Mom has never changed any of the books in there.

And that's exactly where we find her. She is curled up on the loveseat with a blanket, reading a book. She looks up when she hears us come in and her eyes widen when she spots who I'm with. I give her an encouraging smile. "You all right?"

Liz stares past me at Kim who holds her gaze for a beat more before looking at me with a tentative smile. "I'm okay, now."

"Hey Lizzy. Don't worry, were not here to bite," Kyle calls out to her as he sets his hands on Kim's shoulder, all but pushing her to sit in the sectional across from Liz.

"I missed you, shorty." He then makes a point of pulling up Liz into a hug, lifting her off the floor. Which looks almost comical given their height difference. Liz is barely tops five-feet while Kyle boasts a six-foot-two frame.

I grab a few Fijis from the cooler, tossing one to Kim.

"Thanks." Impressively, she catches it even though she's distractedly watching Kyle and Liz hug it out. I start to relax. *Maybe this really will be as easy as Kyle assured me it would be.*

Liz starts patting Kyle on the shoulder. "I missed you too, but you can put me down now. Please." The stab of jealousy I feel at seeing her in his arms agrees with that statement.

He chuckles as he sets Liz back down on the loveseat, tossing the blanket, which fell on the floor when he picked her up, back onto her lap. I hand him a water not missing the sly wink he sends me.

The asshole drops down next to Kim, putting his feet up.

I settle on the floor next to Liz and hand a Fiji to her.

"Did you…" I pause remembering that the others don't know yet about her anxiety and it isn't my place to say anything about it.

She pats my hand and just nods at me.

"Did she what?" Kim asks as she sips her water, giving us both a cautious gaze.

I stay silent as I glance over at Liz. I offer her the most reassuring smile I can muster.

I wish we could all talk about what happened before first instead of diving into something that seems like Liz is still coming to terms with it, but the opening is there, and Kim takes it. I mentally kick myself for giving her no other option.

We all watch in silence as Liz closes the book and places it beside her, tucking her legs underneath her.

She looks like she is buying time, trying to figure out how to open up about her struggle. But just as fleeting as her discomfort was earlier, her determination looks like its steadily taking over, as she squares her shoulders and looks straight at Kim.

Liz shrugs and just throws it out there. "I had a panic attack earlier."

Of all the things she could have opened with, I never expected that to be it.

My gaze jumps to the pair sitting on the couch and I register the look of shock on Kim's face. She turns to Kyle beside her, as if asking for a lifeline.

Kyle sits up, resting his elbows on his knees, looking just as equally baffled yet concerned.

"Are you okay? What do you mean, a panic attack? Why?"

A soft laugh escapes Liz and she lets out a breath, leaning back on the loveseat.

"To answer your questions, I'm okay but I have anxiety. I was diagnosed in the ninth grade. And I am guessing the panic attack happened because I also have social anxiety. I don't do well in crowds or at social events." She picks at the hem of her dress again, which I am starting to recognize as one of the telltale signs she is growing anxious.

"There was just…a lot of people outside."

"This happens even around people you know and grew up with?" Kyle asks her gently.

"Social anxiety in general doesn't really discriminate between people I know or don't. Even in this house I practically grew up in with people I've known my whole life. It is just this intense fear, and I have zero control over it." She lets out a frustrated sigh. "Like a nasty stain I can't get rid of. No matter how hard I try."

Kim sets her bottle on the carpet as she moves to mimic Liz's sitting position, leaning against the armrest. "Is that why you haven't been to games or school dances or parties? I mean, not that I've noticed or anything."

Liz's head pops up at the sound of Kim's voice and a hint of a smile appears on her lips.

"Basically, yes."

Kyle leans over and pats Liz's knee, "That explains a lot actually."

"What do you mean?"

I nod in understanding. "I get what Kyle is saying. You got pretty distant—even with me— back then. It was confusing and yeah, I got a little defensive then because suddenly you weren't up to going anywhere, not even coming over here. I mean I know I didn't make it easy Lizzy, I really didn't, so I take the blame for how I acted to make things worse. I should have asked why instead of blowing you off. I should have asked if you were okay or if something was going on." I shrug. "I didn't understand it back then, but I'm starting to now."

Liz stares at me for what feels like a hot minute, her eyes shining as she lets my words wash over her.

Fuck, please don't cry.

I almost say it out loud and have to tamp down the urge not to continue with the words that are sitting at the tip of my tongue.

I had feelings for you back then, and I felt rejected every time I asked you to go somewhere, and you said no. Maybe I should have gone with that? Though knowing what I know now, I'm sure it wouldn't have made a difference. She was going through a lot then and any confession of mine would have just made things worse for her. Now, looking at this girl I once knew, I'm hit with the realization that she isn't the same person she was back then.

And I don't know what to do with that information.

I can't take back the years we lost or those few months when we let our misunderstandings and miscommunications cause a divide between us. I never told her how I felt and frankly, I'm starting to realize that I never took the time to really get over her. Because the more time I spend with her, the more blurred those lines are getting.

Again.

Both our friendship and the fact that I love this girl is still hanging over my head but even that is still very much complicated.

Right now, I don't even know *what* we are.

Are we best friends again? Friends? Acquaintances? Class-mates? What are we?

After a few more moments of just the two of us staring at each other, I hear Kyle clearing his throat. Both our heads turn in unison towards them. Kim is staring down at her lap, her fingers clasped. She appears to be deep in thought.

Kyle shoots me a look that pretty much says, *Get it together Bradley.*

I give him a small nod, letting him know I get the message loud and clear. He returns the nod before placing a hand on top of Kim's bringing her attention to him. Something unspoken passes between them that makes Kim straighten up in her seat.

She sighs before turning her full gaze to us. "You weren't wrong, Liz."

There's something in Kim's eyes and the way Kyle is rubbing his thumb on Kim's knuckles that has me on alert. I feel like a bomb is about to dropped on us.

Liz's brows crumple in confusion. "You have to be more specific Kim."

Kim lets out a long-suffering sigh and jerks her hands from Kyle's to tunnel her fingers through her hair in frustration. "I *was* blowing you off. We both were."

She nods at Kyle, taking a deep breath, and her words come tumbling out in an exhale. Fast and rushed. "Summer before freshman year, Kyle and I dated."

I sit back on my haunches, completely unsurprised but still somehow feeling a twinge of shock at the same time. Thinking back, I remember how that summer both Liz and I left to go on family vacations. We were gone for pretty much the whole summer. I spent most of it travelling with my parents while Liz went to the Philippines with hers on what I now understood was a last-ditch effort by her parents to fix their crumbling marriage.

How when I came back, it felt like something had shifted in our group. That all of a sudden it was hard to just get everyone together even for a quick hang.

Liz sits up, a frown on her face. "I don't understand. Why couldn't you just *tell* us that?"

There's tension in Liz's tone and Kim takes offense at that. Her head tilts as her gaze narrows.

"You were being weird, Elizabeth."

Liz scoffs. "That doesn't explain a thing."

Kim's frustration turns into anger as she leans towards Liz, an eyebrow raised.

"You were my best friend then suddenly you weren't. He was my best friend then suddenly he was something more. You left me to deal with all that on my own. So, excuse me if I got pissed and pretended you didn't exist."

Liz's head rears back like she's been punched, and she blinks rapidly. "I...I guess I deserved that."

Kyle makes a *tsk*-ing sound and regards Kim with a shake of his head. "Getting defensive is exactly what got us to this place. Cut that shit out."

I put up a hand. "Hold up. Can we go back to the part where Kim said you guys *dated*? As in past tense? What happened?"

Kyle shrugs. "We were fifteen. Too much, too soon."

My mouth quirks up. "And now?"

Kyle chuckles as Kim slowly turns to him, wanting to know the answer to that herself.

"We're figuring it out. How's that?" He waggles his eyebrows at her which makes her laugh, the tension melting off of her.

"Okay now that the cat's out of the bag, how about I break this down since I might be the only one with no hang-ups here?"

Can't argue with that. Man is chill as fuck even when the girls go at it.

"You guys weren't around so we hung out together a lot. Started making out. It got way too intense for either one of us to handle on top of having to keep it a secret. We decided to just avoid any situations where we could slip up."

"Why keep it a secret?" Liz asked softly.

Kim rolls her shoulders back and adjusts herself, so she's facing both of us again.

"We didn't set out to at first. Our parents didn't even question us spending all that time together even without you guys around. Then we started hanging out more with the guys from the team and their girlfriends and when you guys came back, it just felt *off*. When I would ask you to come out with us, you would say no. Brad came once but then made an excuse to go early, like if you weren't there, he didn't want to be either. So yeah, I got upset and stopped asking. I was fifteen, falling for a boy I used to give wet willies to and the one person I wanted to share that with wasn't around."

"I wanted to be, though."

"Yes, but with conditions, Liz. You wanted *us* to hang out. It was like you were punishing me for having new friends. I didn't take that well, obviously."

Liz straightens in her seat. "It wasn't like that at all."

"Then explain it to me. Isn't that what we were summoned here for?"

I feel Kim getting defensive again and it takes everything in me not to speak out of turn. This is something between *them*.

I don't need an explanation as to why Kyle didn't tell me. I can figure that out on my own. I turn to look at him and understood what he wants to convey with just a shrug and a nod. I had only told one person about how I felt for Liz and that was Kyle. I'd confessed my feelings back in the sixth grade and as the years went on, he became the one person I vented to after becoming increasingly frustrated between not knowing what to do about my growing feelings and not wanting to ruin my friendship with Liz. I understand without needing him to say it that he had not wanted to rub it in my face how his friendship with our other friend had progressed into a relationship.

I give him mad props for that.

"Kim—" Liz's voice cuts off in a wobbly whisper as she hugs her arms to her chest. With a determined pinch of her mouth that makes me proud as hell, she looks down at her lap and continues. "My parents were fighting every day. That family trip we took to the Philippines? It was supposed to be for eight weeks, but my dad didn't even make it to two. He flew home early. I was left there with my mom reeling and my brother, who was having violent mood swings. I didn't even know what we would come home to. But we never thought it would be to my dad's stuff gone from the house and him making plans to move his practice to California. That he had planned all along to divorce my mom and move to where Danny was going off to college. I was dealing with all of that and I..." She trails off and rubs her eyes, tears pooling at the corners. I'm overcome once again with the sudden urge to pull her into my lap and kick everyone else out of this room.

Kim leans over the armrest, concern etched on her face. "What is it?"

Liz looks up at us as her tears continue to fall. There's something lurking behind her eyes that I can't quite pinpoint. Is that *fear?* What does she have to be afraid of?

"I broke, okay? Just like you, I wanted my best friends to be there for me. I know now that I should have told you why I wasn't comfortable being around other people. I expected you guys to just know something was going on. To…I don't know, maybe check up on me. It was selfish of me to just assume that, and I get that now, but back then it was hard, and at some point, I started hating you all for having lives without me. Deflection? Jealousy, maybe? I couldn't control anything at home. I couldn't even control my own thoughts or feelings. So, when you guys would hang out with other friends or do your own things, I felt cast aside and lonely until I finally decided that if I was feeling that way, I may as well just be alone."

She looks like she has more to say, but like clockwork, she gets a distant look in her eyes, and she visibly shuts off anything that resembles the girl we all used to know.

Falling back on the loveseat with a weary sigh, she closes her eyes. Once again shutting us out and letting us deal with the aftermath of her words while silent tears roll down her cheeks.

I feel like I've been hit by a semi. Her words, her pain, have that impact. Here I was thinking she had been ignoring me, choosing not to hang out with me, when she had been facing battles all on her own.

I should have known she wasn't okay. We had known each other since we were fetuses, for fuck's sake, and I didn't even think to pull up to her house and check on her? I let my damn frustration at thinking I was being friend-zoned make her feel like she meant nothing to me when in fact she meant everything. Another thought hits me at full force. *What if it is too late?*

Something akin to loss rolls over me. I used to be able to read her. I used to be so attuned to her every thought but now she just seemed like an old movie I watched as a child. I can't quite bring back the same feelings or thoughts I had back then. All I have left is the memory of it all. That realization makes me question whether I ever really knew her as much as I thought I did. I can't shake the sinking feeling that everything might be lost. Yes, we are here to make things right. To talk things through. But what if the friendship and closeness we shared before is long gone? What if we can't get it back?

It's one thing to feel tethered together in this moment but what happens when we're back in our own lives? We spent the last three years apart, accustomed to doing our own things. *What happens now?*

I try to push away the thoughts that are starting to bulldoze me as I take in the room.

The aftershock of what Liz said has had a similar effect on the others. Kim is silently crying, and Kyle is hinged forward, his hands clasped in a fist between his knees.

None of us know how we are supposed to act or what we are supposed to say to make things right and move on from this. We all had a hand in ruining our friendship and we haven't even begun to discuss all the horrible words we said to each other back then.

There are too many things bubbling up inside of me threatening to spill out. I know if I even attempt to say anything right now, everything will come pouring out. I can't decide if it will make things better or worse.

I share a somber look with Kyle, and we both decide it isn't the time.

I have no fucking clue if that is even a possibility anymore.

Liz

I feel incredibly exposed. I didn't tell them everything, but I told them enough that now all my insecurities are yelling at me to get up and get out of there. Escape.

I am in no shape to be here. I am about to crack. I have laid it out for them to dissect and prod, should they choose to. Yet no one does. They simply accept it.

I can't figure out if that's good or bad. I swipe at my tears and channel all the therapy I've gotten in the last three years to controlling my emotions. I will the tears to stop flowing as I ponder the possible outcomes of just outright telling them that I almost died. That three years ago, I was sent to rehab and when I came back, I had become a shell of the person I had once been. I don't know how to get the old me back. She feels gone.

She was *their* friend. Not this person I have become.

But I can't even if I wanted to. I simply have nothing more to give right now.

I am tired and worn out. Now all I want to do is to curl up on my own bed. To be back in the safety of my own room. Away from these people I once thought of more as family than my own parents before they bear witness to my impending breakdown.

As if on cue, a knock cuts through the silence and without waiting for a response, my brother walks in. He scans the group and zeroes in on me.

A crease forms between his eyebrows as he reads the room. Judging by the way his mouth pinches, he knows he has interrupted something. His gaze locks with mine. I can tell he is trying to ask me without asking me if I am okay, but he's torn between not knowing how much I divulged to them and whether he simply walked into a fight.

"Liz, Mom isn't feeling well and wants to go home. You ready to go?"

I simply nod and make a move to get up. Suddenly I feel Brad's hand cover mine and I nearly jump from the sudden contact. I drop my blanket at his feet.

I look down at him from his perch on the floor. He looks up at me tentatively as he rises to his feet. His head tilts and his eyes shift between mine like he is trying to read me.

"I should go...Mom had a couple of mimosas. She's not fit to drive."

He stays silent, still holding my hand and searching my eyes, for what, I don't know.

It's like he's panicking. No. He *is* panicking. I know him. I know by the way his thumb is currently pressing gently on my wrist. In the way his shoulders stay rigid as his eyes do that crazy dance between mine, that he's trying to figure out a way to get me to stay.

It would be futile. Nothing he can say right now will make me want to do that.

I turn to my brother and—as calmly as I possibly can—nod towards the door.

"I'll be right down. Stay and hang out with Summer. I'll take mom home."

He raises an eyebrow at me, and I know he's shocked that I noticed the way he walked in with Summer earlier. I did. I'm happy for him. If there is something going on there, I hope that is enough reason for him to want to stay here. Something other than his helpless sister.

I shake my myself out of my stupor. I match his raised eyebrow and he scans the room one more time, his gaze lingering at Brad's hand on mine before he heads out.

I square my shoulders and get up.

Brad drops his hand, his eyes following my movements as I walk around him to face them.

Kim looks like she wants to say something but doesn't know where to start. She's staring at Brad with a curious look in her eyes like she's also trying to figure out what's gotten him in such a knot. I catch Kyle's eye as he looks away from the door. And it's just now that I realize that he might be wondering what's going on with our siblings too.

"My sister and your brother?"

I have to smile at that, "Yeah. I think they hung out last night. He mentioned hanging out with a friend. I'm guessing it was Summer since they came together."

Kyle laughs. "*Sweeeeeet*. Dan's always been cool. Maybe my sister will learn to have fun more if she dates your brother instead of the losers she usually hangs out with."

Kim sniffs and smacks him on the arm. "Can we focus?"

Kyle puts his hands up and leans back, making a *carry-on* motion with hands.

"Look, I-"

Brad cuts me off with a hand under my elbow, "Can you please stay and talk with us?"

I sigh, not in the mood to argue or explain the many reasons why that isn't a good idea, so I go with what will make the most sense to him.

"Brad. I think we've said more than enough today, don't you think? I know there's still more to unpack and talk about, but we can't all of a sudden just forget like we haven't spent the last three years as strangers. It's going to take more than just one conversation to change that..."

I look over at the others. Give them what I hope comes off as a sincere smile in spite of the anxiety I feel building up inside me. "If we even decide to do that."

I clench my fists to my side to ease my nerves as I address Kim and Kyle,

"I'm really happy for you guys. I am so sorry I was blind to it before, but I see it clear as day now, you guys are great together."

"I know, right?" Kyle grins as he attempts to wrap an arm around Kim who ribs him. A blush creeps up her cheeks as she turns to us, wiping her eyes on the sleeves of her denim jacket.

"Liz is right."

Kyle waggles his eyebrows and whoops. Kim rolls her eyes and gets up to stand as well.

"*What I mean is* we've shared quite a bit today. I don't think we should push each other to do more than that."

She waves a dismissive hand around when Brad looks like he's about to argue with her.

"Besides, like it or not, were stuck with each other for the rest of the year. Thanks to Santos. Let's not force this all at once."

She gives me her signature half smile and before I realize it, I get swept up in a quick hug. She steps back and raises an eyebrow at Brad.

"I think Liz and I need to figure out our own shit too." She gestures towards me. "*When* were *both* ready to."

I don't even know how to react to this complete one-eighty from her. I don't know if it's because I finally admitted to having mental illness or the fact that I complimented her relationship with Kyle—which I have to admit I am incredibly curious about—but she got over our tiff pretty quickly by the looks of it. If I had known this was all it would take for her to acknowledge me and possibly be my friend again, I would have done it a long time ago.

No, no I wouldn't have. Because I'm a coward.

Which is why I need to get the hell out of here.

"Right, Liz?"

I nod in agreement as I look over at Brad. He still has that worried look on his face.

And that's what makes *me* worry. I peer up at him and there is something else in his expression. It is definitely concern, but about what? Maybe for my mom? But she's probably just reeling from all the mimosas she had today. Why would he be worried about that? Or maybe he's concerned that my leaving right now will erase the progress we have made?

I fight against the nerves as I reach out to pat his arm. All I want to do is to reassure him that we are good. That I am not running from this. But he captures my hand in his and keeps it in place on his arm.

"Brad? What's wrong?"

Something passes over his face. Then he blinks and its gone. It happens so fast I don't have time to decipher it. He takes a step back and offers me a small smile that doesn't quite reach his eyes. "Nothing. Kim is right. You're right. Let's not rush. We have time."

My forehead creases in confusion but in the back of my mind, I'm aware my mom is waiting for me. I glance at the door and then back at them.

Now I'm starting to worry about her.

"I should go. My mom doesn't really drink anymore. The mimosas may be getting to her."

Kim picks up her phone from the edge of the couch,

"Do you still have the same number?"

Still reeling from her complete change of attitude, all I can muster is a nod in return.

"Okay, I'll text you."

Brad

I watch as Liz gives us a small smile and a wave before heading out.

I was trying to get Liz to stay so we could finish talking it out, but the girls are right. It's too soon. Just from what was shared today, it already feels like an emotional punch in the gut. I don't think I could have handled any more either, to be honest. Then what Dan said registered, and it all nearly spilled out. I considered telling them what I overheard downstairs.

I know that if I had done that, it would have been my desperate attempt to keep her here and it would not have been fair to her or her family.

A throat being cleared breaks into my thoughts. I look away from the door only to find Kyle grinning with his arms stretched out on the couch and Kim tilting her head at me, her arms folded. She has a weird expression on her face, like she's figuring something out.

"How long?" She demands, pointing a finger at me.

My brows wrinkle as I plop down on the chair Liz just vacated. "How long what?"

I pick up the blanket that fell, trying to avoid her eyes.

"How long have you had feelings for Liz?"

I feel my eyes go wide as I turn an accusatory look at Kyle. "Bro, you told her?"

Kyle chuckles. "No, but you just did."

My head snaps back just in time to see Kim slap a hand over her mouth.

Well *fuck*.

"Oh, my god! *How* the *hell* did I miss that? It all makes sense now."

Kim starts pacing the room and I can only watch in silence. I don't even understand my own feelings for Liz. I'm not about to confess to something I have yet to figure out.

"Like how long Brad? Since when? Oh my god, in the sixth grade when Evan Hudson asked her out to the dance, and you got all pissy and picked a fight with her and she had to buy you that lizard to get you to talk to her again. Was that when? Was that *why*?"

She takes one look at my face and squeals...or I think that's the sound that comes out of her mouth. "Shit, I am right. I *know* I am."

She continues to pace for a few more minutes and Kyle laughs, slapping his knee.

"Can't believe you confessed to being in love with Liz without actually confessing to it."

What. The. Hell. Kyle.

Kim turns around fast and nearly screams, "You're in love?"

I bury my face in my hands, leaning my elbows on my knees.

"Yell a little louder, Kimberly. I don't think Liz heard you from downstairs."

"Oh please, this room is soundproof. No one heard me."

I groan and through clenched teeth, I sound out every word. "The. *Theatre*. Is. Soundproof."

"Oh oops." *Oops*? I look up and stare at her.

I kept that a secret for six years and all she can say is *oops*?

At least Kyle has the decency to look sorry. He grabs Kim

by her outstretched hand. Pulls her gently down beside him. "Babe. Let's take it down a notch. Breathe."

"I can't calm down. This is too..." Her eyes go wide, and she grabs Kyle by the arm, "Wait. Wait just a damn minute. You knew and you didn't tell me!"

Kyle shrugs, "It wasn't my secret to tell."

"Right." She turns to me, "Brad... Does Liz know?"

I shake my head. "Look, I had feelings for her back then. No use bringing it up now."

Kyle snorts. "You still do man."

Kim rolls her eyes, "All I had to do was watch you watching her, and I knew." Then she shakes her head in disbelief. "I *cannot* believe it took me this long to figure that out."

I push off the chair and grab a Coke from the cooler. I want something stronger to get me through the direction this conversation is going but my parents are downstairs, not to mention half of my extended family. My mom won't care if I drink a beer or two as long as I do it at home, but my grandma definitely would.

"So how come you never told her?"

Kim has now turned to face me to continue her interrogation. Her elbows are propped on the back of the couch as she watches me, her chin in her hands.

I would laugh at how absurd this scene is if it wasn't so at odds with how I am feeling.

I shrug, popping open the bottle in my hand using the bottle opener on the side of the cooler.

"Lots of reasons, I guess. At first, it was because I was confused. She was my best friend. I couldn't remember a time when I didn't love her, so it took some time for me to figure out that I definitely felt more for her than just plain affection... especially since it was completely different from how I felt about well... you. In a lot of ways." I grimace, "No offense."

She grins, "I'm not pressed. Please continue."

I take a sip, then another as I think back on how to explain it in a way that makes sense.

"Then I got scared. What if she didn't feel the same or couldn't even picture *feeling* the same way and things got awkward? What if we stopped being friends because of it?"

I pause, feeling the familiar wave of emotions wash over me.

"And then when it got way too hard to keep it all bottled in and I made up my mind to tell her, she got, well...you know."

I search for the perfect word without minimizing what she was going through at the time.

Now that I am actually privy to that information I want to tread carefully and respectfully.

"Distant?" Kyle offered.

I point at him, acknowledging the word. "Yeah...well, I got pissed after that. Every time I planned on telling her, she wouldn't want to go out. I felt like I was being rejected before I could even confess. Then when she came to us that day and told us she wanted to stop being friends? I felt like my fucking heart got ripped out. Took me awhile to get over it."

I down the rest of the soda and toss the empty bottle into the recycling bin. I thump my chest as I let the fizz burn through me, mimicking the tide of emotions threatening to drown me.

"I couldn't exactly go up to her and say hey, by the way, can we maybe try dating?"

Kim looks over at Kyle and sighs, "I guess we really all did have our own shit."

Kyle snorts, "Deadass."

"What about now?"

Kim really isn't going to drop this until she squeezes every last drop of information from me. *Figures.*

I plop back down on the love seat and shake my head at her.

"I don't know, Kim. This is the most time I've spent with Liz since we all spoke last, and I don't even know if what I'm feeling right now is the same damned thing, I felt three years ago or if I'm just feeling whiplash from us all talking like this again."

She sighs, "Fair enough. Do you want to know what I think?"

"I'm sure you'll tell me anyways. So go on."

She rolls her eyes so hard; I swear she probably saw stars back there.

"She's different but still the same with you...and honestly, judging by the way you literally have this whole alpha male thing going on when she's around, it seems like you're already way past being confused. You're so far gone. I'm shocked you haven't been chasing after her this whole time. Like seriously, Brad, what are you thinking? We're not even close anymore and I saw through you within minutes. You need to be honest with yourself before you can even begin to be honest with her. Look at you all wound up."

I cringe thinking back on all the times I hovered over Liz today. All the times I just reached out to her instinctively and acted like the last three years hadn't happened.

I have always been protective of Liz, but something felt different today. I was feeling desperation and fear. And utter *happiness*. Something I haven't really felt in a while.

Clearly it was always there, beneath the surface just biding its time. Maybe it was that through all the years, my feelings for her remained dormant. Then comes this sudden change in our dynamic and now it's pushing to the brim, threatening to spill over like lava.

I need to get a grip and admit it, even if it is just to myself, that nothing has changed.

I feel exactly the same way for her as I did before.

I love her.

As I always have. I just got good at hiding it. Deflecting it. Ignoring the ache, I felt every day that I wasn't in her life anymore. Dating around to try and forget her. Throwing myself into my dream. Trying to stay busy at school to avoid reaching out to her like I desperately wanted to. Looking away when I saw her in school, pretending she didn't even exist when everywhere was a memory of her. With her.

Even up in my bedroom, I still have pictures of her displayed on my dresser. Ones I should have gotten rid of a long time ago but never could bring myself to remove.

"You still have pictures of Liz up in your bedroom?"

Fuck. I must have said that last part out loud.

"HELLO?" Liz sounds surprised as she answers.

"Hey, it's me Kim." I roll my eyes at her. Kim rolls hers right back. The last few days have sucked. Liz hasn't been to school, and I wondered if Liz might be avoiding us. I think I fucked up by pushing too hard last weekend. I've spent the last few days stewing, pissed at myself.

I don't feel comfortable enough in our friendship to text her and ask her if everything is okay, but evidently Kim does.

I have to quell the urge to smile, Kim came rushing into the student council office a few minutes ago. She demanded to know if I had checked on Liz.

When I said no, she took her phone out and called Liz.

And she put it on speakerphone.

"Yeah. I know." Liz's soft chuckle breaks into our eye rolling. Kim covers her mouth to suppress a laugh at the grin that breaks out of my face when I hear her laughter. Doesn't stop her from pointing at it though.

"I hope it's okay that I'm calling and not texting. I'm just checking in since you haven't been to school. Are you okay?"

I can hear the shock in Liz's voice, "Oh yeah... My mom's been sick the last few days. I guess it wasn't the mimosas. I just didn't want to leave her because Danny had online classes for the last two days and then had to take his finals. But I'll be back tomorrow."

"Is Aunt Cat okay now?" Oh shit, that came from me.

"Brad?"

"Yeah, it's me." I scrub a hand over my mouth, annoyed with my inability to keep it cool when it comes to Liz.

"Is Kyle—?"

Kim swats my arm and I cringe, careful not to make a sound but that shit hurt. I have more respect for Kyle now.

"No, he's at practice."

"Oh, okay." The confusion is evident in her voice. "I think she's feeling better now that she can actually eat without throwing up, but she's going to see her doctor tomorrow just in case."

In the background, we hear Aunt Cat calling her.

I frown because again I'm reminded of the conversation I overheard.

"Okay, well we'll let you go but... can we all get together at Kyle's tomorrow for Social Studies?" Kim rushes to ask before Liz hangs up.

"Sounds like a plan. I have to go make dinner; do you guys need anything else?"

Kim gives me a pointed look and I respond, "No but it's good to know everything is okay."

I hear the smile in her voice. "I appreciate you both checking up on me. I'll see you tomorrow. Bye."

Kim taps her screen, shoving her phone in her sweats. She

scans me from head to toe making me feel like a kid who got caught sneaking into the kitchen at midnight to eat ice cream.

Yes, that happened. Once or twice.

Shaking her head, she kicks the door closed with her foot without looking then places her hands on my desk, leaning forward like a cop in an interrogation room.

"We need to talk."

I'M on my way to English class when I see Liz almost knock down a few freshmen as she hurries past them to her locker.

I realize I have never seen her late to school until now. She doesn't even notice that I am standing just a few feet away from her. She fumbles with her combination for a few more seconds before resting her forehead on her locker and huffing out a breath, willing herself to calm down.

Before I know it, I'm already tapping her on the shoulder and taking her backpack from her. She turns her head in surprise and when she realizes it's me, she drags out a sigh of relief.

I tamp down the impulse to pull her sweater up over her exposed shoulder. She's wearing an oversized light blue sweater over a white tank top, with jeans and ankle high boots.

But her hair is pulled up in a messy bun, clear evidence that she was in a rush.

Cute as fuck.

I ignore the tugging in my heart at her doe-eyed expression as she gazes up at me.

"Can I help?"

She nods and steps away from her locker, extending her hand,

"I can carry my backpack if you can help me get this locker open. Please."

I nudge her, "We have English together next, I got it. What's your combination?"

She pauses as she wrings her hands, and I gently grip her knuckles, untangling her fingers.

I wonder if my being here is actually making her anxiety worse. My stomach churns at the thought of me being a stressor for her. She must read my mind because she shakes her head profusely.

"Sorry, it just took me a minute. I'm not used to this"—she gestures between the two of us—"yet."

I force a nod. After the talk I had with Kim yesterday and her urging me to hang out with Liz like I used to in an effort to get to know her again, I'm feeling pretty vulnerable and exposed.

"Your combo?"

"Oh, yeah...uh, right. Um, it's my birthday." A shaky sigh comes out of her, and I notice that her hands were now gripping her arms a little too tightly. "One-one-seven."

Like I could forget her birthday.

"I remember."

I earn a genuine smile from her with that. My stomach flip flops at the sight of it.

Fucking butterflies.

I hunch over and work on the lock. I hear her sigh in exasperation.

"Is everything okay Liz?"

She turns, leaning her back on the locker next to hers. She lets out an uneven breath.

"Yeah, I just don't like rushing to school like this. It makes me restless and when I'm anxious, things go wrong, and I have a hard time focusing."

"What happened?" Her lock comes off and I take a step

back, leaning my shoulder on the locker next to hers as she starts taking stuff out of it. Her mouth pinches in annoyance.

"Danny wanted to use my car instead of getting a rental like he usually does. So, now I have to wait for him to come get me later. And you know my brother, he is never on time anywhere. *That* makes me nervous."

I chuckle, "Can I give you a ride? I mean, aren't we all meeting up later to get started on that project anyways? You can ask him to come get you at Kyle's, if that makes you feel more comfortable, but one of us can always take you home." I put a hand up because she looks like she's going to argue with me. "And before you get pissed about this, I'm telling you that I don't mind, and neither will they."

She relents with another smile as she shuts her locker and holds a few books to her chest.

"Okay, thank you. I really appreciate it."

"Anytime." I tug the books gently out of her grip and carry them for her, nodding in the direction of our classroom and she falls in step with me. "What are friends for?"

Liz

On the car ride to Kyle's, Brad wastes no time telling me all about the game he's working on and what he hopes to accomplish with it before he graduates.

I can tell he's excited to finally be able to share what he's been working on with me. His face grows more animated, the happiness evident in his voice.

It is incredibly fascinating, actually—I've always thought of his as brilliant. Now I have definitive evidence of that and more. I smile at the excitement almost radiating from him. He talks about a breakthrough he recently had on an app he was helping develop for his dad's company. I feel a pang of regret at having missed so much of his life.

Disappointed in myself that I didn't bear witness to all the times he created something that made him so proud and happy.

He keeps looking at me to gauge my reactions and each time his eyes get brighter, like he can't believe I'm actually here with him. I'm hit with the continuing realization that in an effort to protect myself, I failed my best friend. I vow never to do that again. I need to make a conscious effort to be more present for him. To try and match all the efforts he's putting into rebuilding what we lost.

I don't know why I even have any doubts when we fall into conversations just as easily as we always have. It feels like we never even stopped being friends.

It is just *that* easy between us. As it always has been.

I feel grateful that he's making such an effort in catching me up on everything I missed.

I feel the guilt, knowing I may not be able to share just as much with him.

I'm still not ready to disclose everything and that is eating at me. I don't know when or if I will ever be ready to tell him or the others everything, but I cling to the fact that at least we're attempting to restore what once was. I only hope it's not too late.

WHEN WE GET to Kyle's, it becomes a slightly different story.

It starts a little awkward, with me standing in the hallway while they exchange pleasantries. Kim, being who she is, crosses over to me within seconds and engulfs me in a hug so tight that it almost has me in tears. But luckily Kyle does what he does best and breaks the tension. He lifts me playfully off the floor and twirls me so fast that I almost pass out. Brad has to physically wrangle me out of his hold which earns another five minutes of them bantering back and forth until things settle down to a good and easy rhythm. Too good actually.

It takes me awhile to get them to focus because Kim and Kyle are getting too comfortable in their PDA around us. I nearly have to use tools just to pry their lips and hands off of each other. After I show them what I have already outlined and researched for our individual parts in the project, everyone gets to work.

After a few moments, I raise my head from my laptop to rest my eyes. I glance around the room to check if they were still on track and fight a smile when I see Kyle hunched over on the floor across from me by the couch, deep in concentration. People never give him enough credit. Dude is easily the most popular kid in school, with his easygoing personality and affinity for making everything light and fun. Beyond that, he gets straight A's, is kind to everyone, and always works hard at everything. Unfortunately, the kids in our school don't see that. All they see is this star athlete who has led our football team to two straight undefeated seasons. They see the captain of the football team who apparently also has a YouTube channel dedicated to covering his favorite songs.

I shake my head in awe of my friend. I just found out about the YouTube channel today and I can't help but marvel at his many talents.

Kyle is a freaking triple threat. Looks and talent with a good heart.

My two friends couldn't be more perfect for each other.

Kim is a catch herself. She just as easily rivals Kyle's popularity and looks.

And as far as personality goes, she is just as easygoing and lighthearted as her boyfriend. Only difference is she saves that side of her solely for those closest to her. She's a ball-buster to everyone else and definitely not one to be messed with. I've heard stories of girls who quit the cheerleading squad because they were scared of her.

If looks could kill, she would have you on the floor in seconds.

I look above him to where Kim is sitting on the couch. Her mouth is pinched, her laptop between her raised knees as she types up her part of the project. I know Kim struggles with school, and that's why I pretty much did most of the work for her part because I didn't want her to stress out about it. I may not know what's been going on with her for the last three years, but I *know* her. The easier I make it for her, the less pressure she puts on herself. I don't know if her situation at home improved since we last spoke about it, but life in her family has never been easy. Both her older sisters were overachievers at school, both graduated at the tops of their respective classes. Something Kim wasn't inclined to do. Her talents lie elsewhere. The need to meet her parents' expectations gets to her sometimes and the pressure to be a good example for her younger brothers has made it significantly worse for her.

For the third time today, I admire the knit sweater she's wearing over her dark distressed jeans, knowing my talented seamstress of a friend made it. She shows me the small shop she has on Etsy, selling custom made jewelry. She talks about her dream of starting her own fashion line after graduation. I can't help but gush and tell her I'd be her first client. Which then launches her into a description of the pieces she will create for me. The unexpected grin that crosses my face gets the attention of Brad, who is sitting on the floor next to me. He nudges me, an eyebrow raised in question. I just shake my head, embarrassed at getting caught and nudge him back. I get back to working on typing out my research.

The nerves never go away for me. I'm still feeling at odds with how well we all just gelled again like nothing ever happened. It's as if our misunderstandings, our fights, and the confessions we made to each other just a few days ago are nothing but a memory only I carry with me. I really hope I get over this nervous feeling I have around them so I can ask about what's going on between Kyle and Kim. It looks like it's getting serious, and I am itching to know the details. The timeline between their breakup and reconciliation is distinctly eating at my Type A-brain. I'm dying to know what happened.

I expel a breath, forcing my focus and attention back into outlining the phone interview I had with my mom's agent about the importance of diversity in literature.

I become so engrossed that I don't notice Kyle jumping to his feet and rushing to me in a state of panic.

"Lizzie..." Kyle says, in barely a whisper.

It took a few moments before it registers to me that he's talking to me. If he wasn't standing so close, I doubt I would have even heard him.

I look up, momentarily distracted by Brad getting up at the same time. Then Kim. Kyle puts his phone in front of Brad like he's asking for help to explain what's on it.

I become slightly annoyed but work on schooling my facial expression into something more neutral. We really needed to finish this part of our assignment.

The progress report is due in two days.

A slight frown touches my lips because now Kim is also reading whatever is on Kyle's phone, her eyes wide in alarm. I'm still in the dark, waiting for someone to clue me in.

"*Yes*?"

Kyle drops to his knees in front of me and rests his hands gently on my shoulders,

"Aunt Cat is in the hospital. It doesn't sound good. Summer texted me because you weren't answering your phone. Dan wants me to take you. Right now."

THE DRIVE to the hospital is excruciating. My phone had died before the end of the school day, so I couldn't even see what Summer had texted me or the number of times she attempted to reach me. As soon as Kyle dropped that bomb on me, my brain went on autopilot. I manage to not break down, but I am so out of it that I start walking to the door without a word to anyone. Kim has to hold onto me and direct me to Brad's car. I didn't even grab any of my stuff, but thankfully Brad did. He had Kyle drive so he can stay with me in the backseat.

I want to call my mom. Hear her voice. Talk to her. But I know she won't answer.

I felt it in my gut. There is something terribly wrong with Mom. Dan couldn't even bring himself to tell me and had Summer try to reach me.

I start to feel the fear and trepidation build up inside me, but I will myself to stay calm.

Brad continues to hover over me protectively, switching back and forth between asking me if I am okay and what he can do for me. I just keep shaking my head in response, hoping he will just leave me alone to my thoughts for now.

Kim, who's up front in the passenger seat, keeps looking over her shoulder at me. I know she's trying to catch my eye. I continue to gaze past her and stare ahead.

I am so far gone in my head; I don't even notice when we finally arrive at the hospital.

As soon as Kyle parks the car, Kim gets out and meets me at my door. She slings an arm around my shoulders as she steers me to the front of the hospital where we find Summer waiting for us out front. I look up and realize we are not in the emergency room.

What's going on? Where is my mom? Where's Dan?

I try to say that out loud, but my voice betrays me. I start to sway, and Kim's hold tightens.

"What's going on? Is Aunt Cat, okay?" Kyle's voice is strong, but it turns raspy as he says my mom's name.

That's when I notice Summer's red rimmed eyes. Her hair is sticking to her face like she has hastily swiped at tears to cover up the fact that she has been crying.

She attempts to smile at me, but she fails as her mouth starts to quiver.

She peers over her shoulder, "I'll let Dan tell you. I'll take you upstairs."

We follow her to the line of elevators at the end of the hall and as she punches the floor number. *Ten.* I realize we are headed towards the part of the hospital where long-term care patients stay. I remember this from the time Mom had a bad case of influenza two years ago and stayed at the hospital for a few weeks.

Kim still has her arm around me. For the first time in the last hour, it hits me that none of them have left my side from the moment they heard my mom was in the hospital. That thought has me reaching for Kim's hand on my shoulder and squeezing it. Hoping she knows just how much I appreciate them being there for me even if I can't find the words to voice it out just now.

AS THE DOORS OPEN, I see the familiar shape of my brother pacing back and forth in the waiting area. I start to run to him but freeze to a standstill at the sight of him charging towards me.

Dan's face is scrunched up in anger, his shoulders rigid with tension and his hands are fisted to his sides. And he looks *furious* as he makes his way to me.

Summer makes a beeline past me to him and holds a hand to his chest, stopping him before he reaches me. Suddenly Brad is at my side, his hand on my elbow.

"How could you *not* tell me that Mom has cancer?!"

I take a mental step back as my mind struggles to make sense of what my brother has just yelled.

My mouth drops open in shock as I watch my brother continue to shake with rage.

"Are you fucking kidding me, Elizabeth? After all we have been through, you keep this shit from me? How could you not tell me?"

Then like pieces of a puzzle, my consciousness starts registering his words. They start to fall piece by piece as my brain fights to put it together.

I feel my whole body start to shake. My knees unbuckle and I feel Brad wrap an arm around my waist keeping me upright. I start to lose control of my senses. My vision starts to blur, and my hearing fails me. I know words are being said to me. By Dan. By Brad. By Kim.

But I am still stuck trying to finish this puzzle in my head.

Cancer. He said cancer. He said I kept it from him. Cancer? Mom has cancer? How could I keep a secret I don't know? Cancer? Mom doesn't have cancer. She is fine. She is healthy. She is okay. She doesn't have cancer. So why is he yelling about cancer? Cancer?

Mom has cancer.

"She didn't know."

Aunt Rose? Somehow her voice breaks into my raging thoughts, and I turn with everyone in time to see her walking out of an elevator.

She stops in front of me and cradles my face in her palms, swiping at my tears with her thumbs. That's when I realize I'm crying.

"I am so sorry, honey."

"Mom, what's going on?"

She leans back, placing her hands firmly on my shoulder. She turns to Brad and sighs.

"Let's sit while we wait for the doctor to come out and I'll tell you what I know."

Brad

I listen as my mom recounts the sequence of events from when Aunt Cat first found out she had cancer (two years ago), to when she started treatment (two years ago at this very hospital), to when her doctor informed her that her cancer had progressed (last week) and she would not recover from it.

I listen to Mom, but my eyes are fixed on my best friend. The devastation my mom's words inflict play out on Liz's face.

The shock. The horror. The fear. The anger.

I do nothing but helplessly stare as silent tears roll down her cheeks and she shakes from the range of emotions. I yearn to be beside her comforting her but as soon as Mom assured her brother that Liz did not in fact know their mom is dying, Dan's anger for his sister melted away and he scrambled to sit beside her and hold her. Now they sit side-by-side with their hands clasped together.

I sit back and lean my head on the chair opposite them.

I'm seated next to Summer, Kim, and Kyle, all of us wearing identical expressions of hopelessness and distress. We sit here quietly watching our friends fall apart at the news of their mom's diagnosis.

I stare at the ceiling and clench my fists on my lap.

All I want to do is take Liz out of here. Away from everything hurting her.

Or at the very least, take her out of her seat and into my

arms. I want to hold her and tell her I'll be there for her. That I will always be there for her.

But time and place. And this isn't it.

"I don't understand why Mom would keep this from us." At some point Liz has found her voice and the heartbreak is so palpable in it. Her grief unmistakable.

I scrub my face with my palms, and my heart shatters for her. With every sniff and quiver in her voice, I'm being sliced open, her pain seeping into me like it's my own.

I wish there is a way I can spare her from all of this. I'd do it in a heartbeat.

Mom shakes her head, her voice hoarse with grief at the impending loss of her best friend, "Let's make one thing clear, your mom's intention was never to hurt you."

She puts a hand on top of Liz and Dan's joined ones. There's a tremor in her voice.

"You two have been through so much in the last few years. All she wanted was to shield you from more pain. She was doing what she could to protect you both while hoping the treatments would work."

Dan's head has been bent this whole time, but it snaps up and jerks towards Liz. He kneels in front of her and starts rubbing her arms. I sit up, wondering what I missed.

Then Liz starts...hyperventilating. It takes me a second then it hits me: Liz has cues. I read up on anxiety last night so I could understand and support her better. I read that people who suffered with disorders like she does have cues that signal an impending anxiety or panic attack. Before it even happens, Dan has read her cues and knows what she needs.

Mom's head turns slightly towards us, a strange expression on her face. She quickly turns away and takes out a bottle of water from her purse. She hands it to Dan.

That's when another thing hits me. My mom has known this

whole time what my best friend has been going through. She's kept it from me. I have always wondered why she never pushed for me to fix my friendship with Liz like she does most things. It was because she was afraid that she might accidentally let it slip. I don't know whether to be pissed at her or appreciate how much she loves Liz enough to safeguard her secret.

I choose the latter.

I know and don't have to guess how much Mom loves Liz. She's always saying how Liz is the daughter she never had. Usually with a twinkle in her eye and a knowing look in my direction. My stomach starts churning, the acid rising as my own anxious feelings grow. I would be fucked up if it was my mom in here. I can't believe this is Liz and Dan's reality.

I still didn't know all the details, like where Aunt Cat is right now and how she is doing.

Or how Dan managed to find out.

All I know is that she's dying.

And it will happen soon.

Liz

My breath hitches as I watch Nurse Zjan do her routine check on my mom.

Checking her vitals, getting a blood sample and making sure the various bags of fluids and medication that are currently being fed to her through IV are doing their jobs.

I bite the inside of my cheek as I struggle against another cry-fest.

The day nurse, whom I have come to adore, gives me a sad smile as she adjusts the nasal cannula that's providing my mom with oxygen.

It has been nine days since we first found out about our mom's cancer.

Brad's parents pulled some strings with the help of our dad's connections here at the hospital and got Mom her own private suite with extended visiting hours.

Dan's currently at home getting a much-needed shower and change of clothes. He's been alternating with Aunt Rose, who is spending every Tuesday and Thursday night here at the hospital. Danny stays Sunday, Monday, and Wednesday nights; I volunteered to do Fridays and Saturdays. This weekend will be my first alone.

Last weekend, Aunt Rose stayed to make sure my mom got everything she needed. But Dan promised me that this week, I would get my turn.

Dan fought tooth and nail to be here more than three days, but Aunt Rose insisted that she would not let us do that. She wanted to do right by her best friend and make sure her kids still stayed kids. I love Aunt Rose, but I agree with my brother. We need to be here for mom. She has been suffering alone this whole time to make sure we didn't suffer. This is the least we can do for her. I just wish she would wake up and talk to us already. *Before…*

I shut my eyes tight, willing that thought to go away. I am not ready for that.

Will *never* be ready.

I refuse to dwell on it now when I need to make the most of the time, I still have with her.

Mom…please wake up.

"Can I get you something, anak?" Nurse Zjan asks me in a quiet voice as she takes a seat on the couch beside me. When I first met her and she called me anak, I almost broke down. My mom calls me that sometimes. It translates to "my child" in Tagalog, a term of endearment Filipino parents call their kids. Nurse Zjan is a Filipina in her 50s who doesn't look a day over 35. She has grown fond of Dan and me. She even brings us fruits and snacks from Seafood City, each time making excuses about buying too much, but I know why she does it. She sees two young siblings taking care of their dying mother and because she is a mom too, she wants to take care of us in her own way.

I open my eyes, knowing they are glistening with unshed tears, and shake my head.

"I'm okay, po."

She pats my cheek but doesn't push which I just love about her. She knows there is nothing anyone can do to make this situation better for any of us.

"I'm just a button away. Press it if you need me." She gets

up, checking Mom's bed pan under the bed. "Leave this to me, anak. You have other things to worry about."

I nod my response. The first day we were here, I took to dumping the bed pan out in the bathroom every hour because I needed to do something with my hands. But Nurse Zjan caught me. She gently told me it was her job then brought me towels and a bowl, showing me how to give my mom a towel bath. It's as if she knew I felt a need to do something for my mom. Every day since then, I find a fresh set of towels and a bowl in the bathroom waiting for me. Even when she is off shift, it's there. I'm guessing she made sure the other nurses on rotation know.

My phone vibrates in my bag, and I realize I have not checked it all day. Fridays are usually a short day for me, so I opted to just take the day off of school. I wanted to spend more time with Mom and give Dan a break.

I hit the side button and punch in my passcode. I wait as it takes eons to load because I'm frugal and haven't upgraded my phone since middle school. Besides until recently, only my parents and brother ever texted or called me. With the occasional texts from the students, I tutored.

Most days, I forget I even own a phone.

I sigh at the number of messages I have. I appreciate their concern, but my mind has not had time to process this new reality yet. I'm already struggling with my anxiety and depression. Getting more overwhelmed. At the same time, I feel guilty for my lack of efforts. Brad texts me every day, and so does Kim. Kyle texts me every now and then but mostly just gifs or one liners intended to make me laugh. I'm guessing it's because Summer probably updates him. She has taken a semester off school and is here with Danny most days.

Feeling like an awful sister for not checking on him more, I make a mental note of asking him how it's going between them. I don't remember even asking him how they started.

I start swiping and reading my messages, actually pausing to smile at Kyle's gif of the day which is of a man peering over a bush and making a face. I can imagine him doing just that like he had when we were kids whenever he would get it in his head that it would be fun to scare Kim or me. Each time, it earned him a beating from her.

Man, how times have changed.

The last few days at school, they did their best to engage with me. To check up on me like I had accused them of not doing before. But I would just smile, nod, and mutter an excuse about catching up on schoolwork. At school, I have to wear a mask—I refuse to have a meltdown there. If they kept hovering like that, I knew I would—could—break at any moment. I started skipping lunch and just hanging out at the library. I cancelled all my tutoring sessions for the next few weeks. I lugged all my books and notebooks in my backpack so I could avoid stopping at my locker and inviting conversation. I communicated through email about our Social Studies project and responded to text messages—usually hours later—with one-word responses.

I didn't have anything more to give than that.

But I do feel the guilt and miss how carefree we were as kids. Hanging out at Brad's house, having sleepovers and staying all hours of the night just content to be with each other.

A few days ago, if you'd asked me, I would have said that was a possibility again, but now as I look over at Mom, I grasp that it really isn't.

That first day after Aunt Rose had sat us down in the waiting room, Doctor Levin came out and explained to us in detail what the next months were going to look like for Mom.

If she even lived that long. The good doctor made sure to emphasize that it was a big *if.*

I don't have the mental or emotional bandwidth needed to

repair broken friendships when I have to focus all of what I have into taking care of Mom and giving her what she needs while supporting my brother through this.

I'm filled with an overwhelming sense of guilt as Dr. Levin's words wash over me again. I never should have gone to school that day and insisted on driving her to that appointment. Instead, I took Mom at her word. She drove herself only to end up passing out and hitting her head hard on the steering wheel. She had unbuckled her seatbelt at some point but thankfully, she was coherent enough to park off to the side of the freeway. She was even able to text Dan her location and the word HELP before she eventually fainted. Dan didn't even make it back in time to find her because someone had already called 911 when they saw a woman passed out in her car on the side of the road. Just as he was starting to freak out because he couldn't get ahold of her, Dad called him to let him know that the hospital had called him.

She still had him as her emergency contact.

He then informed Dan to check on Mom first before letting me know.

Oh, and by the way, Mom has cancer.

That is why I am currently ignoring all the texts and calls from my father.

I huff and angrily delete Dad's newer messages without reading them.

I hastily delete his voicemails without listening to them as well.

Because he had the gall to drop that bomb on my brother on the *phone*. Then continued to tell him not to call me until he'd spoken to the doctor.

Like, *why*? To *protect* me? When that did the exact opposite and insinuated that I'd kept my mom's illness from my own brother.

I was upset with him. No, scratch that. *I'm still very much pissed.*

An emotion I never want to feel for my parents, yet here I am angry at both for keeping secrets *again.* For always *always* keeping Dan and me in the dark only to stab us with the truth later on. How did they still not understand that it would have made everything ten times easier had we known all this before?

Poor Danny. He is trying his best to stay strong for me. He has only let me see him cry once. Since then, he has spent his days driving me to and from school—thanks to Mom's accident, he's become paranoid about letting me behind the wheel —then going back and forth to the hospital to watch over Mom.

Thanks to Aunt Rose, I only have to be home alone three days out of the week but that in itself is torture. I hate how quiet the house is without Mom blasting music as she writes in her office downstairs, or her singing karaoke on her many writing breaks.

It's only been over a week, but I'm already missing her eccentricities that I once thought were annoying. Now I would do absolutely anything to get those back.

The way she leaves the TV on in her room on as she records her Filipino *teleseryes* because she refuses to believe that even with the TV off, it will record properly or that there is a thing called On Demand where the episodes are stored automatically after airing.

"You can't be too safe. Technology is only great when it works Lizzy," she would say to me whenever I rolled my eyes at her and attempted to explain how it works.

A gasp comes out of me as a memory unexpectedly hits me.

It was three weeks ago, when she had last repeated those words to me. She had taken the weekend off from writing. She was bingeing a show in her room wearing one of her signature robes and face masks. She patted the spot beside her in bed and invited me to watch with her. I declined saying I had to finish an essay due on Monday, then I went on a spiel about On Demand and how it works.

It was a Saturday for crying out loud. Why didn't I just cuddle with her and shut up?

What if that was the last chance, I had to do that?

How could I have been so blind to my mother's pain and suffering?

I lived with her. How could I have not known this was going on?

That she was terminally ill?

A sob almost chokes me and now the tears fall on my phone as it lays forgotten once again on my lap. I cry so hard that my body starts vibrating as sob after sob wrecks through me.

I climb up on the hospital bed and curl up next to her in a fetal position, falling sleep after a few moments from the utter exhaustion of it all.

I WAKE up to the sound of whispered conversations. I stifle a groan at how heavy my eyelids have become as I struggle to open them. I feel someone shift beside me. I jolt upright in surprise to find six pairs of eyes staring at me.

I don't know when they came in or how long I have been sleeping, but at some point, my brother came back with Summer, who is sitting on the chair beside him as he perches on the side of Mom's bed. Aunt Rose is also here, nestled beside Mom on the other side. Brad and Kyle are lounging on the couch. Kim is sitting with her knees curled up, beside me on the guest bed.

Wait. *Wait. I'm on the guest bed?* How did that happen?

A blanket falls off my shoulder and I realize someone had tucked me in as well.

"Lizzy, you okay?" Dan has somehow made his way across the room in seconds. He's kneeling in front of me, my hands in his.

"Did you move me to the bed?"

Aunt Rose beams at us from across the room, "Brad did, honey. We got here first."

I tilt my head in response as I take in the room. Everyone is still staring at me. Brad looks away just as my eyes meet his. He's hunched over in his seat, his gaze on the floor.

I tear my eyes away and frown down at my brother, "What time is it?"

He checks his phone, "Almost four."

My eyes bug out, and this time, I groan.

When Nurse Zjan was making her rounds, it was barely twelve. I remember this because she offered to bring me lunch when she walked in and found me there curled up beside Mom. Which means I slept for three hours and missed lunch.

As if reading my mind, Kim goes over to the small table where the kitchenette is. I notice the table is full of paper bags and drinks. She grabs one and hands it to me.

"Here. Kyle and I brought Dick's. I figured we could all use some." Her eyebrow quirks up at the dirty pun. Given the situation she lets her unintended joke fall flat and just smiles.

I placate with her a small smile of my own.

Regardless, I'm grateful she's trying.

I open the bag and pause.

"Have you guys eaten?"

Kim sighs dramatically, "Noooooo. Brad was making us wait for you."

Aunt Rose lets out a chuckle as she brushes Mom's hair out of her face.

"We just didn't want you to eat by yourself." She adds, helpfully.

Kim leans in and whispers, "Brad looks like he wants to poke my eyes out."

I peek over her shoulder and yeah, I guess the look on his face *could* be described as just that.

Dan snorts as he gets on his feet and grabs a chair next to Summer.

Summer rises from her seat then bends down to whisper something in his ear. I watch Dan nod and look up at her with the gentlest expression I have ever seen on his face.

My brother is falling in love.

Summer squeezes his shoulder then gets to work on sorting burgers and fries on paper plates. Kim pivots back to help her sort and Brad gets up to help hand them out.

I rub the sleep out of my eyes and use the scrunchie on my wrist to put my hair up while everyone gets their food. I mumble a thank you to Brad who hands me a bottled water.

I expect him to sit back on the couch with Kyle but instead he sits beside me with two paper plates. He takes the paper bag from me, placing my burger on the plate with fries on it and hands it back to me.

"Eat."

I blink at the tone of his voice. It is both gentle and forceful. A hint of worry furrows his brow as he patiently waits for me to do what he says.

So, I take a bite of the burger and raise my eyebrows in inquiry. When he continues to say nothing, I take another.

The edges of his lips perk up in amusement. It's such a sudden change that I end up staring at his mouth longer than it would have been polite to do so. He looks startled for a second before he busies himself with his own burger.

I look away and not for the first time this week, watch again as Summer dotes on my brother. I can't believe it took this long for them to find each other when they practically grew up together. They seem so perfect together. She manages to make him smile and even laugh despite our circumstances. *I'm so glad he's not alone in this.*

I look around and realize that I'm not either. Kim and Kyle are whispering and smiling at one another while they eat. I know they undoubtedly have better things to do, but instead they're here with me. Came without me asking.

And Brad. Well… I wouldn't expect anything less from him.

I glance at him through the corner of my eye and feel my heart lodge in my throat.

He checks up on me the most. He postmates me food every day, always accompanied by a text saying he just wanted to make sure I have one less thing to worry about.

I've noticed the slight changes in Brad's personality too. He's a lot more intense and serious now. More protective, probably because of all the stuff happening in my life right now. He for sure isn't going all big brother on Kim.

Kim's voice pulls me away from my Brad-infested thoughts.

"Liz. Why is Hunter Davis texting you?" I feel Brad stiffen beside me as we both turn to look at Kim waving my phone around. "More importantly, why is your phone so ancient?"

Hunter? My mind goes blank for a second before I remember he's a junior I started tutoring last year.

Shoot. Did I forget to tell Jessica about his session today?

I roll my eyes and motion for her to throw it at me. "Because it still works?"

Kim tosses it at me, and Brad leans back so I can catch it.

I unlock my phone and tap on Hunter's message, ignoring another missed call from Dad.

"Hey beautiful,

Jessica told me about your mom.
If you need someone to make you smile.
Shoot me a text, I got a milkshake with your
name on it."

I scoff.

Hunter is hilarious. Always going on about milkshakes. I hope he's not bugging Jessica like this. She was gracious enough to sub for me and take over my tutoring for a month.

Still, I wish she hadn't told Hunter. Now I'm wondering who else she told.

I toss my phone on the bed. I look up to find I'm being stared at expectantly like I was supposed to read that out loud or something.

Well, except for Aunt Rose and Summer.

Aunt Rose is massaging mom's legs and Summer's on her phone. They have better things to do than wonder why someone's texting me.

I frown, "What?"

My brother looks slightly amused albeit curious, "Who is Hunter?"

I'm searching for an appropriate response when I realize he's not even looking at me, he's looking at Brad. I turn my head and find Brad looking at my phone intently. Then his eyes bore into mine and the intensity behind them is, well...for lack of a better word. *Intense.*

Kyle chuckles from behind Brad's shoulder and answers for me,

"Football player. Running back."

My brother's amusement turns into bemusement.

"Why the fuck—sorry Aunt Rose—is he texting you?"

Aunt Rose rolls her eyes as she gets off the bed and leaves the room.

"Curse away. I'll be right back, just going to ask for an update."

I take the opportunity to get up. I check on Mom, tucking her blanket tighter around her.

I squeeze her hand, hoping to get one back but she just lays there, motionless. I lean in to kiss her cheek and whisper to her that I love her.

"So?" Dan raises his eyebrow at me.

Why can't he drop this?

"He heard about mom."

My brother grimaces, "So why is he texting you?"

Now it's my turn to look amused as I turn to sit back down on the guest bed.

"He's one of the kids I tutor. He's just being nice."

"He's single. And gorgeous." Kim announces from the couch.

Kyle narrows his eyes at her but then she whispers something to him that makes him grin.

Her mouth quirks up as Kyle leans back on the couch, arms outstretched behind his head. They were both excited about this for some reason.

"Did he ask you out?" My brother is somehow glowering at me now.

And right beside me, Brad's mouth is pinched. His back is as straight as a rod.

Okay, well, this escalated quickly.

The tone in Dan's voice catches Summer's attention. She finally glances up at her boyfriend and scowls. "Leave Liz alone. She's allowed to have friends."

"Thank you, Summer. Take the older brother protective hat off, Dan. Like I've told you before. I don't date the guys I tutor."

I'm seriously getting annoyed by this conversation. This isn't the place or time for it.

I stare my brother down and hope he gets the message. But he gets distracted by Summer as she continues to quietly chastise him.

That shut him up.

"Well, that's a shame." Kim admonishes. "You tutor a lot of hot guys."

That doesn't even constitute a reply, so I ignore it and go back to eating my burger.

Kim however is still really riveted by this.

As if she is trying to get a rise out of me or something.

"I wasn't going to say anything but..." She exchanges looks with Kyle. "I think he likes you."

Kyle snorts and winks at me, "Facts. Kid's been carrying a torch for Liz since she helped him pass the tenth grade."

I shrug as I ball up the wrapper, "That's kinda my job."

As I start to get up to toss my trash out, Brad stills me with his hand on my knee. He takes my plate and gets up wordlessly to the kitchenette. He tosses my plate into the trash along with his uneaten burger then he leans on the counter, a stoic look on his face and crosses his arms.

His face remains passive and unreadable as he stares at Kim.

He is in a mood today. What is his problem?

I work on slow, steady breaths so I don't end up snapping at my selfless, caring friends who are sacrificing a Friday to keep me company.

Wait. It's Friday.

"Hey, don't you guys have a game to be at?"

Kyle shakes his head as he stretches and pulls Kim to his side. "I got the pass to skip practice today."

Kim pulls her legs out from under her and snuggles closer to Kyle. "We got…"

Her response gets cut off when the Vital Signs monitor hooked up to my mom starts beeping loudly. *That can't be good.*

I shoot to my feet and run over to my mom and Dan runs out, yelling for help.

Within seconds, I feel Brad next to me. I'm trying to read the monitor but can't make sense of it—it's all blurring together. *Is she flatlining?*

My knees start to shake as the panic starts to rise in me. I climb onto the bed and check the cannula, her IV lines, and even her pulse. I can't find anything wrong.

Everything seems to be hooked up correctly.

I can feel her breath coming out of her nose. It's shallow but she's breathing.

I check her pulse again; it's faint but it's there.

"Mom? Mom. Mom. Mom." I can feel my eyes stinging with unshed tears, but I can't let them fall. I need to be strong for her. I edge closer to her and place my palms on her cheeks. "Mom. What is it? What's going on? Mom. Open your eyes. Mom PLEASE."

I can hear the nurse's crash cart rolling into the room and the sound of footsteps closing in from behind. I hear Dan yell at me to get off the bed. But I vehemently shake my head. I grasp my mom's hands and find them cold as ice. *Is she cold? That's it. She's cold.*

I pull the covers up to her chin but then I feel Brad wrap an arm around my waist trying to lift me off the bed, but I resist.

I am not moving from here.

Not until my mother wakes up.

Not until that damned machine stops beeping like crazy.

Not until she stabilizes.

But I'm not strong enough to resist when both my brother and Brad pull me off the bed.

Dan sets me on my feet. He bends down to look at me. My eyes are jumping around the room following the nurses and doctors who have run in.

"We need to let them do their job Liz."

I nod. I can only nod. Why is he so *calm*? *How can he be so calm?*

I tear my eyes away from his and look over at Mom.

But I barely catch a glimpse of her behind the sets of shoulders surrounding her.

Is this it?

A frantic Aunt Rose comes running into the room and Dan goes to meet her. They speak in hushed tones, but I don't try to insert myself there.

I'm hanging by a thread. I am so close to a break down. I can feel it.

I might lose my mom today.

My lips start to quiver and a sob escapes in a tremble. Every part of me starts to shudder.

I feel Brad's hands curl around my shoulders, and I let him lead me to the couch.

Kim pulls me down next to her and Brad hunkers down in front of me.

I lean my forehead on Brad's shoulder. He slings an arm around me and cradles me in.

I let myself go and sob into his chest just in time to hear the unmistakable sound of my mother flatlining.

Brad

A unt Cat died.

Flatlined. Just like that.

I had never seen someone die before, at least not in real life.

For all the time I spent playing video games, you would think that would have numbed me in the face of actual death, but my reaction is the complete opposite.

I will never take a second of my life for granted ever again.

I will never forget the moment when they called her time of death. The guttural cries that were coming out of Dan as he collapsed on the floor, nearly pulling Mom down with him.

The way Liz switched off at the sound of her brother's sobs.

One second, she is in my arms, losing herself in pain and grief. The next she wrenches herself out of my grasp and with slow breaths crosses the room to Dan. She takes him in her arms like her pain comes second to his. Not long after, she turns to ask Summer to take him outside. Dan's break is so intense that it takes three people to pick him up. Summer and Kim hold him on one side while Kyle holds the other.

Mom has composed herself enough to take care of all the arrangements needed including calling Liz's dad and Aunt Cat's family.

The doctor tries to talk to Liz, but she is impassive. She walks right by him to the private bath. Moments later, she comes out with a bowl of warm water and rolled up towels.

Then simply stands there and patiently waits for the nurses to do their thing.

They try to tell her that she can't touch the body, but she ignores them all until an older nurse rushes in. She speaks with the doctor then sits with Liz on the bed and helps her lift Aunt Cat.

My heart shatters as I watch the girl I love bathe her mother one last time.

And like a coward, I walk out of the room, unable to bear witness to it.

I AM sure as hell not going to chicken out today.

I pull my gaze away from Liz.

She is seated on the first pew sitting at the end of the row with her brother and Summer. I am on the third row with Kim and Kyle.

I hinge forward, elbows on my thighs and bury my face in my hands.

I focus on taking slow breaths to keep from crying.

My heart feels like its permanently lodged in my throat.

My chest has a tightness that's downright excruciating. It's nothing compared to the sharp twists in my gut that flat-out feel like knife stabs when I look at Liz or even think of her.

I know my pain can't compare to what Liz is feeling. She lost her mom.

Or how my mom, who's sitting on the first row on my side with Aunt Cat's family, is feeling. She lost her best friend that day. I'm reminded just how selfless my mom is as she holds on to Liz's grandma. Between grieving and throwing herself into funeral arrangements so Liz and Dan wouldn't have to worry about it, she's spreading herself thin.

God, I love my mom.

I look up to check on the other woman who has my heart.

I have spent the last three hours watching Liz just sit there with her hands clasped on her lap and her head hung low.

From here I had the perfect vantage point of every shallow breath and throat bob from her. She's hanging on by a thread.

I know she's trying to stay strong because Dan is losing it. I knew this because not once has she even tried to approach her mom's casket. As if she knows it will break her.

She ignores everyone who approaches her to offer their condolences and kept her head down. Even when Kim goes to her, she says nothing. I have yet to attempt to go to her.

The only time I see her actually acknowledge someone is when her dad walks in.

With his new girlfriend.

I grit my teeth to prevent from audibly growling.

I don't know what happened between Uncle Will and Aunt Cat but bringing his girlfriend to his ex-wife's funeral seems like a pretty shitty thing to do.

"What should we do?" Kim whispers from beside me.

Kyle nudges me, "I think you should go to her once we're outside."

I shake my head. Originally, I had planned to give her and her family space to grieve, but after seeing her in the state she's in right now, I know I need to go to her sooner than that.

Kyle and I offered to help carry the casket outside but my mom made arrangements for people from the funeral parlor to do it so Aunt Cat's family and friends can focus on saying their goodbyes.

I check my watch.

In an hour, the procession will start, and Liz would lose her only chance to say goodbye to her mom. To see her face one last time. I need to go to her soon.

I needed to go to her now.

It only takes me four steps to get there. I kneel beside her and take her hand.

She startles at the contact. As soon as our gazes lock, the mask she has put on shatters and her beautiful brown eyes glisten with tears, her pain swimming in them.

I huff a breath, clutching at my own self-control and stiffly nod towards the casket.

She bites her lip but gives me permission to take her to her mom.

I move my hand to the small of her back and gently nudge her until she's close enough to see her mom. I have to close my eyes at the sight of Aunt Cat.

This kind, caring, funny, beautiful woman who cared for us like she was our own mother, who instilled so much of herself into the girl of my dreams and loved my mom like they were sisters, is gone. *Forever.*

A gut-wrenching whimper comes out of Liz and my eyes fly open just in time to see her launch herself on top of the casket and start bawling.

Every piece of me breaks as I finally let my tears fall.

I feel a hand on my shoulder and Dan comes into my periphery.

I step aside so he can be with his sister.

I meet Summer, Kim and Kyle at the bottom steps. Kim reaches for my hand and squeezes it while with the other, she holds on to Kyle, who has an arm wrapped around his sister.

After a few moments, Uncle Will strides up the small steps. He wraps his arms around Dan's and Liz's shoulders. The knife inside me twists as we listen to them say their final goodbyes.

~

"I'm not having a party, Mom."

Mom glares at me from across the room.

I abandon all pretense of studying and throw my textbooks on the floor.

I don't bother hiding the scowl spreading across my face either. *Fuck it.*

I'm pissed that she even thinks I want to celebrate anything, even my eighteenth birthday, at a time like this. Aunt Cat's funeral was just a few weeks ago.

"Your cousins are already coming Brad."

"No."

"Bradley Dean—"

"You can full name me all you want Mom. It's not happening."

Mom rests her forehead on the doorjamb, her hand still resting on the knob.

Her voice breaks as she turns her head just enough so that I can meet her eyes and the intensity of the emotions battling on her face punches me with guilt.

"Honey, don't you think we should take every opportunity to celebrate life?"

I sigh, "Mom, I get. But I just don't think it would be respectful to have a party when we just lost...I can't do it Mom. I don't really care about my birthday." I reach under my pillow, grabbing the phone I shoved in there a few minutes ago. I check it again, knowing full well I won't find a response until much later when Liz goes to bed.

I level her with a look, hoping she gets it. Hoping she isn't offended.

Hoping she will just understand. "I only care about making sure Liz is okay."

Then something weird happens. My mom grins through her tears and marches to my bed.

"You're still in love with her."

My mouth pinches but I pretend I don't understand what she means. Maybe, just maybe she will drop this because I have zero intention of discussing this with my mother.

Something must pass over my face in my attempt to remain expressionless because she's smirking at me now. "I knew it. Cathy knew it. Hell, even your dad knew it."

You've got to be shitting me. Seriously. *Can the floor just swallow me whole right the fuck now?*

She sits on the edge on the bed and now it's her turn to level me with a stare.

"I guess the real question is, does Liz know how you feel?"

I shake my head, sinking back on the pillows. I cover my eyes with my arm in an effort to keep my mom from seeing the emotions I'm trying to keep hidden.

"Oh honey…"

I cut her off. I've been meaning to say this to her for awhile now.

"Mom. I know you orchestrated this whole group project thing with Mister Santos."

She opens her mouth to say something like she already has a whole speech rehearsed to justify her meddling, but I hold a hand up to let her know I wasn't done. I could care less about her making Mr. Santos put us in a group but what I do care about is getting to the bottom of something that's been eating at me for weeks.

"I also heard you two at the party Mom. You and Aunt Cat. In the sunroom."

A disconcerted gasp comes from her but then I hear her sigh.

"How much did you hear?"

The tone in her question makes me rise up on my elbows to meet her resigned gaze.

"Not much. Probably just the tail end of you trying to convince Aunt Cat to tell Liz and Dan about her illness. It sounded personal so I left before I could hear anything else. I really didn't put it together until that day in the hospital."

She lets out a breath and I swear that look on her face is relief.

Okay that's weird.

"Mom? Is there something else I should know?"

She tilts her head at me and places her hand on my knee, "Cathy had good reasons for keeping her illness from her kids. And Will agreed to it for those very same reasons. Now... and this may be oversharing on my part, but I need you to understand that family has been through a lot more than anyone should. Liz most especially. Since you kids are trying to fix your friendship, I hope you can all stay patient with her. If you love her, be there for her. She needs you more than you can possibly understand right now and as much as I want to tell you why, it's not my place." She pulls her gaze away from mine and starts blinking back tears, "You two have something special and maybe only one of you realizes that right now but honey don't give up on her."

Like I could. I don't even know how I managed to spend the last three years without her.

All I know is that she needed me, and I wasn't there for her.

I won't make the same mistake again.

Liz

I half-listen to Kyle and Kim as they bicker over his grammar and her spelling as she types out their parts. All four of us are in Brad's room, working on our Social Studies final.

I'm sitting with my knees pulled up on the floor. I'm leaning on the bed, a plush blanket wrapped around me. Brad is lounging on his bed above me with his iPad, working on the art we are including in our project.

Kyle and Kim are sitting side by side at Brad's desk. On it are two huge monitors with an impressive CPU, if you can call it that. It is completely transparent with rainbow lights that mirror his keyboard. He mentions that he built it from scratch.

Brad refused to let Kim use it because she teased him about it. He cleared some space for her at the desk and now she is using his MacBook since she was banned from the desktop for insulting it. I can't help but smile remembering the fake outrage on Kim's face.

They won't let me do anything else but sit here and be present. The second I walked into his house, Kyle grabbed my bag and Kim wrapped me up in this blanket. Brad ushered me up the stairs to his room. I was so shocked that I didn't fight it.

Then I was sat down, and Brad put a plate in front of me. Brad had ordered pasta, pizza, wings, and by the looks of it, he bought every salt and vinegar chip he could find at the store. It made me feel special that he knew these were my comfort foods.

I fight another smile. I'm glad I came today. It's a semblance of normalcy and I desperately need it. Kim finally convinced me to come hang out with them to work on the project and not just have them email me their parts. Which was perfect timing because Dan flew to California with Summer for the weekend. Dan is officially moving back home so they have gone to pack up his stuff and drive back in his car.

The thought of being alone at home right now, with every inch of it reminding me of Mom, is nothing short of harrowing. I don't trust myself not to spiral into a depressive episode. Aunt Rose invited me to stay here with them for the weekend. Kim found out, invited herself, and then Kyle came too.

Now for the first time since middle school, we are having a "sleepover".

It couldn't have come at a better time. This Sunday is Brad's birthday.

One he apparently doesn't want to celebrate.

I am determined to play my part in changing that.

The last month since Mom's funeral has been awful. I've been going through the motions at school but when I am at home, I digress back to the person I have fought so hard not to become again. Dad has put me back in therapy to avoid a relapse. He's been looking into relocating his practice back to Seattle to be closer to us. With Olivia.

I sigh and cross my legs underneath me.

To my surprise, Olivia is nice. Now that I have gotten to know her better, I'm able to be happy for my dad. She was gracious enough when I apologized for lashing out at dad when he brought her to Mom's funeral. She was instrumental in getting dad and me to reconcile.

I just wish Dan would meet him halfway also. Dad is all we

have now that Mom is gone. But he's still salty about how everything went down.

He still hasn't forgiven Dad for helping Mom keep her cancer a secret from us. He blames Dad for all the time he has lost with Mom. Which is undeserved.

If anyone should be blamed, it's me. It should be me.

I am the biggest reason they kept this from us.

They feared me relapsing. They were protecting him—us—because of me.

"Lizzy?"

I look up to find my friends patiently waiting for me. I realize it must be my turn to start dictating my part for Kim to type out. I make a move to get up, but Brad takes the folder from my lap and tosses it to Kyle without a word.

"We're going to take a break, El."

I twist my head surprised at Brad's sudden use of the nickname he gave me when we were seven. He stopped using it when we were in the sixth grade and reverted to using Lizzy like the others.

He simply smiles at my surprise and gestures to the door, "I guess you missed it when Kyle said let's head downstairs to the game room?"

I return his smile and nod, "Sorry I was just thinking about how nice it is to be hanging out with you guys again."

"Aw Lizzy."

Kim crosses the room to me in a flash and envelops me in her signature tight hug.

"We are always going to be here for you."

She leans back and scrunches her nose up in the cute way she does when she's trying not to cry, "What do you say we kick the boys' asses in Monopoly?"

I pretend to think about it, "Make it Mario Party and you got a deal."

. . .

I TOSS the controller four hours later and watch Kyle do another victory lap around the room. He just beat us for the second time, this time on Mario Kart and he is not being quiet about it. Kim is not happy about losing again as she folds her arms and sticks her tongue out at Kyle. She turns her head away, ignoring his request for a kiss.

I feel Brad nudge me, "What are we going to do with those two?"

I turn my head, resting my cheek on the couch and face him. "Hope for the best?"

He chuckles and leans in close. I feel his breath on my nose.

My heart starts to race at the unexpected closeness, and I have to focus on trying to draw air into my lungs. I look up and immediately am taken aback by the heat in his eyes.

Whatever he's about to say gets forgotten in the moment as we both look up to the sound of Aunt Rose walking into the room.

"Sorry for the interruption but I wanted to check in before I head to bed."

I give her a quick nod when I meet her eyes. I plan to pull Brad aside and talk to him about his birthday party.

This is another reason I am determined to stay here for the weekend because apparently, I was the deciding factor in his decision.

I hate to think that he would be willing to cancel anything on my account.

Besides, he has it wrong. He is my best friend. No matter the circumstances, I want to celebrate his life. Even though I don't go to parties, I already missed his last three birthdays. There is no way in hell I'm missing his eighteenth.

Aunt Rose lifts a pleased eyebrow at me, her gaze travelling around the room.

"So, girls are we all set for tomorrow?"

I nod again because I suck at lying but thankfully Kim responds for the both of us.

She gives Aunt Rose a thumbs up, "We're good. I've already sent the invites. And tomorrow Kyle and I will go pick up the stuff Liz ordered from—"

"Mom." Brad's terse voice cuts her off.

"Yes, honey?" Aunt Rose looks amused, her voice dripping in honey.

"What is this?" Brad runs his fingers angrily through his hair.

"Well. You said *I* couldn't throw you a party, but you never said *they* couldn't."

"I said no party, Mom. Period."

Silence descends on the room and even though Aunt Rose still looks amused, I am not.

I sigh, "Can we have a second alone, please?"

Brad's head jerks towards me and I can feel his eyes boring a hole on the side of my face. I ignore him as I wait for everyone else to leave. Thankfully they heed my request.

Aunt Rose mumbles a quick goodnight and ushers the two out of the room, but I can just imagine them with their ears pressed to the door.

As soon as the door closes behind them, I feel the air rush out of me.

Instantly I regret not asking Kim or Kyle for backup on this. I don't know why I'm suddenly afraid of being alone with Brad. Maybe it's because I know he isn't happy about any of this or that he might feel betrayed that we did this behind his back.

But it feels strange. My palms are sweaty. I work on not

focusing on the tension crackling in the air between us right now.

"El?"

I turn so I'm facing him. I lean on the couch's armrest, pulling my knees underneath me to buy a few extra minutes so I can think about how to say this in a way that won't betray the number of emotions currently racing through me.

"It was my idea."

I succeed in shocking him. He stays silently staring at me, his face crumpling in confusion.

When Aunt Rose casually let it slip, that Brad had cancelled his party, I begged her to tell me why. When she did, I knew I had to do something about it, so I solicited Kyle and Kim's help. I don't know Brad's friends. They know everyone.

If he is decidedly against having his family throw him a party, then he can't exactly say no if we throw him a surprise one. Well, two surprise parties. One for his friends, another for his family. Especially if the reason why he didn't want to do it in the first place is the one planning it.

"But…why?"

I roll my eyes at him in mock frustration, holding out each finger as I count the number of reasons off the top of my head, "Because I want to."

"Because I'm trying to make up for lost time."

"Because regardless, you're still my best friend."

"Because this is your last chance to celebrate with all your friends before graduation."

I sit up and raise an eyebrow, "Do I need to go on?"

He stares at me in shock, then he relents and lets out a resigned sigh.

"I should have known my mom would play the Liz card."

I feel myself soften at his defeated expression, "Will you please just let me do this?"

He gives me the sweetest smile. It makes my heart beat a little faster.

What is going on with me today?

"Will you be okay? You know Kim. She's bound to invite more people than she should."

This guy. How is he so selfless?

I nod, "All the more reason to have it here so I can make a quick escape."

"You'll let me know if it gets to be too much?"

"*Bradley.*" I emphasize his name, the way I do when he starts to be a bit much.

"It's *your* birthday. You should enjoy yourself and hang out with your friends. Who I'm guessing you already don't see much of these days?"

Ignoring what I said, he shakes his head, "Nope. Either you promise to or no party."

I narrow my eyes at him borrowing a move from Kim's playbook and playfully smack him in the arm, "Yes. Okay fine. I will."

He holds his pinky out and I wrap mine around his. "Deal."

I MISS MY MOM. Every day the pain and grief are there. They never go away.

But losing her has taught me something—that I need to stop hiding and start living.

It is just after eleven and as I look around Brad's backyard at all the people laughing, dancing, and having fun, I'm struck with just how much I miss her and how much I wish she could see me now.

Living.

Just like she always wanted me to do.

113

Aunt Rose had only two rules tonight. One, that no one besides the four of us were allowed past the first floor. Two, that if anyone drinks, they can't drive themselves home.

I'm doing this for Mom. I'm doing this for Brad. I remind myself for the fifth time tonight.

I shake the intrusive thoughts away as I focus on not tripping over anyone's feet. I make my way around the throngs of people milling around the makeshift dance floor.

Party-planning is definitely one of Kim's talents.

What she has managed to accomplish in just a few days is nothing short of impressive. With the help of Aunt Rose and her AmEx, they have succeeded in turning half the backyard into a club. There's even a DJ and everything. The other side of the backyard has been transformed into a tropical paradise, equipped with tiki torches surrounding the pool, floaties, and an impressive buffet. I helped with ordering the food and will help make lunch tomorrow but that's about it for my contribution.

Kim has also somehow managed to invite a ton of people from our grade as well as some underclassmen. I guess it helps that Kyle is basically a god at our school.

Everyone wants to be where he is. So here they all are.

He is currently in the middle of a huge group of guys from the football team cracking jokes and shooting shit.

I leave Kim on the dance floor. I make an excuse about needing a drink after she begs me to dance with her and her friends. I have spent the majority of the evening with them and now I need a break. It isn't that I didn't like them. They are all pretty nice considering they're probably annoyed that I've been monopolizing Kim's time for the last few weeks, but I just don't have anything in common with them. And I definitely don't feel comfortable dancing in front of this many people.

My social meter has reached its limit and I needed a breather.

I made a deal with Brad before the party started. He promised me that he would spend time with his friends, and I promised that I would come find him if it got to be too much for me.

He doesn't need to know that I have no intention of doing so. He has thrown himself into taking care of me these past few months. It's about time I take care of him and put him first.

Tonight, I won't make him worry about me.

Tonight, he deserves to have fun. With his friends.

With his girlfriend?

I can feel my back stiffen at the thought and my face heats up remembering what we walked into earlier. Kim and I had ventured back into the house so she could pee and fix her makeup. We stopped short when we caught sight of Brad sitting closely together with a leggy blonde in the main sitting room that he had turned into a gaming station.

I recognized her from school, but I didn't know who she was.

Kim said her name was Courtney and that she was a junior in the Drama Club.

They were so engrossed in the game they were playing they didn't even notice us walk by.

That was when I realized I had never once asked Brad if he has a girlfriend.

Guilt hit me in full force for taking up so much of his time, along with something else I didn't want to acknowledge.

Jealousy? Why on earth would I be jealous?

It's been a while since I've even felt anything remotely close to this way about Brad.

It was back in the seventh grade when he started dating some girl for a few weeks. I don't even remember what her name was, but I'll never forget the emotions it stirred in me.

Jean. I think that was her name.

But since it hadn't lasted very long, I hadn't spent too much time dwelling on why I felt that way. It was also around the time I was dealing with my parents fighting intensifying.

He is my best friend. That's all it is. *Or I think that's it.*

I've dated other guys but none of them have evoked this kind of feeling before.

As we walked past them at the gaming station, it felt different. Like I was angry and nauseous at the same time.

My stomach wouldn't stop churning and my teeth clenched at the sight of them together.

Thankfully Kim really had to go and dragged me upstairs, so I didn't get caught glaring at them, or worse, shoving *Courtney* off the couch.

I sigh, wrapping my hands around my bare arms.

It is way too chilly to be wearing a dress and definitely not a dress this short, but Kim insisted. It isn't too bad in the backyard with the tiki torches but as I go around back to the kitchen, I start to feel the chill all the way down to my toes.

As I push open the door and step into the kitchen, I realize it might be from something else entirely. There had been people in here drinking earlier.

Now it's basically empty. Except for one person.

Hunter.

Drinking a beer.

Looking absolutely wasted.

I turn back around hoping I can quietly slip out again before he sees me.

"Elizabeth!"

Crap. I hastily paste what I hope is a bright smile on my face.

"Hey. Hunter." I realize I say that with a biting tone and grimace inwardly.

My sour mood has nothing to do with Hunter and everything to do with my mounting social anxiety and the conflicting feelings currently waging a war inside me.

He grins and stalks around the island to me, swaying a bit. "Hey you."

There's something to the look in his eye that gives me goosebumps.

And not the good kind.

Then he proves its warranted by crowding in to my personal bubble and I feel my Spidey senses tingling. He looks like a predator going after its prey as he looks me up and down.

His gaze lingering on my chest and then my legs.

He has definitely already had a few drinks and from the smell seeping out of his pores, I'd bet my GPA he has smoked a joint or two at some point tonight.

I take a small step back and he follows.

My smile drops because he's never been this forward with me.

Before I realize it happening, he's... hugging me.

My arms dangle at my sides. I'm unsure how I'm supposed to react. He's almost a foot taller than me and weighs twice what I do. Plus, all that muscle.

I'm not strong enough to push him off.

"Please get off me." I mumble through his chest, trying to wiggle out of his grasp.

"You look like you could use a hug."

Is he smelling my hair?

I expect him to release me after that but his hands move from my shoulders down to my waist and now he's pulling me closer to him.

I stiffen at the unwanted contact, but my arms are now trapped by his and I am unable to push him off even when I try to.

I try to shove him off using my shoulders. He doesn't

budge. I feel the sense of alarm building and the panic rapidly rising in my voice as his grip tightens around me.

He ignores my muffled pleadings.

I strain until my head is halfway over his arm and I start yelling.

"Hunter! Let me goooo!"

"It's just a hug."

I know screaming is pointless because of the music blasting in the backyard and the sounds of video games reverberating outside this room. No one would even hear me.

I do it anyway.

"Get off of me!"

His hands start to move dangerously close to my butt, then he dips his head to my neck.

I feel his breath on my skin as the fear officially invades every part of me.

I struggle fiercely against him.

"Stop that!"

"Just a quick kiss."

Fuck. No.

I start to raise my knee to hit him in the groin when he gets yanked off of me.

I gasp as I nearly fall back from the force of it when I feel the warmth of familiar hands grip me by the arms and Brad's chocolate-brown eyes lower to my line of sight.

I nearly faint from relief.

Except they look different than they normally do. Scary different.

Thunderous brown eyes are a more accurate description now and I blink, registering both the rage and worry in them as I get wrapped up in the safety of his arms.

"Fuck, you're shaking." Brad whispers furiously, rubbing my back gently.

Shaking? Did he say he was shaking?

No that's me. I'm shaking. I fist his shirt, clutching as I try to swallow my gasps.

Then I hear Kyle angrily yelling as he cusses his teammate out from behind Brad.

"Didn't I tell your ass my friend was off limits?! Then you fucking decide to force yourself on her?"

I lean back to find that Kyle has Hunter twisted by the arm and up against the island. Hunter doesn't even seem at all bothered by it or even appear like he's present. His eyes are now completely glazed over and he's still sporting a big stupid grin on his face.

"Pretty. Tutor girl is pretty."

He's slurring now as he blinks rapidly, keeping his gaze on me.

I shut my eyes at the sight of him leering at me.

Faded. He's faded.

"Just one kiss."

I hear rustling like he's struggling against Kyle's hold.

Brad starts to pull back as if to pounce on Hunter too. I wrap my arms around his waist to keep him in place as another shudder runs through my body.

"Oh my god! What is going on?"

I hear Kim running in, her heels clacking on the marble floor, but I can't risk loosening my hold on Brad in case he's tempted to throw down on my behalf.

His chest heaves against my cheek. I look up to find him glaring at Hunter. Brad's teeth are clenched, eyes blazing as he struggles to stay calm.

"Party's over," Brad bites out looking over his shoulder at the rest of the football team now crowding into the kitchen. "And someone take that piece of shit out of my house before I break his fucking neck!"

It's closer to one in the morning now but the adrenaline from earlier still hasn't worn off.

Brad all but carried me upstairs into my room and ordered me to change into pajamas and then left to go break up the party.

An hour later, I hear the three of them trudge up the stairs.

Kim checks on me before heading into her room.

Apparently, she had started dancing with a guy from the hockey team which got Kyle all riled up, so he went inside the house. Kim chased after him and when Brad saw I wasn't with them, he got worried, so they all went looking for me.

Kim suggested looking in the kitchen because I had mentioned getting a drink.

They split up. Kim went upstairs to check my room. The boys went to the kitchen and that's when they walked in on Hunter forcing himself on me.

I ask Kim if Brad's upset and she just nods with an apologetic look on her face.

Even though she assures me he isn't mad at me, I still felt at fault.

I have succeeded in ruining not only his party but also his birthday.

This was why I didn't socialize. I don't know why I even try. It would have been just fine if I had let them throw the party without me and just flown with my brother to California.

Or stayed at home. Or hell, even stayed up here.

Why I had to insert myself where I didn't belong, I really don't know.

A knock on the door breaks into my thoughts and Kyle's head pops through the open crack.

"Hey...how are you holding up?"

I shrug.

Kyle shoves the door open and leaves it that way. He strides inside the room to plop down beside me on the bed. He slings an arm around me and pulls me close.

"I'm sorry we didn't get there sooner. I hate to think about what could have happened if we hadn't." He scans my face as he draws a frustrated breath.

"Are you mad at me?"

He pulls back, clearly confused. "Why *the fuck* would I be mad *at you*?"

I shrug again. "Ruining the party. Because of me you guys had to kick your friends out."

"Liz. You're our friend too." He chuckles lightly, "Besides the party would have ended soon anyways. Aunt Rose had us swear to a midnight curfew remember?"

Yeah, but don't high school parties usually run late?

I guess I wouldn't know. This was my first.

And my last.

As if reading my thoughts, he shakes his head and tugs me to my feet.

"It's pretty fucked up for this to happen but don't let it keep you from having fun because I promise you that I've got your back. You will never be in that position ever again."

I scoff.

I doubt I will ever go to another party. Probably not even in college.

I just don't fit in like that.

Kim raps on the door and I feel the tension simmer in the air between them.

"I texted Brad to come meet us in the game room, but he said he was going to sleep."

She's holding the small box in her hand that has the cake I

bought earlier to surprise Brad with after the party. He must be really upset if he can't even come down here for a bit.

I glance up at the ceiling wondering how he's doing.

I turn back to my friends and find them looking in opposite directions, completely avoiding each other's eyes. Kyle's mouth is pinched, his brows meeting.

Kim looks like she's about to burst into tears.

I sigh, taking the cake box from Kim.

"I think you two need to talk this out."

Kim runs her fingers through her hair and looks at Kyle, tears forming in her eyes.

Kyle groans in desolation when his eyes meet hers. Before I can even blink, he's already crossing the room to Kim. He pulls her in for a hug.

I lead them out of my room and nod towards the stairs.

"I'll go check on the birthday boy. You guys get some rest. We still have that lunch with Brad's family in a few hours."

That's all the push they need to leave. I watch them walk down the hall, arms around each other's waists, to Kim's room.

Brad

A soft knock interrupts my count. I drop the weights on the mat and draw a heavy breath.

I should have known she wouldn't take no for an answer. I should have just gone down there when Kim texted. Now I have to face Liz and I'm not even remotely ready to do that yet.

I'm positive it's her because only she would knock instead of barging in like the other two.

"Come in." I work on keeping the anger still coursing through me out of my voice.

I want to grab my keys, find that prick and beat his ass.

But *fuck* I have to be better than that. I'm eighteen now. I would be charged as an adult.

Because I know that when I see him, a few punches won't be enough.

That's the only thing that kept me from doing it.

So instead, I'm pushing my body to the brink of exhaustion and pain. I work out the frustration and rage. I desperately need an outlet for this shitty feeling of absolute helplessness, of not being able to protect her when that's my fucking job.

Now I feel like I also failed her by leaving her alone in the aftermath.

I should have gone and checked on her.

Instead, here she is checking on me.

Good going Brad. Way to be a selfish asshole.

I sit up on the bench as I watch her walk in.

My heart races at the sight of her. Then breaks at the memory of how she felt in my arms earlier, shaking and gasping for air.

She has her head down as she shuts the door behind her and crosses the room with soft-padded footsteps. She's holding a small box in her hands. The guilt punches me again. This is probably why they wanted me to come down. She has been waiting to give this to me.

"Are you okay?"

"You okay?"

We speak at the same time.

She looks up, a shy smile on her face.

"Happy Birthday." She holds the box out to me.

I swipe my shirt hastily around my neck and arms before I get up and take the box from her.

Now I regret my decision to work out. She looks adorable in silk pajamas, her hair in a side braid and she smells amazing. Freshly showered with a scent all Liz, a hint of lavender and vanilla while I undoubtedly smell like a dirty gym sock.

"Thanks El." I open the box to find a small lava cake.

My favorite.

There's only one place this could have come from.

I turn the box to check and sure enough it's from Thea's. A small bakeshop downtown.

I beam at her, "You remembered?"

She rolls her eyes at me, "How could I forget? You told your mom you hated her because she wouldn't buy this for you once." She wags her finger at me, her eyes twinkling with laughter. "You. Made. Her. Cry."

I chuckle and rub a knuckle on my brow, "I was eight."

She shakes her head in amusement, but then she stops and her gaze rakes over me then quickly to my gym equipment.

"When did you start working out?"

I shrug, surprised by the abruptness of the question but I humor her.

"Freshman year. I needed a physical activity to release tension, an outlet, when I'm frustrated as fuck."

Her eyebrows rise and I realize she might have mistaken that as innuendo.

I open my mouth to refute it, but she walks away and plucks a small weight from the floor. Her sudden mood shift is as blatant as the way her shoulders are suddenly rigid. She plays with the weight in her hand, avoiding my eyes. "I'm sorry I ruined your party."

Before I realize what I'm doing, I've closed the distance between us.

Crooking a finger under her chin, I force her to meet my eyes.

"I will only say this once, then I never want to hear you say anything like that again, okay?" Liz's eyes grow wide as I basically loom over her, my voice tight with unchecked anger.

She nods her head tentatively at my words.

I pause taking the weight from her hand and place it on the bench behind me. I then turn my whole attention to this beautiful, kind, selfless girl I'm so desperately in love with.

Who instead of hurting from what happened to her is worried about hurting me.

"The only thing that mattered to me tonight was *you*. I don't care—have never cared—about the party. I care about *you*. All I wanted to do tonight was hang out with *you*."

I make sure to put emphasis on the *you* so there's no confusion.

It's about damned time she understands just how much she matters to me.

Undeterred, I go on because now that I've started there's no stopping as the words come spilling out of me. My threadbare grip on self-preservation snaps and I'm a dam breaking with the force of every wave of emotion coursing through me.

"Do you not understand what you mean to me? How for the last eighteen years, friends or not, you have remained the single most important person in my life? How no one in the last three years has even come close to you? How you consume my every thought and dream? How much I want to skin that piece of shit for what he did to you? What he could have done to you? That I will kick the crap out of him if he ever so much as looks at you?"

I huff out a breath, trying to power through despite my heart painfully lodging in my throat. "So please don't insult me by thinking or saying a party would ever trump you. Nothing—no one—will ever come before you."

Liz's breath hitches as she visibly swallows, the weight of my words pinning her in place.

I can practically hear the wheels turning in her head. As her eyes bounce between mine, I watch as she pieces together what I've said.

My gut clenches when her forehead crumples in what seems like confusion.

I expel a breath. My words don't seem to penetrate those ironclad walls.

I force myself to look away.

I want to keep going, I want to tell her that I love her. That I want her. Only her.

But there are only so many times a guy's heart can break in a single day. Two is my quota.

I roll my shoulders back and drop my hand from her chin.

I walk around her to place the cake on my desk.

I'm about to tell her to go back to her room and sleep when I feel her fingers close around my arm, pulling me to a stop.

"*Brad.*"

Her voice makes me pause.

"*Brad.*"

There it is again.

Creating a sliver of hope in me.

I have never heard her use that tone with me. It's gentle, coaxing.

It's as if she's throwing everything into how she's calling out to me.

Letting it speak for her.

I don't dare turn around. I don't trust myself not to cut myself open and hand her my heart.

What happened tonight has exposed me raw.

I can no longer hide behind the guise of friendship and if she doesn't feel the same way?

There's no going back to the way we were.

Not even to the way we were before we stopped talking.

Because to me, *she is it. The One.*

Yeah, I know, I only just turned eighteen, but I've always known that she's the one for me.

Knowing someone your whole life can give you that clarity.

"Brad." This time her voice comes out stronger.

Air rushes out of me when I feel her fingers travel down the length of my arm, leaving a fiery path of goosebumps in their wake, down to my fingertips.

Liz tugs me until I'm facing her.

She tightens her grip on my hand, compelling me to look at her.

The confusion is still evident in it, but her face reflects a number of emotions that give her away. She isn't as oblivious as I thought.

Maybe—just maybe—she feels the same way. Or at the very least feels something.

"What are you really trying to say?"

Her voice quivers like she's trying to pull herself together.

I know what she's asking. What she wants to hear.

But I have become paralyzed by the moment, aching for something else.

I search her face for any indication that she isn't ready for this, but I see none of that.

She doesn't shy away from how I'm looking at her right now.

Not even when my eyes lower to her lips.

I hear her breath quicken but she doesn't let go of my hand or move away.

Instead, she moves her gaze lower too.

I take that as my green light. I curl my free hand around the back of her neck, pulling her closer to me. I slide my thumb over her chin, tipping it up and before I lose the nerve, I do what I've only dreamt of doing and kiss her.

Right here in my bedroom.

On my eighteenth birthday.

Happy Birthday to me.

A startled gasp causes her lips to part, but I reign it in. As much as I want to devour these soft lips that have dominated my every daydream, I resign myself to taking it slow.

Because there is still a chance that she doesn't feel the same way about me.

And if it comes to that, then at least I won't wonder what she tastes like because now I know. *Fuck* if it isn't better than I imagined. She tastes like my every hope and dream.

She shivers, then as she places a hand on my bare chest. I'm reminded that I'm not wearing a shirt and I've been sweating so I pull back. I rest my forehead on hers.

My breath fans her face when I whisper to her why I stopped. "I'm sweaty and I probably stink."

She snorts and I lift my head to find her scrunching her nose up at me, trying not to laugh.

Do I smell that bad?

Great. Just how I wanted our first kiss to be.

I say that out loud.

She snatches her hand from my chest. It goes straight to her stomach; she clutches at it as she dissolves into laughter. Her other hand is still tightly enclosed in mine.

I groan and lean back on my desk, "Really El?"

She composes herself and clamps her lips to keep from laughing more.

"I'm sorry but you should have seen your face when you said that."

I shake my head unable to keep the smile off my face.

I fucking love this girl.

A switch turns on inside me. I'm lit up in every way and I'm no longer a saint, so I tug her until she's in between my legs.

The unexpectedness of it catches Liz off guard and has her stumbling towards me.

I steady her by clasping my hands around her waist.

Given my position, she's nearly at eye level with me now. She plants her palms on my chest as her wide eyes meet mine and I feel the heat just radiate off her.

Her pupils start to dilate at our proximity. We're mere inches apart.

I forget all my reasons for stopping before and close the distance between us.

This time there is no slow pace and I let myself get lost in the kiss.

She matches my pace, another reminder of just how well-matched we are.

Equal parts, giving and receiving.

Never taking more, always seeking each other out.

But like always, she has the upper hand. She has control. I am completely at her mercy. I groan as our tongues finally meet in a dance that makes it seem like we've been doing this more than just twice in the last ten minutes.

I still don't know whether she feels as strongly about me as I do for her.

But at this moment, I know I have a chance.

A chance to prove to her we are meant to be.

Because Lizzy doesn't let just anyone in.

Like she lets me in.

Hell, she just gave me the damn key and is telling me to make myself at home.

She is home.

This time she breaks the kiss, patting me gently on the chest.

"You should take a shower." She whispers against my lips.

I grimace. I must stink bad if she broke that kiss. Because, fuck, that kiss was phenomenal.

She puts a finger between my brows, smoothing the creases.

"You smell fine, I promise. But it's just that it's really late and I still want to give you my birthday present."

I grin down at her, "You mean the cake wasn't my gift?"

She snorts this time in annoyance, "Give me more credit than that Bradley. You'll devour that thing in a minute. I got you something better than that."

I tap her bottom lip. "How could you possibly give me anything better?"

Smooth.

She looks away, a light blush staining her cheeks.

"Please for the love of God, shower and put a damned shirt on."

I sport a permanent grin on my face now.

130

Chuckling, I let her go to stride over to my dresser and grab clothes before heading into my bathroom to do what I'm told.

AFTER THE FASTEST shower I have ever had in my life, I walk back into my bedroom only to find Liz curled up on the edge of my bed, sound asleep.

She's one roll away from falling off, her tiny feet sticking out.

Like she's afraid to venture past that side.

Given that we spent a good twenty minutes making out, she's right to be cautious.

Luckily, I took a cold shower, and it woke me up. There's still a lot we need to talk about. I still haven't told her the extent of my feelings.

She needs to know that just as much as I need to hear where she's at.

Her mom just died. She still needs time to process that and grieve.

And I know things are a little rocky for her at home with her brother and Dad not getting along. Not to mention the trauma she experienced tonight.

I grit my teeth, feeling the anger rise in me again. I force myself to unclench and lower myself down to the floor to take a moment and just look at her.

I brush strands off her face, warmth ballooning in my chest at just how much she means to me. I'm not about to pressure her into more than she's ready for, but I'm not going to shy away or pretend anymore either.

Not after that kiss.

Especially because *she kissed me back*.

I'm going to lay it all out for her. Let her know I am willing

to wait for her but that I want to be the one holding her hand—
and hopefully kissing her—through all of this.

I rise, about to take her in my arms and carry her to her
room when her eyelids flutter open. She gives me a sleepy
smile and points to the corner of my room.

"Can you do me a favor and look in your closet?"

She yawns, rubbing her eyes as she moves to sit up
motioning for me to go.

Seeing as how she's seconds away from falling asleep
again, I move quick.

I stalk past my desk, tv and gym equipment and fling open
the door.

I switch the light on.

Right in the middle of my walk-in is a huge rectangular box
with a bow on top of it. The words "From L" scrawled on the
box in Sharpie.

And when I read the words on the box and see the picture
on it, my jaw drops open in shock.

My heart starts to race, excitement building inside me. In
my head I'm already planning where to set it up and all the
things I could do with it but first things first.

I can't believe she got this for me.

I can't believe she spent this much on me.

I jerk around to face her. She's sitting with her knees up, her
chin resting on top of them watching me. "Do you...do you like
it? Is it the right one?"

I breach the distance between us, taking huge strides to get
to her faster.

I pull her up in my arms, trying to be as gentle as I possibly
can but needing to express just how much it meant to me that
she knows me enough to have gotten me just what I wanted and
needed.

"I love it. I lo—I love it. Thank you."

I grimace inwardly. I almost slipped up and told her that I love her. This isn't the time to do it. I look over at the clock on my bedside table. *2:31 AM.*

She feels heavier in my arms like all the strength she has is gone. She's clearly exhausted, and the adrenaline from what happened earlier must be causing her to crash yet she is still powering through for me. That means more to me than a two-thousand dollar 49-inch curved gaming monitor, although I am beyond grateful for it.

I set her back down on the bed and I have to ask. "Isn't it too much?"

She shakes her head, yawning. "Think of it as four years' worth of birthday presents."

I sit beside her, wrapping an arm around her. I let her rest her head on my shoulder.

"How did you get that up here without me noticing?"

She laughs softly, rubbing her eyes as she curls up next to me.

"Kyle snuck it up for me after the party started."

I hear her yawn again and when I peer down at her, I find her eyes are closed.

I stifle a laugh, "Hey. Let's get you downstairs and in bed, okay?"

She shakes her head and whispers against my neck, "I don't want to be alone."

Her words pack a punch. For all her bravado, Liz is incredibly fragile right now.

My heart hurts for all the things she's had to go through wishing I could take some of it from her, if not all of it. I grab the back of her legs and carry her around my bed.

I ease her onto my pillows and grab the remote on my bedside table to click the lights off.

Climbing in next to her, I nestle her against my chest and

hold her like I've always wanted to.

Feeling her chest rise and her breath growing even, I watch as she relaxes and falls asleep.

With a content sigh, I hug her close following her into slumber.

~

THIS FEELS LIKE DÉJÀ VU.

Running downstairs right before a party. Running late because I overslept.

But this time is different because I woke up in a state of panic after realizing Liz was gone.

I'm feeling desperate. I need to see her. Now.

I have to find out if what happened between us was some fever dream brought on by a rush of adrenaline.

I woke up to a call from my mom, telling me that she is on her way home with Dad and that I should probably head downstairs because my friends are all setting up for the party. Which means she didn't leave. She's still here.

That has to be a good thing.

I even check the closet to make sure I didn't dream up her gift either.

I can't wait to unbox it.

Fuck, I need to see her.

Thank her again for that damned gift. Kiss her again if she'll let me.

But probably have that talk first. Put my cards down on the table for her.

I try not to get annoyed that my mom went against my wishes and still planned the lunch with my cousins because all I want to do right now is drag her upstairs for a talk.

Hopefully some more making out. Because damn it now

that it's happened, I'm addicted.

Well maybe, two things, I also wanted to set that monitor up and see what my game will look like on it.

It comes back to me, all of a sudden. I was in the car with her, on the way to Kyle's, same day we learned about Aunt Cat's cancer. I ended up telling her something I had never shared with anyone. Not even my dad.

For the last year, I've been working on an RPG game. I had been itching to buy a curved monitor for the graphics, but my mom nixed the idea. Even though we could afford it, she wanted me to earn the money to pay for it, next summer. Citing the fact that I already owned two monitors, she couldn't understand my need for this, but Liz did.

Liz knows how much this means to me and my dream, so she got it for me.

I scan the rooms as I pass them by.

I cringe seeing that the makeshift game room I set up last night in the living room has already been cleared.

Once again, I slept through it all. I didn't lift a finger.

I push open the door to the kitchen.

Liz is the first person I see.

She looks up when I walk in, and her face breaks out in a smile.

I mirror it back to her.

"Happy Birthday! Sleep well?" Kim greets me bringing my attention to her.

I nod and search Kim's face for any indication that Liz told her about what happened.

I find nothing. If she knew anything, she would be bouncing off the walls right now.

Kim is entirely focused on her task, looking away before I answer her question. She is too busy doing a side-stepping dance, squeaking as the pan in front of her sizzles and pops.

"Happy Birthday B!"

Kyle raises his elbow for me to bump as he's fingers deep into rolling what looks like spring rolls and that's when my eyes sweep the room.

Kim is lobbing the rolls into the fryer.

Liz is chopping up ingredients and throwing them into a huge wok full of stir-fried noodles and vegetables.

That's when it hits me: they're making lunch for the party.

Not just any kind, but the kind Aunt Cat used to make for me because it was my favorite.

Pancit and lumpia.

Filipino stir-fried noodles and spring rolls.

For the party. For me.

This is why Liz got up early without waking me up.

Why Kim and Kyle didn't wake me up either.

When did she learn how to cook?

I can't believe they're going through all this trouble for me.

Swallowing hard, I roll up my sleeves to help but Liz shushes me away.

"This is too much. You guys should have woken me up. I could have helped."

Kyle snorts, "Don't make it weird man. It's only a big deal if you make it."

Then he winks and nods his head toward Liz who looks up right at that moment and catches the exchange. She rolls her eyes and shoves a bowl of lumpia base into Kyle's hands.

"Roll faster, Anderson."

Liz turns to me and shakes her head slightly, letting me know that she hasn't told them anything. Then she turns around to wash her hands.

And with the dishtowel on her shoulder, she dries her hands. She walks over to the microwave, taking out the lava cake she gave me earlier along with a fork.

Handing me the plate, she flicks a hand toward a stool.

"Sit. Eat. Your birthday is a good excuse to have cake for breakfast." Liz grins.

That smile has me spellbound and it takes me a minute to realize Kyle's talking to me.

"Do what she says. Liz is bossy today."

That earns him a smack from Kim who turns around with a tray of lumpia in her hands.

She places it on the island. She smiles fondly at Liz who's caught up showing Kyle how to properly roll the lumpia with raw egg whites, so it won't unfold.

"I still can't believe you cook now."

Liz gives her a small smile that doesn't quite reach her eyes,

"I had to learn if I wanted to eat something other than pizza and takeout."

Kim mimics the frown on my face, leaning forward on the island.

"What do you mean?"

"Mom was pretty busy the last few years. She was focused on finishing her book series."

Liz shrugs, mouth pursed. "I guess we know why now."

Kim wraps an arm around her and squeezes her shoulder. "Thank you for teaching us how to make these."

I focus on taking a bite of the cake and ignore the urge to go around the island and take her in my arms too. I watch her turn off the burners and load two foil pans with pancit. Then she immediately starts piling lumpia onto a tray.

"Can I have some of that?" I give her my best smile hoping she'll give in.

Her mouth quirks up in a smile.

Without looking up from her task, Liz grabs a piece of lumpia and hands it to me.

I don't know what possesses me to do this because were not

alone and Kim has already started watching us curiously. I lean over and take a bite of it right from her hand.

Startled, Liz looks up at me, the tongs she's holding on her other hand falling to the floor.

Kim nearly deafens me with her scream and knocks Kyle right off of his seat.

"I'm too young to lose my hearing babe." Kyle grumbles as he straightens himself back on the stool. Oblivious to the rest of us, he gets back to work rolling.

Kim's mouth stays open in shock as her head ping pongs between Liz and me.

Liz and I are staring at each other. Then she blinks and breaks eye contact, placing my half-eaten lumpia on my empty plate.

Picking up the tongs from the floor, Liz turns away to wash them in the sink.

My gaze never leaves her. I'm paralyzed equally by frustration and embarrassment.

Kyle finally notices the tense silence and his eyes bounce between the three of us.

"What the fu—?"

My mom chooses that moment to walk in, all smiles. She hangs an arm around me and kisses me on the cheek. "Happy Birthday bud."

I sling an arm around her waist and squeeze it.

"Thanks Mom."

She gives my head a pat before going around the island to where Liz is busy washing the utensils and pots they used.

With a disapproving cluck of her tongue, she pats Liz's hand to get attention.

Liz gives her a small smile and drops the pot she's scrubbing back into the sink.

Liz is actively avoiding looking at me now. I can't tell if it's because I caught her off guard or because of what happened between us a few hours ago.

"Sorry Auntie, we made a mess. Just wanted to clean up."

My mom flings a hand to the door, "You've done more than enough. You kids get ready. We have a little over an hour until everyone comes back from their tour in Seattle." She reaches out to squeeze Liz' hand, "I've made these countless of times with your mom, I'll finish up here".

I don't need her to tell me twice. I'm aching to talk to Liz alone.

But my mother raised me right so I ask, "Do you need me to do anything Mom?"

With a firm shake of her head, "Go on, run a brush through that mop on your head."

Kyle snorts. Liz ducks her head as she makes for the door. Kim intercepts her by hooking an arm around Liz's.

I follow them out the door, with Kyle close behind me, tapping on his phone.

Kyle speed walks until he's walking beside me and nudges me.

"Hey so I spoke to Coach Wilde this morning about that asshole Hunter. He's called a mandatory team meeting after school tomorrow and that he's talking to Principal Gardner about it."

Rage boils inside me just at the mere mention of his name.

He whispers as he cranes his neck to check if the girls are listening.

"Which means PG will call her in to talk."

"You should have told her first man. We don't know what's going on in that mind of hers."

Kyle gives me a knowing smile, "You mean after all that time she spent up in your room this morning, you didn't talk about it?"

I groan, causing the two girls to stop on the second-floor landing and turn around.

"What's wrong?" Liz frowns as her gaze hops between Kyle and me.

With a chuckle, Kyle motions for them to keep going up the stairs. "He ate too much cake."

Kim's eyebrows shoot up, not buying Kyle's BS excuse.

With a hand on her hip, she points up, "Game room. Now."

This time, it's Liz's turn to groan, "I really want to shower and change Kimmy."

Crap. Do not think about Liz and showers. Do not go there.

Something in my face prompts Kim to grin and shake her head.

"Unless you two want to spill the beans right here right now on these steps."

Resigned, Liz rolls her head back and tugs Kim. "Let's get this over with."

TREATING us like were on trial, Kim has Liz and I sit on the loveseat together while she paces in front of us. Her hands are clasped behind her back.

Kyle sits on the floor, leaning back on his elbows, looking like he's about to fall into a fit of laughter. Like we're a damn comedy and all he's missing is a bowl of popcorn.

I glance at Liz when she sighs for a third time. She's leaning her head back on the couch with her eyes closed and arms crossed. She looks exhausted.

Need to wrap this up quick and get my girl to take a nap.

The fact that Kim thinks what's going on—or what she thinks is going on between Liz and me—is up for discussion is starting to grate on my nerves.

"Kimberly. Say what you need to say and then we're done

here."

Kim twists around at the tone of my voice and Kyle sits up, the laughter dying in his face.

Liz's eyes snap open and she turns her head to look at me.

Kim lets out a long-suffering sigh and with her hands imitating a puppet. She looks me straight in the eye, "Look I know what you're going to say…that's it's none of my business yada yada yada blah blah blah."

I fight back a smile. As annoyed as I am, Kim is still one of my best friends and always so entertaining. It's hard to stay mad at her.

She senses this, and the sides of her mouth rise up.

"First things first, then we'll get to the good part."

She turns her attention to Liz, "I'm really sorry about last night. I should have gone with you to get a drink. First rule at a party, no girl should be left alone and it's all my fault."

Liz's arms tighten around herself and because I can't last a single second without touching her again, I ease an arm around her and pull her close.

I feel her stiffen. Not wanting to push, I start to take my arm back, but she relaxes, leaning in.

"It's not your fault Kim. I don't even know what possessed Hunter to do that. He's always been nothing but friendly to me. Maybe it was my fault. I chose to ignore his texts and come-ons instead of just flat out telling him I'm not interested. I made him think there was a chance that I was."

My stomach starts to churn, like a cocktail of jealousy, fury, and the strong need to protect my person. Because that's what she is.

My person.

But even if she isn't and she decides she doesn't feel the same way, it still doesn't matter. No one has the fucking right to touch her—or any other person—like that without her consent.

I'm pulsing with a combination of all three. She clearly thinks she's at fault for what that piece of shit did.

I rub my forehead as I share a look with Kyle. He looks just as disturbed as I am about that.

We are both unsure about who should be the one to say it and I shake my head saying I can't.

I clench my teeth trying to keep from unleashing another barrage of repressed emotions.

Kyle doesn't need to be told twice, he gets up and crosses the room to Liz.

Sitting on the table in front of us, he hinges forward, hands clasped in front of him.

"Lizzy. No one has the right to touch you without your consent. And I'm being generous with my wording right now. I'm pissed as hell. Don't ever think for a fucking second that getting harassed and assaulted is your fault. Am I clear?"

Liz looks taken aback.

I don't blame her. Kyle is lighthearted, always a joke on hand. As tall and imposing in build as he is, he never takes on a stern tone even when technically he is the oldest out of the four of us. He usually lets things roll off his back.

That draws Kim closer to us and she bends and whispers to him, "That was hot."

He spares her a sideways glance and a wink. "Later." He says that like a promise.

I choke back my laughter. Leave it to these two to break the tension.

He turns back to Liz, "Will you do me a favor?"

Liz nods but I can already see the tension seeping out of her.

"If he even so much as looks at you. *Tell*"—he cocks his head at me—*"us."*

Liz's eyes widen in shock, "I don't want to cause any

142

trouble."

Kyle's expression turns almost violent.

Because of how easygoing he typically is, I tend to forget how commanding his presence can be.

"He should have thought about that before committing a crime. You do know that's what he did to you right?"

Liz looks to me, pleading for help with her eyes. I shake my head.

"I agree, El. I should have called the cops last night."

That thought has been smashing around my head since last night and I curse under my breath. Last night, all my focus was on getting Liz out of there. What I should have done was pull my phone out and call 911. Then watch as they hauled his ass out of my house.

Kim reaches over and brushes Liz's hair out of her eyes, "They're absolutely right Lizzy. Admittedly, we were all running on fumes last night but one of us should have called."

She pats Kyle's shoulder. "Tell her babe."

Kyle looks at me for a beat and I nod.

He takes a deep breath. "I called Coach this morning and told him."

Liz gasps and sits up, her eyes widening to saucers now.

Kyle holds a hand up, "It had to be done. I should have talked to you first, but I cannot, will not have someone like that on my team. I spoke to a bunch of the guys last night before they left and they're all in agreement. None of us want him around, and"—he straightens his shoulders, a firm indication that he isn't backing down from this—"none of us are comfortable with him being around our girls either. We want him off the team."

Taking a deep breath, he drops the bomb on her, "Which means...tomorrow it will be all over school. Principal Gardner will likely—no, definitely—call you into his office."

Liz is sputtering in disbelief.

Her eyes are dancing around the room and she's clenching her hands in front of her.

Then she pulls her knees up in one swift motion and hides her face between them.

Fuck.

"But...but I can't." Her voice is muffled so we can barely make out what she's saying.

"You can't what, El?"

She shakes her head, seemingly shrinking in, making herself smaller than she already is.

All of us look at each other.

"I'll go with you, Liz." Kim whispers, as she sits on the armrest on Liz's other side.

She starts threading her fingers through Liz's hair.

I don't know what magic Kim's fingers have because within seconds of her doing that, Liz's shoulders droop. Liz uncurls herself, resting her head on Kim's knee, her eyes closed.

Without a word, Kim continues to thread her fingers through Liz's hair until she relaxes completely.

Just as I think Liz is about to fall asleep, her eyelids flutter open. She leans back on the couch, pulling her legs up again. She gives Kim a grateful smile, resting her chin on her knees,

"My mom used to do that. Always calmed me down."

I make a mental note of that.

She's whispering but her voice is crackling with so much pain.

It feels like someone's ripping my heart out.

A tear slips out of her. She sighs, and resting her cheek on a knee, she turns her gaze upward.

"I miss her. I don't know how to be strong without her."

She sniffs and instinctively we all reach out for some part of her.

Kim starts running her fingers through Liz's hair again.

Kyle reaches over to squeeze her knee.

I cup her cheek, tracing it with my thumb.

As if that's what she was waiting for, Liz breaks down. Her chest starts heaving with every sob like she has been holding it in until she felt safe enough to let go.

With that my heart goes straight down the garbage disposal.

The other two let go, allowing me the space to gather her into my lap and hold her.

I nestle her head between my neck and my chest, my cheek resting on her head.

Rubbing her back, I do my best with every gentle squeeze and whisper of assurance to let her know that she's not alone, to let her know she is safe.

Because damn it, she is.

Not just because I'm never going to fucking leave her again but because I suspect the other two feel just as strongly as I do. We failed each other before and we learned from it.

I don't need to look at them to feel the love and protective energy radiating from Kim and Kyle right now.

What happened between us didn't destroy us like it should have.

Instead, it only strengthened our bond and friendship.

We have each other for life.

Liz's gasping sobs turn into gentle cries and her body starts to slack, the heaviness in her easing with each slow and staggering breath she takes until she finally stops crying altogether.

It takes her a few minutes to compose herself, and when Liz gently pushes herself off my chest, a tissue box materializes from Kim's direction.

Liz mumbles a soft thank you. She's patting her cheeks and nose when her head shoots up. She looks up at me, apparently realizing just how close we are to each other.

Her cheeks turn a soft pink, and she eases off my lap, back onto the other side of the couch.

Kyle snorts, once again breaking the tension.

I'm still reeling from feeling her break down in my arms to notice that Kim is getting started.

"Too late Elizabeth." Kim scoffs as she leans over to brush Liz's hair out of her face.

I forget how motherly and protective Kim had been of Liz before. These last few weeks have reminded me of just how much.

Liz is the only one out of the four of us born a different year.

Kyle's birthday is in June, Kim's in August and mine is in November.

Liz's birthday is in January and so for now, she's a year younger than us although we're only months apart.

Patting Liz's head, Kim throws me a smirk.

"Still can't believe it took you six years."

Liz rubs her eyes, a frown playing on her lips. "What do you mean?"

Kim glances back at me. She must not understand the look I'm trying to convey which is *Abort! Abort now!* because she just tilts her head and shrugs. That damned smirk still firmly on her face.

"To tell you that he's in love with you?"

I groan because that's the only thing I can do right now. I rock my head back on the couch just as I feel Liz turn slowly to me. I hazard a look at her.

The impact of what Kim said and what happened earlier slowly dawns on her.

Thanks, Kim. *Thanks a lot.*

I hope Kim gets this message as I glare at her.

Kyle intercepts the message and shoots up to his feet.

He tries to wrangle Kim out the door, but she stammers, her eyebrows shooting up.

"Good going babe. You gave him the gift of confessing for his birthday."

"I did? But...but all the touching and she fed him lumpia. Shit." Kim sputters, "Happy Birthday? I swear we have a better present for you. Give him the headset, Kyle. Quick!"

Kyle picks Kim up and slings her over his shoulder.

"Later babe." Patting her bottom. "Let's go get ready for lunch."

"I'm sooooorrrrrryyyyyyyyyyyyyy!"

I watch them leave and stare at the door as it shuts behind them hanging on to a few extra seconds like a life raft. Of all the scenarios I made up in my head about finally confessing my feelings for Liz, somehow this was never one of them.

I feel Liz move beside me. She's sitting with her legs crossed under her, facing me.

Her face is still damp, and her eyes are swollen from crying.

She swipes at the damp tendrils of hair on her face.

Fuck if she still isn't the most beautiful thing I've ever seen. I throw her my raft.

"We can talk about this some other time El."

I can tell by the way her nose scrunches up and her eyes shift between mine that she is trying to read me. Trying to come to terms with finding out how I feel about her.

Reaching over, I tenderly place a fingertip on the side of her mouth.

"Is it really that hard to believe after...you know?"

"It's not that." She blinks rapidly and I relish in the pink staining her cheeks, "But in love? And...and Kim said six years...I'm trying to wrap my head around *that* part. So since...?"

"Sixth grade."

I try to be as nonchalant as possible even though my heart is racing a mile a minute.

Her arms drop. I can almost see the wheels turning in her head as she makes sense of those two words. She looks unconvinced but not surprised.

"But you dated those girls in middle school, and we weren't even speaking for three years and I'm almost positive you dated Aly Peters last year and probably others. How...how can you —" She stops to catch her breath as the words tumble out of her. I take advantage of that moment to hold my palms out to her. She lets out a long breath, but she relents and puts hers on mine.

"This isn't how I pictured this happening, but I need to put the brakes on this right now, okay? Not that I don't want to talk about this. I do. But we have this thing happening downstairs and I don't know about you, but I hear the food is excellent."

I tease her even though I don't mean any of it. Well except the food part but the rest, I really didn't give a flying fuck about. All I want is to take her upstairs to my room.

Lock the door and talk about this. About us.

Hand her my heart, hope she gives me hers.

Then set up my new monitor and show her my game.

In more ways than one.

Liz's hand flies to her mouth and she nods, "Your family is waiting downstairs. I should get dressed and do something about my face."

Hesitating she adds, "We'll talk about this soon though, right?"

I can't resist so I pull her into my arms. I place a soft kiss on her temple that has her sighing into me. I tighten my hold on her for a few extra seconds before releasing her.

"Tomorrow. After school?"

She nods and before I get tempted to do anything other than

give her another chaste kiss, I tug her up and place a hand in the small of her back, guiding her outside.

I nod towards the guest rooms, "I'll meet you downstairs."

She looks like she wants to say more, as she looks over her shoulder at me, pausing outside her door but then she smiles and nods before walking in.

I have a big stupid smile on my face because she didn't say no.

She didn't say she didn't feel the same.

She let me hold her and kiss her.

But until I hear the words coming from her, I have to keep waiting. Stay patient.

I FIND myself staring at Liz from across the lanai—just like I have been for the last three hours.

Having had to play host to my cousins, I haven't had a chance to get any alone time with her since we all came down to the party.

I decide today that pink is my new favorite color.

On her.

She's wearing another pink dress.

It looks amazing against her beige skin and jet-black hair. She is still wearing it down but now she had it slightly pulled off to the side with a pink clip. She's laughing at something my cousin Missy is saying.

I catch her eye, and she stops mid-laugh and stares at me, a curious look on her face.

Knowing I just got caught staring at her *again*, I try to play it off as simply looking around but then her gaze travels down the length of my body and back up again to my face. I feel the heat of it coursing through me.

It's the same exact way she looked at me early this morning when she was telling me to put a shirt on. And now we are both silently staring at each other across the backyard.

A light blush is creeping up on her cheeks and before my mind even decides it, I'm already halfway across the backyard headed to her.

"Hey."

"Hey...hi?" Our height difference has her looking up at me, her head tilted in question.

I grin down at her because she just looks so damned cute looking up at me like that, even though what I really want to do is to lean over and see if she'll meet me halfway.

Her response is a smile that's slow and wide. I'm a goner.

A warm sensation pools around my chest at the sight of it.

I gesture at the buffet table across from us.

"So, everyone told me they loved the food you made."

She blushes again, dipping her head to stare at her toes in her platform sandals.

I am not lying. Every one of my cousins raved about her cooking to me.

Even though she made enough for at least twenty people, and there are only ten of us here, all the chafing dishes are now empty.

Luckily Dad also grilled hotdogs and burgers to tide over my ravenous cousins.

If they didn't love Liz before, she definitely won them over today with lumpia and pancit.

Another cousin, Sierra, chooses that moment to come back around and whisper, *"Marry her."*

I can't help but wink at my giggling cousin as she walks away.

I tap Liz's nose, "Thank you for doing that, by the way. I

realized when we were all eating earlier that I never thanked you."

Crinkling her nose, she gives a little shrug.

"It's the least I can do. You've been taking care of me this whole time."

I cup the back of her neck and give it a gentle squeeze.

"El, that's my job."

She swats my arm, challenging me, "Well, then this is mine too."

Then her eyes widen as much as my grin does at the double meaning her words hold.

"Yoooo Lizzy." Kyle strides up to us, breaking the spell.

Got to love his impeccable timing.

"Why is your brother blowing up my phone?"

Liz frowns then groans, "I left my phone somewhere in my room. Sorry...he gets a little carried away and overprotective." She holds a hand out to Kyle, "Can I borrow yours? Mine is probably dead. I never charged it last night."

He unlocks his phone and hands it to Liz.

Dan answers on the first ring because no sooner than Liz dials his number, she says,

"Hey Danny, it's me—"

Liz rolls her eyes at whatever her brother is saying then all of a sudden, she goes very still. Her gaze jumps to Kyle then to me. Biting her lip, she swallows hard.

"How am I supposed to tell you if I haven't seen you yet?"

Shit.

I glance at Kyle who seems to register at the same moment as I do what their conversation is about. I reach out and curl a hand around Liz's wrist, hoping she'll give me her hand.

Liz shakes her head at me, shutting her eyes. Shutting me out.

She just stays silent listening to her brother. We start to hear the distinct rumble of Dan's voice. Kyle nudges me, his brow furrowing. It's obvious Dan's yelling at her. We get it, Dan is pissed about this, we all feel the same way, but damn, he shouldn't be taking it out on Liz.

But then her eyes fly open, "I'm seventeen, Daniel. Not twelve. I know what that means."

Her eyes start to blaze with anger.

In a deadpan voice, she whispers, "I promise I would know if I got raped, Dan."

My grip tightens around her wrist as her words jab a knife inside me.

Pursing her lips, she hits the end button and shoots a quick text.

Handing the phone back to Kyle, she turns to me.

"I'm sorry. I have to go."

"What happened?"

"He said he's swinging by to pick me up. He's coming straight here after dropping Summer off so he should be here soon." Looking over her shoulder she scans the backyard. "Where's Kim?"

Kyle looks up from his phone, "She went to get Brad's gift from her room. I just texted her and told her to wait for us in yours."

Liz's face drops, "You guys don't have to. Enjoy the party."

I drop her hand and nod towards the sunroom doors leading to the back staircase.

"We'll follow you up."

Hesitating, she glances behind me at my cousins who have started a game of cornhole.

I shake my head at her, and thankfully she doesn't fight me on it.

Liz

I follow Dan into the house, locking the door behind me.

I rest my back against the door and watch as he kicks his shoes off. He strides into the living room barefoot, ignoring his slippers. Sighing, I kick mine off too, placing our shoes on the rack. If mom were here, she'd rag on him for being careless.

Growing up half Filipino, it's engrained in us to take our shoes off before entering the house. It amazes me that he still did it given his current state. I expected my brother's anger, but I wasn't prepared for his silence. He barely spoke to me on the way home.

When he picked me up, he didn't even bother getting out of the car until he remembered his manners and yelled a quick Happy Birthday to Brad before we pulled out of the driveway.

If Dan had been paying attention, he would have noticed just how much Brad and Kyle don't care for his whole Big Brother bit. I shot Brad an apologetic smile as we drove away and the smile, I got in return sent butterflies flying incessantly in my stomach.

Until now, I was still feeling the aftermath of it.

Might as well get this over with.

I slide my feet into my slippers, tossing my bag on the bottom stairs and follow Dan into the living room. I find him burning a hole on the carpet as he paces back and forth.

I curl up on the sofa, wrapping myself with a blanket,

wishing I had said yes to Brad's offer to borrow one of his sweatshirts. I could have wrapped myself up in his scent to get me through another Dan interrogation.

The guilt continues to prick me at the back of my neck and is starting to give me a full-on migraine. There were so many opportunities this weekend where I could have told them why Dan acts like this. How it's not really my brother's fault.

But at the same time, I know that once they find out what I did, it will change everything. Change how they look at me. Feel about me.

Given the current revelations swirling in my brain right now, it's not a risk I'm willing to take. I am still trying to wrap my head around everything.

My brain and heart are both literally working on overtime.

From missing Mom to what happened with Hunter—what could have happened.

To finding out Brad had...has feelings for me?

To him kissing me...twice.

To me kissing him back. To it feeling right.

How it felt when I woke up this morning in his arms.

Like it's where I'm supposed to be. He feels like home.

For the first time in a long time, I woke up at ease. Safe. Happy.

Something shifted between us the second he poured out his frustrations to me this morning. Suddenly he's looking at me differently, touching me differently.

And I like it. I didn't even notice it when I started doing the same. Touching him differently. Seeking him out. Looking at him as more than just...Brad.

It feels like we're constantly being pulled to each other.

Our senses heightened to always know where the other is.

Even when he wasn't anywhere near me, I was aware of him.

Without looking up, I could tell you exactly where he was.

Find him looking back at me.

I would register his joy before I heard his laughter.

Feel his presence before he came into my line of sight.

It was a superpower that I never knew I even possessed until the moment his lips touched mine. And I wanted to do it again.

It should have been awkward. Kissing my best friend. But somehow it felt like it was the most natural thing in the world to do.

Then when Kim accidentally let that slip—he has been in love with me? For six years?

I should feel weird about that too, but I don't. Love is something I have always associated with Brad. Sure, I've never said it to him before, but I know I feel it.

He loves me. I love him. I know that much.

We're best friends—of course we love each other.

But *in* love? How do I even know if I'm in love? How can he be so sure that he is?

He's had girlfriends before. He's kissed other girls and possibly done more than that, so how am I supposed to reconcile that with what he's saying he has always felt about me?

How can I know that what he's telling me is true and it's not just something that was borne out of the guilt he feels about the last three years? How could I?

What if we try this, make it official, and we mess it up?

I'm so consumed with my thoughts that I don't notice that Dan had already started his inquisition.

It's not until he says, "Are you sure he didn't…" that I realize I've missed everything he has said up to that point.

"Yes. He just hugged me, okay? Then Kyle and Brad were there literally within minutes. Nothing happened. I feel like they're more shaken up than I am."

I do my best to school my expression into a calm one no matter how much I wanted to cry right here, right now.

I wish Mom was here.

Dan must be feeling the same way because he glances at Mom's picture on the side table beside me. He's not equipped to help me deal with something like this. He's feeling angry and protective. Mom would have understood what I needed. She would have known the right thing to say and do.

Dan musses up his hair in frustration, resting a shoulder on the wall facing me.

"You need to talk to Dr. T about this, Liz."

I nod. I've started meeting with my therapist once a week again, usually via video chats.

Mostly so Dad and Dan can stop worrying about me. Not that it really helps. They still do. Dan still hovers. Dad still calls and checks in with Dr. T.

It's not that I don't feel anything about what happened. I did. I do.

Maybe it just hasn't quite sunk in yet. A part of me still feels like it's my fault for not saying I didn't reciprocate his feelings. But honestly, I thought he was just a shameless flirt. I didn't realize he actually wanted to be with me that way.

Before last night, Hunter had never been anything but nice to me, so when he did what he did, a small part of me felt like I deserved it. But Kyle's right.

He didn't have a right to touch me like that.

Unless I wanted him to.

Like with Brad. I don't know what changed or how it did because when Brad did it, it felt right. It felt like he didn't even need my permission to do it.

In fact, I want him to do it without asking me.

Like at lunch today, I kept hoping Brad would kiss me again.

With Hunter, I just felt gross and violated at the mere thought of him touching me like that.

Last night, after Brad left me in my room, I ran straight into the bathroom and threw up repeatedly until there was nothing more left in me.

I took a long shower, trying to scrub off how Hunter felt on me.

On my waist from where he grabbed me, I scrubbed so hard, I left marks.

I feel sick just thinking about it again.

But maybe because of what happened with Brad, I'm able to compartmentalize everything that happened over the weekend. Brad's feelings take precedence over anything else. I don't know if that's a healthy way to think and maybe there's some avoidance happening, but it's how I feel at this moment.

I look up at my brother and decide that maybe this is something I can talk to him about. Hopefully without him overreacting.

I know he likes Brad. Dan grew up with him too.

Maybe he can help me figure all this out.

I can even ignore the jabs that are sure to come because this is important to me.

"Brad kissed me."

You know those cartoons where a character's eyes bug out in shock? Like *ppoing-ppoing*?

I was expecting something like that to happen. Maybe even hoping for some validation that I wasn't as clueless as I appeared to have been for six years.

Instead, I'm rewarded with my brother's stoic mug staring back at me.

Dan folds his arms and simply waits for me to continue.

Okay. I guess he wants to hear more before formulating a more appropriate response.

"I kissed him back." I look away, knowing I'm turning as red as a tomato. "Twice."

"Before or after you gave him that monitor you dipped into your trust fund for?"

"Before."

My head is seriously starting to really hurt now.

I lay back against the couch and rub my temples.

I hear Danny sigh and leave the room. A few minutes later, he comes back, and I feel him nudge my arm. He hands me two pills and a water.

He waits for me to drink it before taking the glass from me and setting it on the table behind him. He sits next to me, contemplation written all over his face like he's trying to figure out what to say next. I'm perturbed. He isn't normally like this.

Last year I started dating this guy from Valley High that I met at the Academic Decathlon. When Dan found out, he took the next flight out to have a talk with a guy I only had a handful of dates with. It was the most disturbing thing to find my brother had browbeaten Alex in the living room. We barely finished our scheduled date after that before we both agreed to end it.

So, to see my brother like this is strangely uncharacteristic of him.

Not a single comment to offer, no advice to shove down my throat or veiled threats of dismemberment.

"Elizabeth."

Or maybe it's just wishful thinking on my part.

I wrap my arms tightly across my chest, preparing for the onslaught to come.

He adjusts himself so he's facing me and braces an arm on the back of the couch.

"I'm sorry,"

Eyes wide, I tilt my head confused. Definitely the last thing I thought he was going to say.

"For?"

An exasperated sigh leaves him and for the first time in a while, I can see the control slipping from him. Like he's letting go of something.

"Honestly? For everything."

"I don't understand—"

He shakes his head and puts a hand up. "Let me get this out."

He rubs his face in frustration and I can tell he's struggling to find the words.

"First, I'm sorry for the last few years of me just being too—"

"Overbearing?" I offer quietly.

He nods, a grin pulling at his mouth. "I was going to go with a word that starts with an A and ends with hole but that works too."

"What is making you say this now?"

He rubs a knuckle across his chin, looking embarrassed, "A few people have called me out on it. Summer has been noticing it. The second she found out I took your car keys; she gave me the dressing down of the century. I planned to apologize to you tonight before I heard about what happened to you. Then that went out the window until your boyfriend talked to me."

"How did you even find out about it?"

His jaw tightens, "One of the freshmen I was on the basketball team with was at the party. Senior now. Well, I ran into him at the Dick's downtown, and he told me about it."

Damn, I should have known. Dan and I are only three years apart, and went to the same high school, of course he would know some of the kids in my grade.

Then what he said next finally registers in my overwhelmed state of mind.

My boyfriend?

"I don't have a—wait do you mean Brad?"

Dan's grin is fully out now, amusement dancing in his eyes. He shoots me a look that says he knew about the kiss before I even told him about it.

"He called me shortly after we spoke on the phone. He wanted to talk to me before I took you home but didn't want you to know, so when I got there, I texted Brad instead of you."

I distinctly remember being told by my friends to change into sweats from the short dress Kim had styled me in. Kim pointed out that it might make my brother even more mad about the situation. And when I came out of the bathroom, both Brad and Kyle were gone.

Kim told me they were upstairs just setting up the VR goggles she and Kyle had gotten Brad for his birthday and that the boys would come down once Dan got there to walk me out. I remember thinking that was strange but didn't think too much of it because Kim had already launched into a cross-examination about what was going on with Brad and me. I didn't even question it because it had felt good to talk to Kim again and I needed her advice.

Which I got in spades. The gist was *Date him.*

"Liz. I overreacted. I should have waited until you got home to talk to you about it or waited until you were ready to tell me about what happened. I just panicked, okay?"

I glance at my brother, sighing at the pained expression on his face. I remind myself to thank Brad for once again doing something I should have done myself but was too afraid to.

I owe my brother my life. He's the one who saved me.

"I know. I'm sorry—"

Dan shakes his head vigorously; he once again puts a hand up to cut me off.

"*No*. It's not your fault. I've let my fear of losing you lead me to controlling you. I let you lock yourself in your room because it made me feel better knowing there was less of a chance of anyone or anything hurting you again that way. And it wasn't just me. Mom let you do it. Dad let you do it. We all failed you by letting you hide from life when what we should have done was encourage you to live it."

My breath catches in my throat.

"Like you are now."

Tears pool at the corners of my eyes. My brother is echoing our mom's words.

The same words that have carried me through the last grief-stricken months, knowing I'm finally doing what Mom wanted.

"Did Brad tell you all that?"

"Not in so many words because why would he? It is painstakingly clear that you still have not told them about…" He trails off. Not once in the last few years has he been able to put into words what happened to me. What I did. But I think, just like everything else, it's time for us to face it head-on and not mince words about it or skate around the subject.

I did what I did. I broke and my brother saved me.

"My suicide attempt?"

Dan shuts his eyes, sucking in a breath at my choice of words.

I choose to push past it for now. I'm not ready to dissect all the reasons why I still haven't told my friends. I don't want to hash it out right now and add it to the many reasons my head currently feels like it's about to explode.

"So, what *did* Brad say?"

Dan frowns in a way that tells me this isn't the last time we will talk about this.

"That I need to loosen the reigns completely and trust that you know what you're doing."

I raise an eyebrow, sensing there's more to it than that, "And?"

He smirks warning me that I may or may not like what he says next.

"He has every intention of taking over from now on."

"I hate to ask, but what exactly does that mean?"

Dan chortles, prompting me to smack his arm. "Just that our boy finally manned up. It took seeing another guy manhandle you to finally get over his fear of you rejecting him."

I straighten up, letting the blanket fall off my shoulders.

I stare at my brother. Shellshocked.

"Wait…did you know? Did *everyone* know?"

Guffaw. That's the only way to explain the sound that is currently coming out of my brother's mouth. I smack him repeatedly with a pillow until he holds his hands up in surrender, calming himself down enough to continue.

"I don't know if everyone did but yeah, it's so obvious that if you weren't my sister, I would seriously ask you to get your eyes checked."

He makes a show of shaking his head at me. He's all seriousness now.

"Devotion. I used to think the word was overrated, like who does that, but then lately seeing Brad practically worship the ground you walk on? Come on Liz. How did you not know?"

"But…I…." I realize I'm sputtering again but he's right. I don't understand why I didn't notice it before. But now that everyone has so nicely pointed it out, it all makes sense.

Everything becomes so glaringly obvious.

My mind starts playing specific memories like a montage.

How he reacted when he first heard about Hunter.

How he held me after Mom died.

How he helped me say goodbye to her.

How he has taken care of me these last few months.

All the small gestures of love, all the things he did for me without asking for anything in return.

Not just lately but always. He has always given and never asked.

Three years ago, how crestfallen he was when I told him I didn't want him in my life anymore. The heartbreak was written all over his face and I was so stuck in my own pain that I never saw his. Never acknowledged it for what it was. I claimed I knew him better than anyone else and I never once saw how much he truly loved and cared about me.

How much it hurt him when I cut him from my life without so much as a backwards glance.

My hands fly to my mouth as more memories play in my head, my heart pounding hard against my chest. I'm positive Dan can hear it too.

"Oh. My. God."

"I'm happy for you, Liz."

My hands drop in my lap.

"Wait—you're not mad? No threats or veiled insults about his manhood?"

Dan looks away for a moment and when he looks back at me, there's hesitation in his eyes.

"How do you feel about him?"

My brother looks at me like what he has to say next rests solely on how I feel about Brad, but I'm stuck trying to process everything.

The guilt causes my stomach to churn.

I place hands over my chest and stomach to try to ease the pressure I have building inside me. I feel like a complete fraud. Why do I deserve someone as selfless and patient as Brad?

I took for granted that he had always been there.

A constant. Even in the three years we were strangers, I knew in the back of my mind he was my safety net. There when I needed him. Regardless of the state of our friendship.

I don't deserve him. He deserves someone better.

Can I allow myself to be that selfish again?

What if I mess it up and I end up losing him again? This time there will be no going back to the way we were.

If I let myself do this, we could alter our whole friendship into something fragile.

Something I could destroy.

As if he knows exactly what I am thinking, Dan reaches out and places a hand on both of mine. I hadn't even realized I had curled them into fists, bunched in my lap.

"Lizzy. Stop it. Do not let the guilt and self-doubt you carry around with you keep you from this. I hate to see you turn your back on love and a happy future with Brad."

"Future? You think we have a future?" I blink and have to smile at that, "Okay who are you and what have you done to my big brother?"

He shakes his head at my lame attempt at a joke.

"I'm serious Liz. I will deny I ever said this but"—Dan clasps his hands behind his neck, stealing another glance at Mom's picture behind me—"I don't believe in soulmates. I feel like geography and luck have more of a hand in helping choose your partner in life than fate or destiny do. It's just shit they use to sell movies and books. That was until I watched my little sister get taken care of with such..."

"Devotion?" I offer in a shaky whisper.

He looks straight at me as he continues, unwavering in delivering his message.

"Devotion. I always suspected he had a crush on you back then, but these last few months, the way he's catered to your every need without you asking for anything? The way you don't seem to notice you do it for him too. It's unnerving as an older brother to witness. And if I hadn't seen it myself, I would rag on him the way I have on all the losers you've dated but I trust the kid. I trust Brad."

Dan runs a shaky hand through his hair, a defeated look on his face.

"True love. That's what I see when I look at the two of you. I know you're young but he's not some guy you just met. You've known each other your whole damn lives. I have to resign myself to the fact that my kid sister has already found her soulmate and I get to sit back and watch." He looks back at me, failing to suppress a scowl, "Just don't get pregnant or get married yet okay?"

I shake my head at him, trying to make sense of everything he just said.

"Who knew you could be so profound, Daniel?"

He chuckles, pulling me into a hug.

"It's time to stop hiding, Elizabeth."

It's not until much later that I realize that my brother never did wait for me to answer his question.

Breathe in. Breathe out.

Focus. Five things you can see.

Graffiti on the bathroom stall door.

Fluorescent lighting.

More graffiti on the bathroom walls.

Does that one say Jessica loves Kyle? I wonder if Kim has seen that one.

Wait. Right. Listing things I can see.

My shoes. My backpack.

Is that five or four?

I rub my chest, focusing on slowly breathing in and out. I need to calm myself down before Kyle wonders what's taking me so long in here and barges in. I still can't believe he insisted on chaperoning me to the damn bathroom.

Apparently, it wasn't enough to come and pick me up this morning and drive me to school. Kim and Brad had a student council meeting this morning, so they appointed him to be my official shadow guard.

I love my friends but maybe they also need a talking to on the whole overprotective thing.

I'm not dumb, I know what happened to me would be fodder for gossip, but I only have to see these people for a few more months. They can think and say what they want about me. The only ones whose opinions matter are of my friends, and they are already quite literally and figuratively my armor. No one will risk messing with me knowing who my friends are.

Everyone is terrified of Kim. They all worship Kyle and there isn't a single student in this school who doesn't respect Brad. I highly doubt anyone would dare to do anything but simply gossip about me. I choose to not care about it.

I have never lived my life in search of anyone else's approval.

I may have low self-esteem, but I've learned to live with my shortcomings in a way that means there isn't anyone in this world who can use my faults against me but myself.

I reach into my backpack and pull out the little pouch that has my emergency migraine prescription. I grab my reusable bottle. Even though Dan has agreed to loosen the reigns a bit— he even gave back my keys last night—this is one he refused to budge on. He still insists on regulating my prescriptions. I was prescribed migraine medication after I developed chronic migraines from my attempted suicide and because the attempt involved overdosing, Dan still doesn't trust me with meds.

I kick open the stall door while quickly downing the pills with a few sips of water.

Tucking my bottle back in my backpack, I wash my hands then lean on the sink to give myself another quick pep talk and a few more seconds of alone time.

I can do this. I've been through worse. My friends have my back and I have Brad.

The only thing giving me any stress today is knowing that at some point I will have to talk to the principal, but other than that, I can't wait for school to end.

Brad texted me last night asking if I could hang out and talk after school, which of course I agreed to. We need to figure this thing out between us.

Smiling, I remember the selfie he sent me of him posing in front of the monitor I got for him. And at the memory of his texts that came again this morning reminding me about our "date." He'd gone on to say he wished he could've been the one to pick me up and that he'd been thinking of me. I still haven't seen him and it's almost time for lunch.

I saw Kim earlier today because we have PE together. A giggle escapes me thinking about the way she scanned the gym pointedly while she talked to me. At how she glared at the two juniors who quite literally stopped to scan me from head to toe. I had to hold on to her arm to restrain her while she yelled obscenities at them.

Patting my cheeks, I roll my shoulders back and head out of the bathroom

Stepping out into the hall, I mentally prepare myself to tell Kyle to please let me walk to my next class in peace when I find him already gone.

In Kyle's place is Brad with his head down, scrolling on his phone. He hasn't noticed me yet which gives me time to really look at him. His brown hair is tousled in a way that tells me he has been running his fingers through it all morning. He's wearing a dark-gray t-shirt that hugs him just right with a black and forest green flannel over it and dark denim jeans.

With one hand in his pocket, his legs are crossed at the ankles.

He's leaning on the wall opposite where I stand, looking like he's been pulled straight from one of those teen movies with that cute boy you fell in love with and sent a love letter to.

I don't think he even knows how beautiful he really is. I notice a few girls checking him out as they walk past him, and I can't help the twinge of jealousy I feel in my gut.

Then I blush when I remember he only has eyes for me.

The ten-minute warning bell rings, prompting him to raise his head. The second he sees me, his eyes light up and if I hadn't already spent the last five minutes working on my breathing, I may have gone into cardiac arrest simply at the sight of it.

Brad pushes off the wall with his foot and as I step back to let someone pass me, I feel a hand on my elbow.

"Hey, can we talk?"

My chest tightens at the sound of Hunter's voice, but I can't look away from Brad, not now when his jaw tightens as he sees Hunter touch me.

I stiffen and angle my body away from Hunter, so his hand drops from my elbow. My eyes stay glued to Brad as he angrily crosses the crowded hall to me. I put my hand out just in time to meet his chest to put some distance between him and Hunter.

In a flash Brad pulls me gently to him, turning me around so that my back is on his chest.

"I strongly suggest you back the hell away from her right now."

Brad's growl makes me flinch and I feel his hold loosen on me as his arm circles my waist.

"This doesn't concern you man. I just want to apologize to—"

Hunter's gaze drops to Brad's arm wrapped around my waist.

"I—I didn't know you were *seeing anyone*, Elizabeth."

My eyebrow raises at the way Hunter's tone is laced with accusation.

I glare at him. "Why is that any of your business?"

I don't deny my relationship status and I don't appreciate the insinuation he is making.

God, I want to slap that look off Hunter's face, but I don't want to risk leaving Brad's hold. He's breathing hard; it would take very little to set him off right now and I have to tread carefully to avoid escalating this. I'm not about to let him get into trouble for my sake.

"Do you actually think the fact that you thought I was single excuses your behavior?"

Hunter takes a step back at the anger in my voice, his hands curl into fists, and he looks discouraged. "I've never done that before. I was faded and drunk. I like you. I thought all I had to do was kiss you and you'd let me. I can see now that that was a big mistake."

He is still eyeing Brad's arm around me, so I place a hand on top of his, letting Hunter think what he wants to think because to hell with his misplaced accusations.

I feel Brad's arm tighten around me and I can feel how close he is to his limit.

I look up at him, his jaw is still locked tight, his lips pursed in a thin line.

I pull on his arm and lace my fingers through his. I squeeze his hand until he looks down at me, his eyes blazing with barely controlled anger, but his gaze softens around the edges when he sees the reassurance on my face.

I glance back at Hunter. "I am not interested in *you*. Not now. Not ever. I hope you never treat another girl the way you treated me. Now please leave me alone."

I don't wait for his response, I tug on Brad's arm, forcing him to walk away with me.

His head snaps back, feet rooted in place as he continues to glower at Hunter.

"If you want to keep holding my hand, you're going to look away and not make me drag you down this hall."

I look over my shoulder and see Hunter dip his head and walk in the opposite direction.

With an exaggerated pull of breath, Brad maneuvers his arm to rest around my shoulder so my hand dangles from it, still gripping his. I'm both amazed and confused as to how he managed to put me under his arm with such finesse. He leads me down a less crowded hallway, and I stop to untangle myself from his hold. I prop a hand on my hip, tapping my foot for dramatic flair.

"What was that? You know better than to act like that Bradley. What's gotten into you?"

The anger dissipates from him as his shoulders relax and his lips turn up sheepishly.

"I'm sorry. I just flashbacked to last night and saw red. It won't happen again, El."

He reaches for the hand on my hip, threading his fingers through mine.

"Can I walk you to class while I convince you to have lunch with me after?"

I bite my lip, overwhelmed with the effortless way he manages to calm me down.

All the anxiety from the confrontation with Hunter has already faded away.

I know for a fact that the only reason I was even able to

stand up to Hunter was because Brad was there. He has the innate ability to quiet the voices in my head and still the panic that is constantly rising inside me until it dissolves into nothing. Making me feel more confident with myself.

I feel Brad squeeze my hand. I blink realizing he's already walking me to Physics.

I hold our hands up, "Feeling handsy today?"

He winks at me, "You said I could hold your hand if I walked away. I intend on taking full advantage of that privilege."

I bite back another smile, not wanting him to know just yet how much I love the feel of his hand against mine.

Warm, gentle, and safe. Just like him.

"Okay that was cute, I'll have lunch with you."

A laugh shoots out of him, "That was easy. I thought for sure you were going to make me work for it."

I shrug, "Oh, I will. You owe me answers, remember? And I've added two things to my list."

"What two things?"

"Well for starters, what did you tell Dan? Second, I need you to call off the bodyguards."

We stop just outside the lab. He looks down at me, concern etched on his face.

"It's just until the rumors die down, okay? Besides after what that di—he just tried to pull right now; I'm even more convinced it won't be the last time he tries to get you alone again."

I let go of his hand and squeeze his arm.

"Brad. I appreciate the sentiment and I know you're doing this to protect me but wasn't it just yesterday when you had a chat with my brother about his overprotective ways? Don't you see that you're doing exactly what he's been doing?"

He sucks in a breath and looks away, signs of frustration

marring his features. I squeeze his shoulder again to get his attention.

"How about this? If you promise that you won't pick a fight with Hunter, then I'm going to shut up and be grateful that my friends love me enough to want to act like my bodyguards."

His brow wrinkles but there's a hint of teasing in his eyes as he gazes down at me.

"Your friend? Is that what I am? I could have sworn you just implied you weren't single."

I purse my lips in an attempt to stop from smiling again but he catches me in the act.

He closes in and swiftly kisses me on the forehead.

"We can save that talk for later after school."

With a tilting grin, Brad takes a step back then another until he's walking backwards from me. "I'll come back to get you for lunch."

With another wink and a wave, he turns the corner and he's out of my line of sight.

I lean back on the wall, my hands on my flaming cheeks. I trace my fingers up to my forehead where I still feel the imprint of his lips, like he somehow branded me as his.

Another realization hits me, my heart has not stopped racing since the moment I stepped out of the bathroom and these damn butterflies in my tummy have not grown tired of flapping around yet. And it's all because of the boy I've known my whole life.

Seriously, what is he doing to me?

Brad

"How much longer do you think they'll be in there?"

Kim sighs, rolling her eyes as she taps on her phone next to me.

"I don't know." I grunt, annoyed that I'm not in there to give Liz support.

Halfway through lunch, I got a call from Mom saying she was on her way because she received a call from Principal Gardner about Liz.

Uncle Will has appointed her Liz's guardian until she turns eighteen in January.

To say Mom was mad is a complete understatement. She's completely livid that I didn't tell her about the incident in the kitchen between Hunter and Liz. After I basically kicked her and Dad out of the house for my party claiming we didn't need chaperones. Words like grounded and no more parties were shot at me as my mother blasted me.

They pulled Liz out of last period an hour ago and Kyle was called in along with Coach shortly after. If I was hazarding a guess, Hunter is in there as well.

I feel Kim's gaze on me as I run my fingers through my hair again, tugging on the ends in frustration.

"What's up with you?"

I send her a look that I hope shuts her up but instead she

raises an eyebrow at me. She shifts to scoot closer to me, crossing her arms petulantly as if to say, *You asked for it*.

We've known each other since we were eight. I brace myself knowing she's about to grill me like she's been itching to do since yesterday.

"So…you going to tell me what happened with you two?"

I can pretend I don't know what she means or distract her with prom talk but that would just prolong the inevitable. So, I resign myself with the simplest of truths.

"I kissed her." I say this softly enough that she's the only one who hears. We are seated outside the principal's office and there are nosy eyes and ears all around us. "Twice."

"I know."

"She told you? What—what did she say?"

She quirks another eyebrow and stares at me thoughtfully.

"That you kissed her." She looks away, suppressing a smile, "Twice."

"Kimberly." I'm hoping the warning in my voice is enough for her to heed it.

Rolling her eyes, she slaps her knees. "Fine. But it never came from me, okay? And I think you're going to be pleasantly surprised."

Now it was my turn to raise an eyebrow. *Oh?*

I wait for her to continue, stifling the urge to tap my fingers impatiently on my thighs.

"I think she's just really stuck on the whole six years thing." She shoots me an apologetic smile, "Which is my fault because we all know that when Liz overthinks, it can be hard to get through to her. I think underneath all that, she acknowledges that she has feelings for you too that she didn't even realize were there."

I can't help the wide grin that forms on my face despite the situation we're in right now.

Kim matches my grin and nudges me. "I think you two have been skating around that fact for a while now and you were just quicker to figure it out."

I nod. I've been thinking the same thing too.

I may have panicked a bit at first but last night as I lay in bed, I replayed the weekend over in my head. All I could see was Liz.

Liz kissing me back. Liz looking back at me without hesitation.

And that look in her eyes every time she did?

I'd bet my trust fund it matches the one in mine when I look at her.

The facts are there.

Liz didn't stop me.

She let me kiss her. She kissed me back. Both times.

She let me hold her. She held me back.

She let me in.

She didn't shy away or hide afterwards either.

I just need to give her time to catch up. To figure it out. I just hope she doesn't ask for space to do so because all I've been able to think about is kissing and holding her again.

Kim clears her throat.

Lost in my thoughts, I missed her waving a hand in front of me and the twinkle in her eye tells me she knows exactly what I'm thinking.

"I'm glad were friends again, Kimmy."

Her head bobs in agreement, "Me too."

Kim's phone buzzes and she heaves another sigh as she furiously taps away on in her messaging app.

"Who are you texting so angrily?"

"My mom. She wants me to come home so we can go get a tree. And I'm trying to explain to her why I can't but she's being a—"

She is interrupted when the door swings open and we both look up just in time to see Coach Wilde walk out of the principal's office. He's followed by Hunter and an older blonde woman who bears such a striking resemblance to him she must be his mom.

Kyle follows them out and finally Mom walks out with Liz bringing up the rear.

Coach Wilde heads straight out the door leading to the track and fieldhouse. Kyle sees us out of the corner of his eye and quickly sprints to us, giving Kim a peck on the cheek.

"I can't stay, the rest of the team is waiting for us out on the field. I'll talk to you guys later."

He looks at me quickly, "Your mom was on fire in there... but good luck. She's not happy with any of us."

Giving Kim another quick kiss, he tells her he'll call her, and he jogs to catch up with Coach.

I start to get up, but Kim places a hand on my knee. She tips her head over to where my mom and Hunter's Mom are talking to each other in hushed whispers.

Mom has her hand firmly on Liz's shoulder. Liz still hasn't looked up, her arms crossed in front of her. I can tell she's fighting the urge to bolt. She lightly sways back and forth on her heels, her backpack thumping slightly with her movements.

Hunter unabashedly stares at Liz in a way that makes me want to punch his face, if it weren't for our current audience and the fast track to the principal's office.

But mostly I restrain myself because I promised Liz, I wouldn't fight him. But fuck, I really want to ream his pretty face in and see how he likes being manhandled.

"Don't." Kim grumbles under her breath but her hands are flexing like she's thinking the same thing I am.

Good. Maybe she can take a swing at him for both of us.

Her mom isn't here. She didn't promise Liz anything.

But neither of us do. We sit and wait silently as the adults finish up their conversation.

With a final nod to my mom, Hunter's mom leans in as if wanting to hug Liz, prompting Liz to take a step back. Liz slightly raises her head to acknowledge the older woman politely but declines her attempt.

Hunter's mom looks distressed but doesn't push it as she hooks an arm around her son, practically dragging him out in the same direction Kyle and Coach went.

"Guess we know where he got it from." Kim murmurs.

I can't help it, I snort.

Liz's head snaps up and our gazes lock. A slow smile of relief spreads on her face.

But I inadvertently got Mom's attention too and the ice-cold look she's leveling at me gives Elsa a run for her money.

"Shit. Okay that's my cue to go before *my* mom looks at me like that too."

Kim grabs her backpack from the floor and gets up. She pats me on the head, getting close enough to whisper, "For what it's worth I think the way Liz is looking at you right now is worth the way Aunt Rose is glaring. Good luck Bradley."

Kim hastily waves a goodbye to Liz and Mom then speed-walks away.

Stifling a groan, I get up too and meet them halfway.

I lean in, kissing Mom on the cheek, ignoring the ice in her eyes.

"Hi Mom."

"Hmmm."

Yup. Still mad.

I choose to ignore it and just face her wrath later, turning my attention to Liz.

"Are you okay, El?"

Liz's opens her mouth to respond but Mom cuts her off.

"I have to go but I expect both of you at dinner. Five sharp. We *will* talk about this later."

Mom pats Liz's cheek tenderly, "I'm proud of you. You were brave in there."

Then she levels me with a look so cold, I feel my insides shiver. With a terse nod, satisfied that she has just successfully terrified her only son, she marches away, her red-soled heels clicking on the linoleum floors, each step feeling like it is stabbing me with her disappointment.

I shake my head as the knowledge of my parents upset with me settles on me like a weight.

A resigned sigh breaks me out of my stupor. Liz is watching me watch my mom's retreating back with a dejected look on her face.

I force a smile at her. "Are you okay?"

Her gaze is transfixed on mine, her eyes searching for something I can't quite put my finger on until she shuts her eyes for a brief moment.

Taking a deep breath, her eyes no longer meeting mine, Liz simply shakes her head. Pulling one strap off her shoulder, she digs into her backpack and pulls out her phone.

A chill trickles down my spine, and this time it has nothing to do with my mom and everything to do with the defeated set of Liz's shoulders.

I ease her backpack off of her shoulders and sling it on my arm.

"Talk to me. What's going on?"

She raises a shoulder as if to shrug but without her backpack as a shield, I start to see the way her fingers shake as they tighten around her phone.

Concern pierces me and my eyes scan the rest of her.

I notice her short huffs of breath and immediately I can tell that she's on her way to having a panic attack. I instantly wrap an arm around her and guide her outside to my car.

I settle her in the passenger side before throwing our bags in the backseat of my Rover.

I climb into the driver's side, turning the car on, making sure the AC is at a comfortable 70 degrees before shifting in my seat to face her. I wait for her breathing to slow down and give her space. I murmur her reassurances, letting her know I'm here for her and I don't plan on going anywhere. Sensing that she's coming out of it, I lean over to take her left hand and give it a soothing squeeze. I grab a water bottle from the center console and hand it to her, making sure to uncap it first.

"Drink some water El."

Her eyelids flutter open, revealing a sheen in her eyes like she's about to cry.

Tamping down the strong need to curse, I use my free hand to cup the back of her neck. I focus on massaging the tense muscles hoping I can relieve some of the tension she's feeling.

I'm rewarded with a soft moan that makes my insides quiver and heat blaze through me.

I reach over and turn the thermostat down to 68.

"I'm sorry." She whispers after she takes a long sip of water. She hugs the water close and sniffs, shaking her head with remorse.

Restrained by the center console and the fact that we're still on full display of our schoolmates here in this parking lot, I resist the urge to pull her into my lap.

"For what?"

"Your parents are mad at you because of me."

I take the bottled water from her, putting the cap back on.

I reach over and gently turn her so she's facing me.

"They're concerned for you. I really should have told them what happened. That's why Mom is so upset because *you're family*. She just wants you safe and protected like we all do. She cares about you and hates that this happened."

She doesn't look convinced, so I tip her chin up, "El. What happened in there?"

Her glossy eyes meet mine and she raises her hand to grasp mine that's holding her chin.

"Nothing too crazy. Principal Gardner can't do anything but give him a verbal warning."

I start to protest this, letting her go. I twist around to reach for the door handle fully intending to march back into the school and demand a better outcome, when she pulls my hand back to hers.

"Listen. Hunter didn't hurt me, and it didn't happen on school property."

"Didn't hurt—?" A row of expletives shoots out of my mouth before I can stop it, making her chuckle through the tears pooling in her eyes.

Have they not heard of emotional distress? And I was the one who pulled him off of her.

Yes, fuck, he hurt her. I should have been in that office.

This time, she reaches for me, her hand on my cheek, making me look at her.

"But your mom fought it. She said that there needed to be punishment for his behavior, or it could lead to other student athletes taking advantage of female students because they let Hunter get away with it. She used a bunch of legal jargon that I would not be able to repeat."

Liz leans back but she tucks my hand in between hers. She faces me, her cheek resting on the leather seat while her eyes roam my face. "You should have seen the look your mom gave

Coach Wilde when she said that. He looked like he wanted to pee his pants. Basically, he had no choice but to suspend Hunter for two games and put him on probation for the rest of the season. He's a junior so it will affect him since he's gunning to replace Kyle after he graduates."

I exhale a long sigh of relief. Well, that's something, at least.

I scan her face, her exhaustion evident. I bet it wasn't easy for Liz to be subjected to that. Especially without her mom there with her.

"Are you okay, El?"

She wipes the moisture from her eyes. "I don't know. I feel like I am, but I know I'm not."

Grabbing her phone from under her thigh, I realize she has left my hand to rest there. I pull it away not needing the extra temptation to take more than she can give right now.

"I should call my brother"—she looks out the window and I feel the distance she starts putting between us before she even finishes her sentence—"to come pick me up."

"El."

I've always thought of myself as a person who stays and fights.

While Liz…she's the type to fight long enough to say her piece then flee and right now, she's due for a good run.

I can practically hear her thoughts like they're my own. She's trying to figure out a way to tell me she wants to be left alone but I'm determined to get past those walls she keeps putting back up. I have to reaffirm my intentions to her, so she knows she doesn't need to fall back on that option anymore.

"I need you to look at me. Can you do that? Please."

I hear the rasp in my voice and cringe.

Liz glances back at me and I see the panic setting back in.

She doesn't want to offend me, but the fear is so palpable in her gaze that I know I have to find a way for her to let me back in.

"You want to go home?"

She bites her lip, making me falter for a bit but when she nods her head tentatively like she's unsure if that's what she wants. I strengthen my resolve.

"Because your house, your room is your safe space?"

Liz's eyes widen for a bit with the knowledge that I truly understand her. Then her gaze softens and her answering firm nod is all the push I need as I reach for her hands.

"Do you think that maybe…" I look down at our joined hands and lace my fingers through hers. "I can be your refuge instead?"

Her breath catches and our gazes meet. The air between us practically crackles.

I feel my chest tighten from the intensity in her eyes.

Breaking the connection, I let go of one of her hands.

I turn the thermostat down again to cool myself off and also as an added measure to keep me from kissing her like I desperately want to.

"Brad."

It's the faintest of whispers but I feel it in every bone in my body.

Liz is looking at me like I'm the only person in the world. With all the softness and affection, I've always associated with her. Tilting her head, she gives me that smile that I know she reserves just for me.

"You've always been home to me."

I feel her lips touch my cheek in the most tender way, her breath fanning my face.

She's back in her seat by the time I can breathe again.

Taking my hand, she places it on the gear shifter.

She buckles herself in. "Where do you want to go?"

Running a hand through my hair, trying to think of anything except the warmth of her on my cheek, I put my seatbelt on. Checking the time, I realize we don't have much time before the dinner we have both been summoned to, so I opt for the safest option to avoid being late.

Liz

I chuck a grape at Brad who catches it with his mouth. He winks at me before going back to work on his computer. I set the empty bowl on the floor and nestle myself back on to the pillows, feeling more comfortable than I have in a long time.

About a half hour ago, Brad was in the middle of showing me the game he was working on when he found a glitch. So now I'm sitting in the alcove in his room, reading on my Kindle.

I'm trying to focus on the words in front of me but ever since the tense conversation that happened in Principal Gardner's office and the sweet way Brad took care of me after in the car, I've been having a hard time concentrating.

When we got to his house, my nerves got the best of me. I did everything I could to stall our impending conversation. First, I dragged him to the kitchen where I sliced and washed every piece of fruit I could find. Then I challenged him to a round of scrabble which he won. The bookworm in me is still having a hard time dealing with that.

Then we did homework but since he is as meticulous as I am, we barely had much to do so I convinced him to show me his game.

I can tell by the amused way the corner of his mouth tilted up that he knew I was stalling but he let me. So maybe I'm not the only one who's nervous about all this.

In the car earlier, when he asked me to let him be my refuge, everything that had happened up to that point just melted away. All the stress from Hunter, fear of falling apart, and thoughts of my mom got pushed back to the recesses of my mind while Brad edged himself front and center.

I felt instantly calm. Safe.

But I didn't know how to say that to him or express how I feel because I have never not felt this way about him. How do I explain when I couldn't even put it into words myself?

All I think about and feel when I look at him is *home*. So, I said that.

I feel it coming though. Sensing it in the way his leg has started bouncing. In the frequency of his stolen glances my way. Even though the silence is comfortable between us, he's itching to talk to me but doesn't want to push which makes me feel guilty for putting it off.

I tuck my E-reader behind me. I wrap my arms around my legs, resting my chin on my knees, giving him my undivided attention. Brad's thick brows meet in concentration while his long fingers practically fly across his keyboard as he types away, similar to the way my mom's would when she was writing one of her books and she was in the groove.

I wish she was here to help me put how I feel into words. She was good at that. Finding the right words to best convey even the trickiest of feelings like she often did with her characters.

Feeling the weight of my stare, Brad stiffens then looks up, and a thoughtful expression crosses his face before he rises and crosses the room to me.

He crawls into the alcove with me, easing my legs on his lap.

"El. I think we've done enough avoiding, don't you?"

The weight of that question settles in me like a cement block.

"Six years?" I blurt out. It's been floating around in my head ever since Kim let it slip.

Groaning, he looks down at my legs, tucking them closer to him like he's afraid I'll run away.

"Sixth grade. Evan Hudson."

I choke on my spit. Evan Hudson?

I have not thought about that Zac Efron-lookalike in a long time. Pretty sure he moved to Oregon after middle school. What did he have to do...?

I blink at him, confused, hoping he can explain further, but he still isn't looking at me.

Evan...Evan.

A memory pokes through the haze of comparison and I remember it.

"Because Evan asked me to a dance?"

He gives me a sheepish look.

"I said no."

Then it hits me why he is looking guilty.

"You picked a fight with me. You didn't speak to me for over a week..."

Flinching, he looks away.

"You went to the dance with Sara!"

Now he's actively avoiding looking at my eyes.

"Bradley. Dean."

"Ouch. You full-named me."

I smack his arm and the words fly out in a flurry of repressed anger. "You're damned right, I full-named you. Do you know how scared I was back then that I was going to lose my best friend? And *I didn't even know why*. I had to beg Dan to buy me a gross lizard for you just to get you to talk to me again because—because…you—" I poke his arm on my leg. "Picked. A. Fight. Over. Some. Boy. I. Said. No. To."

"I was jealous." He looks ashamed now.

The hurt sixth grade Liz felt is slowly building up inside me needing an outlet for…

I wrench my legs out from under his arm. There's a bit of a struggle and it happens so fast. One second, I'm wrestling my legs out from under him, and the next I'm plopped gently on his lap as he hugs me tightly to his chest, burying his face in the crook of my neck.

"I'm sorry El…" he whispers, and I can feel him breathe me in slowly.

I shiver at the contact then remember I'm supposed to be mad. I push his shoulders back and level him with my best glare…well, as good as I can muster. My resolve is weakening with him touching me like this and looking at me like…that.

Aunt Rose calls it his puppy dog eyes.

He gives me a look from underneath his lashes that would make grown women weep.

Even back then, he could always make me forgive him with just a look.

When we were eight and he cut the ears off of my teddy bear because he was so upset that I wanted to play with my new friend Kim, not him, he gave me this exact look, wielding it like a weapon.

Folding my arms, I use my hair to hide my face from him so he can't see the smile pulling at the corner of my lips. "You don't play fair."

He tucks my hair behind my ear.

"I have another confession." Shaking his head, he corrects himself. "I have several but…I—uh…I let that lizard lose out in the backyard right after the dance."

"I'm not following…"

He tightens the arm resting on my hip while running his fingers through his hair, lightly tugging on the ends as if buying time. He starts looking guilty again.

"Uh... after we had that fight and you walked in on Kyle and me talking, Kyle saw you coming just as I was saying how I liked you so he covered it up by saying I liked lizards and I went along with it just to see if you would, you know, actually get me one."

I burst out laughing. I can't help it. It is so absurd. So random.

"El?"

I haven't laughed like this in a long time, and it feels good.

Tears from laughter stream down my cheeks at the recollection of those moments from our childhood. We were so damned carefree. God, I miss it.

"Sounds like Kyle." I smack his arm. "You jerk. I can't believe you guys."

He chuckles, swiping my tears away with his thumbs.

"We were twelve. I've grown up El."

Releasing a sigh of contentment, he pulls me deeper into his arms.

"Can you let me hold you while I say what I need to? It'll give me strength to get this all out."

I nod in his chest because this moment suddenly feels fragile somehow and it isn't like I'm not relishing being in the safety of his arms.

I also need all the strength I can get.

"I know you're wondering why I dated other girls when I had—have—feelings for you and I'm not proud of myself either for that. They deserved better. You deserve better."

My breath hitches. I will myself to stay silent and let him say what he needs to.

"In middle school, I was confused. I mean, we've known

each other our whole lives. I didn't know if I was jealous or simply feeling overprotective and possessive about you. I mean I always...loved you. I don't remember a time that I didn't, so what's different about it? But when I started getting angry with any guy who gave you attention? When I started getting consumed with thoughts of you. I started figuring out that maybe it was something else. But then I got scared that I would lose this friendship if I messed it up, you know? Or what if you didn't feel the same way? So, I fought my feelings then."

I nod. I've been going through those same thoughts too.

He tips my chin up to meet his eyes.

"I *was* going to tell you, freshman year, but everything got so weird between us. All of us. I mean, now that I know why everything fell apart then, I wish I'd gotten past my ego and told you how I felt. And the last three years..."

His hold on me loosens as he leans back on the bay window, but his eyes never leave mine.

"I can't tell you how many times I thought about stopping you in the hall or coming over to your house, but I was afraid you were going to blow me off. You barely even looked at me in school. And I was heartbroken, I said fuck it, got pissy about that. So, I did what I thought was right at the time. I dated. Tried to forget about you. Wanted to get lost in someone else. Maybe I even liked some of them, but it never even came close to how I still felt—feel—about you." He rests his chin on the top of my head. "They weren't you."

Guilt slams into me fast. I did that. Because I was selfish.

All the irrational and unsure thoughts I had last night while talking to Dan come rushing back. I feel nauseous, bile steadily rising to my throat, and I break eye contact.

Brad senses my inner turmoil. He quickly sets me back down on the cushions and kneels until were eye level again. "El. Hey. Don't shut down on me. Please."

189

Taking my hands in his, he kisses my knuckles tenderly. Like a magnet, I'm looking at him again through the tears pooling in my eyes.

"I didn't know—I'm so—"

He grips the back of my neck and drops his forehead to mine.

"Don't you *dare* say you're sorry. This isn't just on you. We *both* messed up, but we have to try...*No*, we need to get past that."

His thumb starts massaging the hollow of my throat, "I love you, El."

Brad

I love you, El.

I shut my eyes. The gravity of finally saying those words to her hits me like a two-ton truck.

Both of us are breathing hard, our air comingling in the inches between us. I can kiss her with the smallest of movements, but I don't dare yet. I stole those kisses before I told her how I feel. I want to do this right and in order to do that, the next time we kiss needs to be *her* choice. I've had years to sit on my feelings and really understand them. She has had days. She needs more time. Patience is all I've got here.

Strengthening my resolve, I open my eyes, fully intending to tell her just how much I love her again when my bedroom door flies open.

Liz and I both freeze at the sound. She moves slightly away from me, and I quickly remove my hands from her, standing.

I turn and find my mom with a hand on the doorknob.

I watch embarrassed as the frown on my mom's face grows into a full-on Cheshire cat grin. She works hard to school her features into a stern look, but the corners of her mouth keep pulling up. Immediately I know she's already making assumptions.

"Dinner . . ." She stutters, shaking her head. "Dinner will be ready soon."

I can hear Liz behind me smothering a laugh, but I don't want to indulge my mom.

Giving her a pointed look, I say, "We'll be right behind you."

A well-manicured brow rises to her forehead, and she gives me a look as if to say, *You're not off the hook yet but I approve.* Inwardly rolling my eyes, I muster a smile and nod.

"Twenty minutes." With a tap on the door, she closes the door behind her.

Smooth, mom. Any other mother would demand the door be left open if she walked in on her son with a girl in his room but not my mom.

Not that I'm not thrilled but I know it has everything to do with the fact that it's Liz and nothing to do with how much she trusts me.

I hear giggling behind me, and I turn to find that Liz is laughing again while she zips up her backpack.

God, I love her laughter. She doesn't do it enough anymore but when she does, I feel like the luckiest guy in the world to be in the presence of it.

"Your mom isn't very subtle, is she?"

I allow myself the eye roll making Liz laugh again.

Hallelujah. What else do I need to do to make you do that again?

"No. I'm a little afraid of what she's plotting, now that she's walked in on what she thinks she walked in on."

Liz grins at that, pulling her hair into a knot with the scrunchie she wears on her wrist.

"What do you mean?"

"She made it clear to me that our moms have been hoping…" Rubbing my nose of a phantom itch. I hesitate to finish the thought. Not knowing how to explain it without reminding her of the fact that her mom isn't here or putting more pressure on her.

"I bet they did."

She doesn't look surprised at all.

"Oh?"

"We can talk about my mom, Brad. It's okay to talk about her around me. It makes me feel like she's still here with me somehow."

I give her arm a gentle squeeze before taking her backpack from her.

She eyes my awkward movements, tilting her head in thought.

"Brad?"

"Hm?"

"Thank you for not giving up on me."

Dropping all pretense of restraint, I cup her face. For a breadth of a moment, I simply look at her trying to convey everything I feel and want to say.

She may not have said the words back to me, but I see it in the way she looks at me right now. I feel it in my gut.

I feel it in the way she cups my hands over her face, moving my hands to her hips as she hugs me close. In the way she's squeezing me like she never wants me to let her go.

Fat chance of that.

I feel her sigh into my chest, her shoulders relaxing.

I kiss her hair and reluctantly pull her back. I am still very much aware of the fact that my mom is stewing downstairs, and I don't want to risk pissing her off now that she's calmed down. I value my freedom too much to be grounded right now.

"I'm not going to push for more than you're ready for, okay El? Right now, just take the time to figure things out. Hopefully you can start to see me not just as your friend but as a guy who is hopelessly in love with you."

She sucks in a breath and opens her mouth to speak. I shake my head at her.

"Take your time, El. I'm not going anywhere."

I jerk my head towards the door. "Dinner?"

Liz nods, slipping out of my grasp but she holds her hand out for me to take. I don't even bother to hide the goofy grin that spreads on my face as I let her lead me downstairs.

Mom is going to have a hard time staying mad at me now.

JUST AS EXPECTED, Mom is practically over the moon when we walk into the dining room hand-in-hand, but she doesn't press for details.

I don't say much or contribute to the dinner conversation between Mom and Liz, mostly because I still fear my mom's wrath. It was a really shitty thing for me to not tell her about what happened. Liz is like a daughter to her. The daughter of her best friend who just died. The sense of responsibility she feels must be overwhelming at best.

Mom has yet to bring up the Hunter thing, but I know my mom—she's biding her time. Makes me wish Dad was here to back me up. He had to fly to the San Francisco office last night to prepare for the launch of his new streaming app.

During a lull in their conversation after they talk about Aunt Cat's final novel that will be releasing postmortem, I realize what's coming up next week.

"When's Dad coming home?"

Mom looks up as she pushes her plate away from her.

"Wednesday next week, honey. He'll be back for Thanksgiving—"

Beside me, Liz takes a sip of water smiling at me from over

the rim when her eyes meet mine. I momentarily get distracted and don't hear the rest of what Mom says to me.

"Well?" Mom barks out a short laugh and claps her hands together.

Liz and I both turn to look at her like we have just been caught doing something we weren't supposed to be doing.

Mom gives us an indulgent smile before resting her elbows on the table. She props her chin in her hands and raises her eyebrows at me, silently waiting.

I sigh, running a hand through my hair.

"Mom. It was my fault. I never—"

Mom drags a long pull of breath, holding a hand up to cut me off.

"It happened in my house, right?"

I nod.

"At my son's birthday party, yes?"

Fuck. Another nod.

"To Liz. My best friend's daughter whom I consider my own, correct?"

I don't even bother responding this time. I feel Liz's pinky wrap around mine as my hand rests on her knee. We used to do this when we were kids and one of us got in trouble.

I calm myself down with slow deep breaths. Even though I know I fucked up, I hate that my mom is putting me in a position like this in front of Liz who already has enough to deal with without feeling guilt over this too.

"Mom." I call her with just enough warning in my tone.

Mom flicks a glance at Liz, who has her head down. Liz is staring down at her lap, guilt-stricken, and Mom visibly reigns herself in realizing what her words are doing.

"Liz, honey. Have you spoken with your dad?"

"Dan talked to him about it last night. We decided it was

best if dad didn't get worked up considering he's letting us spend Thanksgiving with our *Lola*."

Her *Lola*, her grandmother, lives in Portland with the rest of her mom's family.

I haven't realized that she won't be around for Thanksgiving break until now. Which means, I won't see her for a week.

"Letting you?" There is an unmistakable edge to Mom's words. "And when is he—your dad coming home?"

No doubt about it, Mom is still pissed at Uncle Will. She has never really forgiven him for breaking Aunt Cat's heart. Or for how he's handling everything since she died. I've heard her vent to Dad about it.

If it were up to Mom, Liz would be here with us instead of living without a parent because her dad can't be bothered to rearrange his life for his kids. Dan is technically an adult at twenty-one, but it isn't his responsibility to parent his sister either.

"Sometime in January. I imagine it's a lot to take care of moving from Cali to here especially with dad's practice and Olivia's business."

Mom hums, tapping her fingers on the table, "In time for your birthday?"

Liz sucks in a breath, looking thrown. "I don't think so."

"Then it's settled. I'm planning the debut."

Liz stiffens in her seat, her back straight as a rod. "I don't want a *debut*, Aunt Rose."

Liz pronounces it *deh-boo*. I've heard her mention this once before.

In the Filipino culture they mark turning eighteen as a rite of passage. They throw a formal coming of age celebration into adulthood called "a debut," similar to a *quinceañera*.

Mom is silent for longer than it's comfortable and I'm about to say something when she quietly states, "Your mom really wanted you to have one."

Liz looks away, a hint of sadness marring her expression before addressing Mom again.

"I know, and I really appreciate the offer, Auntie, but it's not something I've ever wanted. I know Mom only did because she never had one, but it's just not for me."

Thankfully, Mom doesn't push. I reach over and take Liz's hand, my thumb stroking her wrist in comfort. It takes me a few minutes to realize Mom has left.

I only notice when Liz looks up, pulling her hand from mine. She gets up, looking around.

"Is—is Aunt Rose mad?"

Frowning, I push off the table but then Mom comes back carrying a large rectangular box.

She sets it on the other side of our long dining table where it's clear of food and plates.

"Liz. Have you given some thought to going to Prom this year?"

I jerk my head to look at Liz, curious too. I know she didn't go last year. Ever since I figured out, I was still harboring feelings for her; I've been wondering if she would go if I asked her. There isn't anyone else I want to go with. If she ended up saying no, then I didn't see the point in going even though I'm technically obligated to as class president.

"You didn't go last year." I say this as a matter-of-factly because I did in fact wait until the last possible second to leave prom last year hoping she would show up.

Liz purses her lips in thought and shrugs.

"Your mom was really disappointed you didn't go last year. Even when you were asked."

I feel my fist tighten into a ball just thinking about any other guy with her. I can tell mom's baiting me, but I know better than to take it.

I try not to roll my eyes. I just want her to get to the point.

"Where is this going Mom?"

With a snide smile, Mom opens the box to reveal a dress. She pulls it out, enough so we can see it, the skirt draped over the table. Then she describes it to Liz in detail.

I don't know much about fashion, so I tune out most of it.

The dress is an off the shoulder pale pink ball gown with a tulle skirt covered in handstitched flowers running the front.

Liz gasps beside me as she runs her fingers through the fluffy fabric of the skirt and over the embroidered flowers. Her mouth forms an O-shape as she openly gushes at the dress.

"I've seen this dress before…" Liz's brows draw together as she tries to figure it out.

"It was…" Mom's answering smile is nostalgic and sad.

Recognition dawns on Liz.

"My mom's." Liz finishes as she lifts the dress to look at it for a beat before putting it back in the box. She looks at mom in question.

"Your mom?" I lean my back on the wall next to the glass door leading into the kitchen.

"It was her prom dress. Why do you have this Auntie?"

"She gave it to me to pass it on to you. Do you remember when I asked you to come run some errands with me a while ago and I took you to get your measurements done?"

"For your vow renewal that you never…wait—this is what it was for?"

"Yes honey, I had alterations done to it. Shortened it since your mom was taller and adjusted the top since"—Mom smirks, giving me a side-eye glance—"you're a little more well-endowed than your mom."

Do not look at it. Do not look at her chest. I look down at my feet and cross them to avoid anyone seeing that my face is beet red.

I hear Liz laugh and I look up just in time to see her lift the dress again.

"I can't believe she gave this to you, like she knew she wouldn't be around to…"

"It was more like she was hoping I could convince you to go. There's a reason her prom dress looks like a debutante's gown. Your *Lola* had it made in the Philippines for your mother's eighteenth birthday. So maybe instead of a *debut* you can go to prom. In this."

Liz's gaze roams the dress before she places it back in the box and gingerly closes the top.

"I guess I'm going to prom?" She glances at me hesitantly before turning to my mom and giving her a hug. "Thanks Auntie. I love it."

"Don't thank me, honey. It was important to your mom that you experience every part of your senior year since you missed so much. I intend to make sure you do. You can try on the dress at home and if it needs to be further altered, we can get it fixed."

Mom gives Liz a quick hug before patting me on the cheek

"I'm headed upstairs to finish some work. Don't stay up too late, okay? It's a school night."

I wait until Mom's out of the dining room before pulling Liz between my legs.

"So, you're going to prom?" I grin down at her, placing my hands on her hips.

Liz laughs incredulously, "I guess I am."

"Need a date?"

She purses her lips, tilting her head up at me. "Depends. Who's asking?"

"Me."

"Okay."

"Okay?"

"If *you're* asking, then yes, I'll go."

The implication isn't lost on me. It makes me only want to kiss her more, but I control the urge. She hasn't fully made her mind up about us yet. I don't want to pressure her for more than she's ready for, so I kiss the top of her head instead.

I'm so happy. I know I'm grinning like a lovesick fool. I'm so lost on her.

Liz smiles back at me and for a moment we just look at each other.

This is the happiest I have seen her in a long time. My chest tightens, relishing the thought that I did that. I give in to temptation and I place another kiss on her scrunched-up nose.

Liz

I can't think when Brad looks at me like that.

Like I'm everything. Like he can't get enough.

Then he goes and kisses me like he can't stand not touching me for a single second.

I lift my hands up, feeling the need to touch his face, but suddenly fear and uncertainty has my fingers drifting back and forth between us.

Brad's eyes crinkle with amusement and something akin to adoration as he takes my hands in his and places them on his cheeks.

"You never have to wonder if you can touch me or have to ask permission."

Leaving my hands on his face, he reaches between us and hugs me close, kissing my temple. "I've always been yours."

He pulls back, letting our foreheads touch, and drags a deep breath. He folds one of my hands in his and gently tugs me towards the front door.

"Let's get you home, *prom date*."

Or at least that's what I think he said. I'm stuck on the four words that came before that. I let them settle. Repeat them over in my head. Hear them in his voice.

I've always been yours.

Yours. Mine. His.

I let that wash over me.

It hits me like a wave.

Full force. A truth that is as basic as needing oxygen to survive.

I've always been his, too.

Like we were born for each other.

He said he was giving me time to see him like that but why do I feel like, deep down, I've always known it?

That I've been his, my entire life.

That somehow, I was already spoken for without even knowing it.

This is a fact. A basic truth.

I barely dated and when I did, it didn't feel right. This is the *why*.

I hid in my room because nothing felt safe until he was back in my life.

Until I was back in his.

He is home. My safe space. My haven. My refuge.

I see him and instantly, I know I'm safe. I know I'm home.

"El? El? Are you okay?"

I blink and realize I'm already standing on the steps leading to the driveway. Brad is standing next to his car, looking up at me. He's down there carrying my backpack and prom dress while I stand up here lost in the truths that have hit me.

Brad sees something in my eyes that has him quickly placing my things in his car.

He slowly makes his way back to me searching my eyes, because he knows me well enough to sense something's happening.

He doesn't stop until he's two steps down and were at eye level.

He hesitates for half a second before grazing a finger across my cheek.

"Talk to me."

He's whispering like he doesn't want to interrupt but needs to know I'm okay.

My heart is racing as I stare back at him void of hesitation.

"You said I need time to see you."

Brad's eyes widen a fraction, hope stirring beneath his gaze. He visibly swallows and nods. He's afraid to break this moment.

But I'm not afraid. For the first time in a long time fear isn't running a course through me.

I let my fingers touch his chest then I slide them up to loop around his neck.

I keep my gaze steady and locked on his.

"I've always been yours too."

I close the distance between us. I finally kiss him like I've always wanted to but never knew it.

I throw every unspoken feeling and emotion I feel for him into it. Hoping he understands just how much he means to me.

I feel his warm hands grip my waist tenderly then tighter with possession.

With a low groan, he angles his head and takes over, pulling my body flush against his.

Hot damn.

He's been holding out on me.

If I thought yesterday's kisses were something, I was sorely mistaken.

The first time he kissed me, it was sweet, soft, and slow.

Then when we came back together that second time around, it was fast and hungry like we were both trying to desperately soothe an ache.

But those kisses have nothing on this one. If those kisses were something poets write about… Well, this kiss—this kiss is what romance novels are written about.

Deep and full of promise.

He's giving me everything. Confessing his feelings for me, loving me in it.

My head explodes. I swear fireworks explode behind my eyelids. I see stars.

If I hadn't experienced it myself, I would have never been privy to this. I would have blindly gone through life not knowing what I've been missing.

Never in my life will I ever scoff at another romance novel mentioning that ever again.

It happens. It's happening to me.

Panic starts building up inside me knowing that when this ends at some point, I will lie awake at night because of it. The realization of having been so blind to what's been right in front of me. Desperation makes me cling to him.

Sensing my turmoil triggers him to break it.

Brad leans his forehead on mine.

I feel his eyes bore into me. I open mine and meet his.

Instantly I calm down.

Where there was panic, now there's peace.

Contentment replaces loneliness.

I hear a lock click into place inside me.

Finally safe. Finally secure. Exactly where I'm supposed to be.

Warmth takes up residence in that big hole inside me. Where I once felt hollow and empty, I am now whole. My cracks are filled with the rightness of us.

This was what was missing this whole time.

I just needed to open my eyes.

"*I see you.*"

With a soft smile, he lifts his head and brushes my hair off my shoulders.

He whispers, "Finally."

"A LITTLE TO THE LEFT. There. Raise it half an inch. Okay. That's perfect."

I can't contain the squeal that comes out as I do a half-jump. I clap my hands in approval.

I take a step back to admire the Christmas lights that my boyfriend has finished putting up on the rooflines of my house and to appreciate the view of Brad coming down the ten-foot ladder he brought with him to help me put all this up.

Boyfriend. I'm still reeling from the fact that I get to call him that and that I'm his *girlfriend.*

Brad looks over his shoulder and winks. He knows I've been checking him out. He moves the ladder to the other side of the house to adjust the lights there to match what he just did.

The last few weeks have flown by in a blur with Thanksgiving and midterms. It was like I blinked, and somehow December was halfway over. I had completely forgotten about Christmas. It wasn't until my friends dragged me to the mall yesterday to replace my phone that I saw the decorations and trees everywhere.

Mom usually had our house set up for Christmas right after Halloween. I intended to continue her traditions, but I had been so preoccupied that I had even forgotten to put up the Halloween decorations. I know Dan would have done it, but he had been so busy with school that he was only home enough to sleep and shower. Any free time he had was dedicated to Summer. She had all but moved in with us already.

When we were up at Lola's house for Thanksgiving, Dan asked me if I was okay with her moving in. I was so taken aback that it took me a few minutes to blurt out that I thought she already had.

I'm thrilled for my brother but at the same time I can't

completely shake the feeling of grief and regret that Mom isn't here to see us happy like this.

The week we spent at our grandmother's house helped ease some of the grief and regret. It really helped us both feel closer and connected to Mom despite her absence. There were a lot of tears but there was also laughter and love. We were surrounded by Mom's side of the family. It also felt good to be together, just the two of us. Dan and I had both been so preoccupied with friends and school. The most time we spent together was a quick breakfast or dinner here and there, usually with Brad or Summer sitting in the kitchen with us. We finally were able to catch up and talk like we used to before Mom died.

Dan confessed that he had been in constant communication with Summer for over a year leading up to his return home, having reconnected with her two summers ago when he went to a party with his old friends from high school. That at first, she wouldn't entertain anything other than friendship with him because of the distance and his penchant for dating around. So, when he had come back home a few months ago, he had fully intended to pursue a relationship with Summer having already developed feelings for her.

Thank God she felt the same way. I don't know how my brother would have handled it, had she rejected him. He had never had his heart broken or been this serious about any other girl before. Seeing them together made me almost as happy as Brad made me.

Brad is down from the ladder. I feel him slip his arms around my waist, resting his chin on top of my head as we both gaze up at the lights.

"Are you happy?"

I tilt my head back to give him access to my forehead, my eyelids fluttering as he presses a gentle kiss there. I nod in response, letting myself relax in his heat and the warmth of this moment with him.

"Very. Thank you for helping me."

He hums as his arms tighten around me, "I want to run something by you."

I turn my head slightly, granting him permission to rain gentle kisses on my temple and cheek. I didn't know I could be more attuned to Brad than I already was, but it was like as soon as I opened myself up to him, my senses heightened around him even more. It was instantaneous. I know with just with a single look or slight movement from Brad what he wants without him having to vocalize it.

"Okay." The word draws out in a sigh of contentment.

"You have to say yes first."

That gives me pause. I turn in his arms and raise an eyebrow at him. "Say yes?"

"You trust me?"

"Better than anyone. Yes."

"Is that a yes?"

I roll my eyes, resting my chin on his chest. I stretch up to my tiptoes and loop my arms lazily around his neck. "Yes."

"I have something planned for your birthday and you already said yes to it."

I half-laugh, half-snort. "Sneaky. What do you have planned?"

"It's a secret."

He bends to kiss my nose. My eyelids. My chin. Everywhere but where I want him to.

I grip the back of his neck and tug him down. "I don't like surprises."

He smiles against my lips, hovering there.

"You'll like this one."

"So, what exactly are you running by me then?" I murmur, kneading the back of his neck.

"I just want to give you time to process that I'm taking you away for the weekend."

I pull back, my feet meeting asphalt again as I move my hands to his chest and peer up at him. "The whole weekend?"

He smiles down at me, but I can sense he's treading carefully. Knowing I need time to prepare myself mentally for anything that deviates from my norm. Anything other than that could trigger my anxiety. If I didn't already feel so many things for this guy, I would fall for him a bit more with how much care he puts into his every thought and gesture.

"Three nights. Four days."

My birthday falls on a Saturday over a holiday weekend which means we have that Monday off school as well.

I worry my bottom lip. There is an unmistakable question beneath all of this. I see it in the cautious way he's looking at me right now, his eyes full of restrained hope and an understanding.

He is asking me to go away for a weekend alone with him. He's asking without pushing about taking our relationship to the next level. I know Brad will never force me to do more than I'm ready to.

Inadvertently this is already something I've been thinking about more these last few weeks.

"I've already cleared it with both our parents and Dan in case you are worried about that."

I shake my head instinctively but then his words make sense in my fogged-up brain.

I forgot to consider that.

He's right. I would...should have been worried about that but I wasn't. I'm not.

This is *us*. Brad and me. It doesn't occur to me to feel like we need permission to just be us or do things together. We've never had to before.

I realize that I still haven't said a word when he cups my face.

He bends his knees so we can be at eye level. "You can say no."

His eyes do a worried dance between mine.

I laugh at that, "I thought you said I had to say yes?"

His other hand slides up to the small of my back, "It was a dumb thing to say. I was trying to be cute. You always have a choice El."

"You're always cute." I kiss him gently allowing myself to get lost in it before I whisper. "Also, when you're the one asking, my answer is always yes."

Brad

It was a struggle not to break and tell her what we have planned.

An even bigger struggle was to not to be so blatantly obvious about it when Kim and Kyle were around. Kim is the absolute worst at keeping secrets and this is a big one.

I look over at Liz sleeping in the passenger seat with an eye mask on. I stifle my laughter remembering how much she fought against wearing the thing when I first handed it to her. Just like I knew she would, within minutes of being on the road, she fell fast asleep. Liz has never been able to stay awake when riding shotgun in a car.

We've been on the road for almost two hours. I stopped once to get gas and she slept through it all which I had been hoping for so I wouldn't have to field more questions.

The last month has been a test to my willpower. I was at my wits ends with keeping this a secret from her, but I know it's going to be worth it.

I drum my fingers on the wheel as I catch sight of the exit for Leavenworth. I make the turn for it and twenty minutes later, hit the private road leading up to the cabin. I quickly glance over at her again to make sure she isn't awake and seeing where we're headed. The sight of her sleeping peacefully next to me makes my heart want to claw its way out of my chest and into hers.

I didn't even know I was capable of being more in love with her than I already was and here I am practically overflowing with it. I am so fucking gone for her.

I love her with such an intense force that I practically vibrate with it just at the mere thought of her. If I can make her forget all the horrible things that happened last year even just for a few days to celebrate her goddamn existence, then that's what I'm determined to do.

Unsurprisingly, Kim and Kyle feel the exact same way, which is why, unbeknownst to Liz, they're here waiting for us. I pull up to the dirt road leading up to my family's private cabin and spot Kyle's Ford F-150 parked near the annex. The screeching of the tires on sleet and snow-covered pavement must have alerted them to our arrival.

I park my Rover just in time for them to come out and meet us. Kim does a jiggling dance on the front steps as she rubs her hands together to stay warm.

It's at least ten degrees colder up here than it is back home. I make a mental note to text Mom a thank you for packing an extra suitcase of winter clothes for the four of us. It's just like her to know we wouldn't be prepared. It's been a while since we were all up here together.

Liz never pays attention to sports or school events and just shows up when I tell her there's a game. So, under the pretense of an "away" game which she thought Kyle and Kim had left school early for, they drove up here first to decorate and set up.

I grin at them from inside the car and nod towards the back. I pop open the trunk and Kyle makes quick work of taking our bags out and into the cabin.

He comes back out in a matter of seconds and gives me a thumbs up.

I climb out of the car, shooing Kim as she tries to open the passenger door first.

I gently ease the door open and unbuckle her seatbelt.

"El. El, we're here, baby." I pat her arm, giving it a gentle squeeze.

Shifting in her seat, Liz rubs a hand down her face, inadvertently taking her sleep mask off in the process. It doesn't matter anymore since we're already here.

I catch the telltale signs of her figuring it out. Her brows meet as she shoots up in her seat. She locks eyes with me before her mouth falls open at the sight of Kim and Kyle waving from behind. Then her hand flies to her mouth as she gasps when she sees—

"We're—we're at the cabin."

Her voice is still groggy from sleep, but her tone conveys a gamut of emotions.

I hold my hand out to her, rendered mute from her reaction.

She blinks back tears as her gaze quickly flies back to me.

I should have expected it, but I don't see it coming.

Liz's arms come flying around my neck as she hurls herself into my chest. We fall back onto the ground. I grip her waist tight to keep her on my chest and shut my eyes, grateful to the snow for cushioning the fall.

"*Oh my god.*" I hear Kyle's booming laughter as Kim scream-laughs in tandem.

Liz

"You can stop laughing now."

Kyle shakes his head as he throws another log on to the fireplace, chuckling to himself. Again. "No can do, Lizzy. I get to use this for at least a year's worth of teasing."

He waves his phone at me before tossing it back on the floor next to him.

Kim had been recording the "surprise" with her phone and caught the exact moment that I launched myself onto Brad and we fell back onto the snow. She then forwarded it to our group chat that somehow now included Aunt Rose, Dan, and Summer. I have a strange feeling she also sent it to Aunt Jen, her mom, and Aunt Simone, Kyle and Summer's mom.

Now everyone I loved is privy to one of the most embarrassing moments of my life.

I bury my face in my hands and curl up on the end of the couch.

"Cut it out." Kim admonishes before dissolving into yet another fit of giggles.

I hear Brad's silent rumbling of laughter next to me and I groan inaudibly. I'm so embarrassed at what I did.

It's been a few hours and I'm still having trouble looking him straight in the eye.

It took him an hour to coax me into even looking at him again after we got here.

Brad's arm wraps around my shoulders. He gently tucks me to his side, squeezing me until I let my hands fall from my face.

He leans in and whispers, "I love you," pressing a kiss on the shell of my ear.

That does it. I feel the tension leave me as my body relaxes into him.

"This is weird, right?"

Kim's question cuts into the comfortable silence that has descended on us.

Aunt Rose ordered food to be left for us. We had dinner after Brad and I changed out of our wet clothes. Afterwards, we relocated to the living room, just like old times.

We then spent the next few hours just talking, playing board games, and catching up.

It's now past ten and we have finally called it a day, too exhausted to keep playing.

Kim is settled into the nook by the fireplace, her legs crossed under her. Her gaze sweeps the room. Kyle is sitting next to the fire by her legs with a beer in hand while Brad and I are curled up on the couch sharing a steaming mug of hot chocolate.

Aunt Rose has packed the kitchen with a week's worth of food, but Kyle brought booze and beer for my birthday celebration tomorrow.

"What's weird babe?" Kyle leans back to rest his head on her lap and Kim's hands automatically go to his shoulders, massaging.

"To be back here just the four of us. No parents. No siblings. Just us?"

I nod in agreement. It does feel kind of weird. But in a good way.

Kyle takes a sip of his beer then uses it to draw a circle in the air, gesturing to the four of us.

"And were all paired up." He shakes his head. "Fuck yeah. It's weird."

Brad laughs, "I missed coming up here with you guys."

We spent countless vacations with our families here. This place has six bedrooms, big enough for all four of our families. Back when we never wanted to be apart from each other, Brad's parents placed two bunk beds in Brad's room so the four of us could sleep together in one room whenever we were here.

Now, he's got a king-sized bed in his room, and this time, it will just be the two of us staying in there. Kim and Kyle chose one of the bigger guest rooms on the other side of the cabin.

Brad, being the gentleman that he always is, offered me my own room but we both know I won't be doing that. Still, the offer was sweet.

This whole weekend trip is sweet.

When I took off my mask earlier and saw where we were, I almost turned into a puddle.

Some of my happiest memories happened right here. Our families all together. My parents still happy and in love. This was where we met Kyle and Summer after their family moved back in the fourth grade. We all took a weekend trip here to meet them. Kyle's dad, Uncle Nico, was friends with Uncle Dave, Brad's dad, in college.

Maybe why they got along so well. They basically inherited their friendship from their dads.

This was where I learned how to ride a bike. Where we all learned how to swim and fish.

We spent countless winters here sledding and having snow-ball fights.

This was where Kim and I started to bond like sisters when the boys would go and do things with the dads. It would be just us two with all the moms because Summer and Kim's sisters had always wanted to do things outside the cabin.

I can't believe Brad remembered just how much I love this place.

I remember when we were kids, talking about what we wanted to do when we grew up. I would respond that I just wanted to live here forever.

I've always felt so safe and happy here. Looking around, I know I still do.

This. This is my happy place.

Right here. With my three best friends. With my Brad.

I gaze up at him and find him watching me with a smile full of affection and promise. I should have known he would know what I wanted for my birthday before I even did.

I kiss his chin before easing out of his hold and grabbing the hot chocolate mug from the table.

Emotion chokes my throat, but I fight past the urge to start crying again.

"Thank you for doing this." I address the room, looking around at everyone.

Kim leans in and hugs Kyle close to her, resting her cheek on his.

"This was way overdue babe. We're just glad we get to celebrate you together like this."

Kyle tips his beer at me, "Can't remember when I had a better Friday."

I snort, grateful for the distraction from my rising emotions.

"Not even when your team scored that winning touchdown last week?"

He winks at me, placing his empty beer bottle beside him. "Not even then."

I watch as Kyle pulls Kim onto the floor and into his lap, snuggling her close.

My curiosity piques again and I start forming question after question in my head.

"So…" I hand the hot chocolate to Brad. He sits up, a knowing smile pulling at his lips. He senses the direction my thoughts go as he takes a sip.

"How did you guys happen?" I blurt out, burying my face in Brad's shoulder.

Kyle's answering chortle makes me look up just in time to catch Kim shake her head in amusement. She looks over her shoulder at Kyle.

"Uh, funny story, actually."

Brad sets the mug back on the table. He brings me back to his chest, threading our fingers together. We wait for them to continue. Our friends are exchanging looks like they don't know how to explain how they ended up as a couple again.

Kyle eventually just shrugs.

"I fucking hated her ex-boyfriend."

Kim scoffs. "I was dating Zane Miller last year."

Brad groans beside me. "Hell, Kimmy. Even I know that guy's a douche canoe."

"Well…the abs and pretty-boy smile blinded me, okay? Not to mention his—"

Kyle's hand flies to Kim's mouth. She giggles, kissing his cheek.

"So, you hated him…that still doesn't explain—" I gesture to the two of them.

"Long story short. We were both at this party last summer where I caught the asshole making out with another girl after he had the audacity to brag about Kim, so I beat his ass."

My eyebrows rise to my forehead. Kyle is the most laidback person I know and despite his build, height, and the sport he plays, I can't imagine him ever being in a fight.

I glance at Kim who is sporting a full-on blush. She playfully rolls her eyes at Kyle, her expression bursting with affection.

"Well, Kyle didn't know that I had already broken up with the jerk because naturally Zane was still using me to show off to his friends like I was some sort of trophy to be had."

Kyle mutters something under his breath that sounds a lot like, "*Fucker*."

He continues the story. "Kim found out about it and followed me as I was leaving the party. She got in my car when I ignored her. Started screaming at me so I got pissed and thought it would be funny to drive off with her still in the car. *Then* we got to talking and well…I decided I liked her still, so she let me chase her for a few weeks until"—Kyle pats Kim's head—"she finally let me catch her, and, well, you know."

Kyle waggles his eyebrows playfully. Kim swats at his chest but there is tenderness there between them. An understanding. And something else that makes me look away and blush. Even the start of their love story is unconventional, but they wouldn't be Kim and Kyle if it weren't. *Someone make that into a movie, please.*

"Sounds like a perfect romcom."

Kyle winks at me as he jumps to his feet, pulling Kim up with him, "And on that note, good night friends. Don't stay up too late birthday girl. There is still so much fun to be had."

Kyle tosses Kim over his shoulder.

Kim giggles and blows us a kiss. He all but jogs to their room.

"Oh god. I don't even want to think about what—eeww."

I laugh. Brad's arm tightens around me, and I look up.

He wordlessly shakes his head at me.

"I love your laugh. Can I record it and make it my alarm? I'd wake up every single time."

I open my mouth to respond with a quick retort, but I quickly forget it when he tenderly grazes my cheek with his thumb instantly distracting me.

"Seeing you happy is all I ever want, El. Are you happy?"

I can feel my gaze soften as warmth balloons in my chest. The way he's looking at me like I'm somehow the blessing instead of the reality of him being mine makes my insides melt.

"I think this is the happiest I've been in a really long time and it's all because of you."

He answers with that slow smile I know he reserves only for me. He cups the back of my neck and rewards me with a quick kiss that's so tender and slow, I feel tingles all the way down to my toes.

"Let me clean up here. Change into pajamas and meet me outside?"

I WRAP the puffy robe Summer bought me for my birthday tighter around me as I make myself comfortable on the patio daybed while I wait for Brad to join me. I close my eyes and bask in the comfortable heat the fire pit offers against the harsh winter chill.

My phone vibrating under my pillow, breaks into my thoughts and when I pull it out and check it, I realize its midnight.

I have several text messages from Dan, greeting me with happy birthday wishes.

Smiling, I open our thread. I start to send him a text saying I miss him, but my smile dies when I finish reading the last message he sent.

It's time to stop hiding Liz. Tell them.
I love you. Here for you.

I lock my phone and toss it behind me.

All week, I've thought about nothing but this.

All week, my brother has been telling me this.

Reminding me relentlessly and repeatedly about how important it is for me to do this.

Not just for my sake but for theirs.

I know he's right. It's time.

My friends need to know what happened, what I did all those years ago.

That by not telling them I attempted suicide, I am keeping this from them. Lying to them. Brad has every right to the truth. Kim and Kyle deserve my honesty.

I rub my temples, shutting my eyes. Mentally preparing myself for this conversation I need to have with them before we leave the cabin.

But I don't know where to even begin. How to start. What to do.

God, I miss Mom. She would tell me what to do. What to say. She would hold me and put my fears to rest. I desperately want to smell her, see her, talk to her...hug her.

I struggle against the tears threatening to overtake me, feeling myself shake with repressed grief. I become so lost in my thoughts that I don't notice the patio flooding with twinkling lights until I feel Brad's presence.

"El?" I hear his cautious footsteps growing nearer.

I look up suddenly and he climbs in beside me, He holds me close to his chest when he sees the look on my face that I have failed to hide from him in time.

"What's wrong baby?" He lifts my chin with his finger and looks down at me worriedly.

I sniff forcing a smile, deciding to tell him at least half the truth. "I miss my mom."

Brad nods in understanding, seemingly getting lost in his thoughts himself.

I gasp when I finally notice the lights. I sit up, resting a hand on his chest as I look around at all the fairy lights that adorn the wrap-around patio and trees that surround the cabin. Making the whole place look like it came straight out of a holiday card.

It's beautiful. Magical.

"Brad...did—did you do all this?"

Someone scoffs behind us, and I twist around to find Kim and Kyle.

"We did." Kyle looks genuinely proud of himself.

"Remember when we watched that Christmas movie and you wouldn't stop gushing about fairy lights and ordered like ten boxes from Amazon?"

I nod. I don't know where to look but I can't tear my eyes away.

I am in awe of this Winter Wonderland.

Kim's arms come around me and she hugs me close to her.

"You didn't really think we would go to bed without making sure our favorite girl felt special on her eighteenth birthday, right?"

My chin trembles and I'm so close to completely losing it, especially when Kyle comes around and sandwiches me from the other side.

"Happy Birthday Little Lizzy."

I squeeze them both, letting their weight and warmth settle and calm me.

An hour later after Kim and Kyle have officially gone to bed, I snuggle closer to Brad on the daybed. I feel the exhaustion of the day finally hit me. Brad on the other hand is still being uncharacteristically quiet. Normally we sit in companionable silence, but I can tell by the tightness in his jaw that there is something on his mind.

I shift in my seat, resting my chin on his chest forcing him to meet my gaze.

"Hey."

"Hey."

"Are you okay?"

"Yeah." He kisses the tip of my nose then sighs, "I'm okay, El. I just hurt when you do. I hate that you're sad, but I understand why. It just kills me that I can't take the hurt away."

This guy. So selfless. So caring.

"It's a strange contradiction that we feel the most sadness when were at our happiest."

I offer him a small smile. "And I really am at my happiest."

Brad's gaze falls to my lips before he looks back up. His eyes soften.

"Brad. You. Did. That."

Tucking me under his chin, he squeezes me gently then tighter with possession.

"I love you so fucking much, El. I still can't believe I get to hold you like this. Call you mine."

I push back a little, to say what, I don't know.

I know I love him, that I love him more than I've ever loved anyone. But somehow getting the words out, saying them out loud is proving challenging.

I know it's senseless to be scared to say I love you to someone I know I love, but the last time I said I love you to someone, my mom died.

He stops me with a finger on my lips, "I need to say this. I need to do this."

Brad reaches behind him, showing me a small black velvet box in his palm. At the sight of it, my heart fully stops. Finding it difficult to breathe, I try to draw air into my lungs as I struggle against the urge to panic. A box like that can only mean one thing.

His accompanying chuckle manages to break into the fog of my rising anxiety.

"El, I'm not proposing. You can relax."

The air gushes out of me and I realize I've been holding my breath the whole time.

I watch as he opens the box to reveal a rose gold infinity ring with round shaped white diamonds. My eyes fly to his and the tears that I've been fighting against come rushing out.

"It's—it's so beautiful."

"It's a promise ring. A promise that I'll be yours for as long as you'll have me. A promise that I'm yours for infinity. *Someday*, I *will* ask you to marry me, but for now I promise you that I will love and protect you for infinity and forever. Just like when we were kids."

For infinity and forever.

We uttered those words to each other as kids. Determined to be best friends forever.

Little did we know what would become of us. What we are now.

A sob breaks out of me, and I clutch at his chest. "I'm happy. I'm so happy."

I try to reassure him, but the tears just keep gushing out of me. I bury my face on his chest and allow myself to feel everything that I've been suppressing up until this moment.

The warmth of his fingers touches mine as he gingerly slips the ring onto my left hand. Then he sits back and just holds me letting me know I'm free and safe to let myself go.

Brad

Liz's birthday flies by in a blur.

Before I know it, were back in the living room that night following dinner.

Exhausted from the previous day, we all woke up late. After having a quick brunch, we spent the day outside, playing in the snow like we used to when we were kids. Venturing into Leavenworth to take in the sights then coming back here to play video games and trading stories from the last three years.

I suspect we aren't quite ready to delve into our issues yet. Everything that we've shared up to this point has all been surface-level, but one of us was going to crack soon especially after Kyle busted out the vodka and beer. I can tell he's itching to say something, with the way he clams up from time to time then cracks a stupid joke we all pretend to laugh at. The air is almost crackling with the intensity of it looming over us like a thundercloud.

An unspoken promise floats between the four of us that tonight is the night we finally talk about it. Talk about what really happened between the four of us that day.

Which is why I'm currently nursing this beer. I feel it coming.

I can't be drunk for this. Kim talked Liz into taking shots and she's had two already. She isn't drunk yet, but I'm responsible enough to at least be more sober than my girlfriend is.

Liz switches to water when Dan and Summer call, and she drags Kyle to the couch with her. She giggles at something Summer says but I don't hear it. I'm distracted when the light catches on the ring on her finger. I consider myself a feminist. Equality for all. But damn, if I don't revel in the caveman-like feelings the sight of my ring on her elicits in me.

I smother a laugh, taking a sip of my beer. I recall the way her eyes almost bugged out of her head when I pulled the box out.

I don't want to tell her that I did in fact toy with the idea of buying her a diamond ring. Something I could give her that would hold the promise of everything I feel for her, but eventually even I had to admit it was too soon regardless of our history.

Now I'm glad I didn't. Holding Liz last night while she lost herself, I worried that I may have pushed for too much. She's been holding tough for months. Not allowing herself to feel everything that has happened to her. The bad *and* the good.

So, I gave her the space to finally let go.

I meant what I said—I want to be her refuge. She doesn't have to hide what she's feeling with me. Even when it's ugly, I want all of it. I reassured her of this last night.

When Liz finally calmed down, she rose to kiss me, like she wanted to lose herself in a different way, but I held off. Not because I didn't want to because fuck did I ever. I think about being with her in that way constantly, but I knew last night wasn't the right time.

She was spent. Both emotionally and physically. So, I simply carried her to bed.

Told her to go to sleep and within minutes of stroking her hair, she did just that.

I woke up holding her still, in a tangle of arms and legs, this morning. And in that moment, I knew I had never been happier.

I want more mornings like that, to have her be the first thing I wake up to. More nights when she is the last thing I see and hold.

I want to give her my strength, so she doesn't have to be strong for everyone anymore. She can just *be* when she's with me. I want *everything* with her.

"Liz is going to melt with how hot you're staring at her right now."

Kim bumps my knee with the Truly she's drinking. I frown down at her.

I'm on the armchair by the fire, alternating between watching everyone do their thing and the tv. Kim's next to me, on the floor with her collection of beads and strings.

I look back at the animated movie playing on the TV.

We still have a collection of VHS tapes and DVDs here.

The four of us have decided to lean into nostalgia tonight and watch our favorite movies from when we were growing up while we sort of sober up. Liz insisted on watching Rugrats and popped in the orange VHS tape. She reminded us of that one Halloween where the four of us dressed up as the characters. Not surprisingly, she is still mildly obsessed with the 90s cartoon show. She's even wearing Reptar socks on her feet tonight.

Yup, we're all just killing time until one of us breaks.

"Are you calling me hot Kimmy?"

"Ew. No." Kim rolls her eyes, "I'm begging you to spare me from seeing you shooting bedroom eyes at Liz." She shudders for dramatic effect, "You're like my brother. Just gross."

I tip my beer at her and down the rest of it, smirking.

Out of the corner of my eye, I see Liz rise taking the phone with her. She's going out to talk to her brother on the patio. I completely missed what just happened.

· · ·

I LOOK over at Kyle who's now hunched over on the couch, staring at his beer. A complete one-eighty from the guy who was just joking around with his sister.

"Everything okay, man?"

Kyle blinks, jerking his head like he's trying to shake a thought out.

"Yeah. Sorry. I was just thinking about old times, you know?"

"Like what, babe?" Kim shifts beside me to face us while still making work on the bracelet she's making for Liz.

Kyle shrugs. The look on his face gives it away. His jaw is set like he wants to say something but he's unsure how to begin the conversation.

I exchange worried looks with Kim. I guess Kyle is starting us off.

Kim sets her beads aside, not taking her eyes off Kyle.

I lean my elbows on my knees, my hands folded between them, preparing myself.

Liz chooses that moment to walk back in. She stops mid-walk when she sees the looks on our faces. She quietly takes a seat next to Kyle, sitting with her legs folded under her.

Liz reaches over to touch Kyle's arm. "What's going through that mind of yours?"

He spares her a quick glance smiling a little but his hold on his beer bottle tightens.

"I just fucking missed all of this. All you guys."

I hear Kim blow out a slow breath beside me. From the looks of it, she knows where Kyle is going with this. It's something they've talked about before with each other.

Liz moves as if to offer Kyle a hug, but he stops her with a gentle hand on her knee.

"Let me get this out." He shares a look with Kim who gives him a reassuring smile.

"I always felt like it was my job to watch over you guys."

I open my mouth to object, and he shakes his head at me, "Even you B. Obviously I fucked it up. I was too focused on making the team back then to argue over the merits of us suddenly not being friends anymore. Then when I did make the team, I made it my life. Turned my back on ten years of friendship like a jackass."

Kim hugs her knees to her chest. Her chin rests on top of them like she's trying to hold herself together. I extend a hand to her. With a grateful squeeze, she takes it, in her own way offering me her support.

"I know I mess around a lot but looking back, the joke is on me. I've been walking around like I own the school, pretending to be someone I'm not. Buying in to the whole popularity game until it became my job. Became a role I *have to* play. I've started hating the thought of coming to school. Hell, I even started hating football because damn it, I'm growing tired of the same bullshit, day in and day out. No one I know wants to just talk or hang out. Everyone wants a piece of me. Just once I want someone to look at me and see me and not just see what they want to see. Being around you guys again, I realize just how much I lost, how much *I'm* lost." Leaning back on the couch, he stares beyond us and into the fire, "I don't have to pretend here. I can just be me. Not the artificial shit I put up but the *real me*. I don't have to smile all the damn time or try to fill silence with jokes that don't even make sense. You guys don't expect the Kyle show and man, I love it when you guys call me out on my shit. No one has done that in three years. Not until Kim let me chase her around all summer."

He looks up at Kim, his expression tender and knowing,

"I think that's when I figured out that a huge chunk of myself was missing."

In a matter of seconds, Kim is standing in front of Kyle.

She pulls the beer out of his hand, setting it down on the table.

"Don't beat yourself up for something we all had a hand in doing. If we keep holding on to what happened, we'll never get past it. Important thing is, we are here now. Together."

She sits on his lap, a tender hand on his cheek.

Kyle nods and the release at finally saying the words that have been gnawing at him is so palpable in him. His shoulders ease from the tension he'd been holding in. The easy smile is back on his face as he looks around at us, his body vibrating with joy and relief.

His smile falters when he looks beside him at Liz.

"Liz?"

Kim and I follow suit.

Liz is shaking. Her hands grip her phone as she stares down at it.

Her eyes are wide, like a deer in headlights.

I shoot to my feet, at the same time Kim is reaching over to her but Liz's resounding, "*Don't!*" stops both of us, bringing us back down to our seats.

"El?"

"I—I won't be able to get this out if any one of you touch me right now."

Her suspiciously bright eyes meet mine and for the first time I finally understand what's been lurking behind them this whole time.

Fear.

"What's going on babes?"

Kim's hand still floats between them, itching to touch Liz.

I understood. I'm hunched over my seat, wanting nothing more than to hold her, offer her my strength. My fingers are tingling from the sheer force of it.

Liz's eyes shut for a moment and when they flutter open,

there's a determined glint in them. Her eyes still hold the fear, I recognize.

She holds my gaze like she's afraid to look away.

That's when it occurs to me that she's most worried about my reaction to whatever she needs to say. My lips quirk up in what I hope comes off as encouragement even though I feel the familiar gnawing in my gut I felt three years ago when she cut us off.

Unease trickles down my spine.

"I tried to kill myself."

Kim lets out an audible gasp. I hear her but I can't make myself look away from Liz. She continues to stare at me, her eyes shining with tears.

I start trembling. I clench my fists tighter together to keep from falling apart.

"That day I came to find you guys…I was in such a bad place. My parents…they were fighting every day. Mom was refusing to divorce my dad even though he had already pretty much moved out. And Dan, he became distant. Barely even spoke or looked at any one of us until he was never home anymore. I just felt so lost and—"

Liz pushes off the couch, dropping her phone on the floor. She walks around the couch, wrapping her arms around her middle. She looks down at her feet like she can't bear to look at us while she's laid herself bare.

She starts shuffling her feet clearly unsure how to continue.

"Alone?" That whisper came from Kyle. It's an unsteady offer.

Liz nods and she shuts her eyes again, taking a deep breath.

"I went straight home after I told you guys, I didn't want to be friends anymore to my parents screaming at each other *again*. It was so bad; worse than it had ever been. Things were getting thrown and Mom yelled at me to go upstairs the second

I walked into the house. I think at some point one of our neighbors called the cops. I heard Dad leave then Mom. I let myself cry after they left until I couldn't anymore then just sat there for a while…maybe hours. Just feeling hollow. The other details of that day are still fuzzy to me, but I remember getting up and going to my mom's room. I remember just looking around, searching, for what, I don't know. Her clothes were scattered on the floor, and I remember thinking I needed to clean it up, but I felt so tired. I saw her sleeping pills. They were just sitting there, and I—I—needed sleep." Liz throat bobs, "So I took one and sat down on her bathroom floor, but I didn't feel sleepy. I remember looking up at her bathtub, still clutching the pills. I *don't* remember turning the water on, but apparently, I did. I remember feeling frustrated because I really wanted to sleep and never wake up, but the pill didn't work. I was wide awake, and I was sick of it. I felt that distinction. I remember getting angry. Really angry. I think I may have tossed a few more things on the floor and I *remember* the exact moment I gave up. I wasn't thinking about anyone else anymore. All I thought about was that I was done. I didn't want to feel the pain of loneliness or fear or anger anymore. I just wanted to be done. So, I took a few more pills. And then the rest of them…"

Liz's lower lip starts to quiver, tears spilling out of her eyes when she opens them. Her eyes find mine again. I see the pain written all over her face. Feel it mirrored in mine.

"Dan was the one who found me. He said he came home because Mom called him to check on me. He found Mom's door open, her room a mess, got worried. He heard the bath running and saw the water spilling out. He rushed in and found me on the floor, my face in the water, empty pill bottle in my hand…and—"

Liz turns her back on us. Her shoulders slump as a sob breaks out of her.

In an instant Kim and Kyle have her.

They set her down on the couch, sitting on either side of her clutching her hands.

In the back of my mind, I register that it's my job to do that.

I should be there with them, holding her but I can't get myself to move. I don't get up.

I fear I'll collapse from the weight of all of this if I do.

I feel the tears scalding my cheeks before I realize I'm crying too. That we all are.

"Dan took me straight to the hospital. I had to get my stomach pumped out. The doctor… he said that if Dan hadn't found me when he did, I would have died. I didn't wake up for two days after that and when I did, they put me on suicide watch. I didn't see my family right away. I couldn't speak. I was ashamed of what I had done. Then the psychiatrist suggested I go to rehab. They thought I had a drug problem. I didn't dispute it, so my parents agreed with the assessment. They wanted me to get help, but I wasn't there for more than a few days. They realized early on that I didn't have a drug problem. I had depression. So, I started therapy instead…and, well, here I am."

Liz folds herself in the couch, her knees bunched up in front of her.

Kyle looks over at me as he tucks Liz in under his arm. I ignore his questioning gaze.

I hang my head, shame in my inability to do anything, still frozen in shock.

I watch them under the curtain of my hair.

"Liz…do you—" Kim runs her fingers through Liz's hair. "Do you think you…"

"Would I try to kill myself again?" Liz's whisper voices out the fear banging in my head.

I shudder at her choice of words.

A world without Liz isn't something I want to think about.

Kim just nods, leaning in to place a gentle kiss on the top of Liz's head.

"No." There is certainty in that one word.

I utter a sigh of relief.

Liz turns to look at me at the sound and she lets out a deep breath. I feel it in my bones.

"I have depression and anxiety, but I've gotten help. Those thoughts I had back then no longer hold any power over me. I'm stronger now. And trust me...I will never forget the look on my brother's face, the pain in his voice when I saw him after. Never in my life will I do anything that will cause myself or the people that I love that kind of trauma again."

Liz

As I utter those last few words, I know they're meant to reassure Brad the most.

I can feel in the gentle and tender ways they are holding me together that Kim and Kyle trust in me and in my truth that I'm stronger than those thoughts.

Brad on the other hand—he's coming undone.

He's crying which he rarely does. His eyes kept flickering back to me but he's unable to hold my gaze for longer than a few seconds. His knuckles are turning white with how hard he's gripping his fingers. His shoulders look so rigid, I fear they might break from the tension.

Kim and Kyle exchange a look over my shoulder.

I feel the second they decide to give us space.

Kyle gently eases me back onto the couch. Lowering his head, he meets me at eye level. His eyes shine with such tenderness, I feel another onslaught of tears coming.

He gives me a mere shake of his head before he drops a kiss on the top of my head.

"Don't get weird on me but I love you Little Lizzy. I'm proud to know you. Proud to be your friend. Just damned proud of you. Thank you for being brave enough to tell us this."

Then it's Kim meeting my eyes, "My Liz. So fucking strong. So freaking beautiful. I love you with all my heart. You are not alone, you hear me? You will never be alone."

Then I'm in her arms. I feel her shake, feel her tears spilling on the back of my shirt as she continues to caress my hair.

We hold each other for a few more minutes then she's gone. Kyle whisks her away into their room, holding her while she cries on his shoulder.

I lose sight of them behind their closed door.

"I almost lost you?"

Brad's whisper breaks into my trance. I jerk my head to look at him just as he looks up.

I don't realize I'm crossing the room until I'm on my knees in front of him. He's hunched forward so we're mere inches apart. I take his face in my hands and kiss both his cheeks.

"I'm sorry." My hands move to his shoulders, down to his arms then to his wrists as I untangle his hands from the viselike grip he has.

In a heartbeat, I'm getting pulled into his lap. His arms circling around my waist tight.

"El. El...I almost lost you." He buries his face on my shoulder, his breath fanning my neck. I feel his tears hot on my skin. I close my eyes, fighting against my own, trying to remain strong, to let him mourn what I already have.

Grateful that my shame has no place here.

He's simply afraid of losing me. Of what could have been.

He deserves to feel that pain. To be able to lose himself in it in order to get past it.

I love him enough to put his pain before mine.

To understand that my pain is also his to carry. And his, mine.

"You didn't. I'm right here."

I kiss the part of his throat I can reach, running my hands down his back.

"I'm so sorry I wasn't there for you."

His jaw tenses then he's on me, his kiss frantic like he needs to be reassured of my existence. His need is reflected in mine as I become just as desperate as he is. My hands glide all over him like I need to be assured that I'm really here with him as well.

His palms grasp my jaw, and he pulls back, resting his forehead on mine.

"I can't lose you El. You're my everything."

"You won't."

My promise echoes in my head, instantly filling me with a sense of calm and peace I only feel when I am with him. He kisses me again, his lips urgent on mine. My arms circle his neck and I press myself against him needing to feel as much of him as I possibly can.

"I'm never leaving you again." He whispers between kisses, his lips trailing down my neck. "I love you. I love you. I love you."

I love you too. The words sit at the tip of my tongue.

"Morning, short stuff."

I whirl around in surprise, nearly dropping the carton of eggs I'm putting back in the fridge.

With the hand that's clutching my chest, I smack Kyle on his arm.

"You scared me!"

Chuckling he reaches over me and grabs the carton of orange juice from the open fridge, and I scowl up at him.

"I would have asked you to grab it for me but that would take longer"—he grins mischievously—"on account of you needing a stepstool to reach it."

He sidesteps my attempt at another smack and goes to grab a glass from the cupboard.

I put the eggs back in the fridge and take a quick survey of the kitchen, making sure that I have cleaned up all the remnants of making breakfast.

Kyle is leaning on the counter, watching me with a thoughtful look on his face.

"Why did you make breakfast Lizzy?"

"Because my cooking is superior to yours."

I deflect, avoiding his eyes as I start to pull plates down to set the table.

"I won't disagree, but it was my turn to make breakfast today."

I count out the utensils and place them on top of the plates before turning my attention to the tall man interrogating me.

"I wanted to do something nice for you all."

"You don't have any reason to feel guilty."

I look away, bracing my hands on the counter.

Kyle hit the nail on the head with that one. He called me out. There is no use denying it.

I hear Kyle push off the counter and his glass clink on the marble counter. He sighs as he approaches me carefully turning me to look up at him.

"I feel it too, you know. I think I made that clear last night. I know Kim and Brad do...but you? You were going through some tough shit," He squeezes my arm gently before dropping his hand. "There is no reason for you to feel guilty or ashamed."

I nod because I have no way of refuting what he said but I can't help how I feel.

This is my truth no matter how much they try to disprove it.

Last night, Brad tried. In between his frantic apologies and whispered promises, he tried to kiss my fear and shame away. It didn't work.

After he drifted off, I lay awake playing the moment I told them about my suicide attempt repeatedly in my head. The looks on their faces are now scorched into my memory.

The frantic fear in Brad's eyes. The protective tenderness in Kyle's. The anguish in Kim's.

That last one branded me hotter than any other

I need to find a moment to speak with her alone.

Kim has gone above and beyond for me these last few months.

She has always been more of a big sister than a friend to me, and in more ways than one, I have always regarded her as such. I want to reassure her that it's not her fault.

Just like I did with Brad last night.

What happened to me was something that none of them could have prevented even if we had stayed friends back then.

I have depression. I got help. I'm doing better now.

"Elizabeth."

"Hmm?" I force a smile on my face.

"Can you do me a favor?"

"Anything."

Kyle leans on the counter next to me and wraps a protective arm around me.

"Whenever you start feeling like that again, will you tell me? I know it's different with Kim and Brad. I have a feeling that it may be harder for you to let them know when it happens because you're scared of hurting them or freaking them out." He shrugs. "I promise I won't hover or overreact. If all you need is someone there with you, I'll sit there with you. I'll listen if you just want to talk it out. I'll leave when the feeling passes, and I won't say anything to them if that's what you need or want. Just say the word, okay?"

I blink back tears. I've cried enough.

Kyle's right. If it were to happen again, which it hasn't since then, I couldn't reach out to anyone else. Brad and Dan would hover and get overprotective. Kim would freak out and panic. They wouldn't be able to do anything *but* overreact.

Kyle wouldn't do any of those things. He would just be what I needed, whatever that may be. A quiet presence or a sounding board.

I offer him a genuine smile, this time. "Thank you."

He simply nods, pats my arm once then pulls away. His gaze falls on the oven door that's slightly ajar and he gestures to it.

"So, what are we having for breakfast?"

My smile widens. "I remember you guys always loved it when my mom made breakfast up here so..." I trail off as I open the door all the way for him to peek in and see.

I am rewarded with a grateful groan and a fist pump.

Inside, I had stored the garlic fried rice with egg, pork tocino, beef tapa and corned beef I made for breakfast. All covered in foil pans so they will stay warm. I didn't know how long everyone would sleep in. When I initially decided to make breakfast this morning, I figured I'd make crepes or waffles but when I rifled through the fridge, I was pleasantly surprised to see that not only had Aunt Rose stocked the kitchen, but she'd also made sure there were items from Seafood City in here. I shouldn't be shocked as she and mom had been friends for over two decades. The gratitude over her just knowing without asking almost made me weep this morning when I saw the familiar items. I thought back to all those months ago, to the last time I made breakfast for mom. The sheer force of missing her still leaves me breathless. I have avoided Seafood City since she died. Avoided cooking any of her favorites.

God, I miss the twinkle in her eye and sigh of contentment when she ate fatty foods, she knew were bad for her. The way she would wink at me at that first bite.

I just miss her period.

I shut the oven door and turn to grab the plates I have

stacked when Kyle's hand falls on my shoulder. He nudges me away from the counter and turns me toward the entryway.

"Hey...Kim woke me up to make breakfast earlier. I bet she's still awake waiting. Let me set the table and clean up the living room while you girls talk. Then we can wake up Brad."

With a grateful nod, I leave him to it.

Brad

I wander into the kitchen and find Kyle loading the dishwasher.

I quickly glance at the clock on the stove and drag a tired hand across my face.

It's barely eight in the morning. Way too early to be awake on a Sunday.

Stifling a yawn, I lightly rap on the breakfast bar. "Good morning."

He looks at me over his shoulder, his eyes wandering from my hair to my chest before he lets out a chuckle and smirks. "Late night?"

I run a hand through my hair, cursing my lack of foresight.

I should have atleast brushed my hair before coming out here.

I woke up, instinctively reaching for Liz, and found her gone. I panicked a little and after pulling on whatever clothes were nearby, I headed straight out here thinking I'd find her.

I found this knucklehead instead.

"Same as you, bro."

He starts the dishwasher, lazily leaning on his side. His arms cross over his chest and he appraises me with a look.

"Your hoodie is on inside out. And backwards."

I look down and sure enough, the tag is hanging right there.

This time I curse out loud. I pull the jacket off and curse again. I forgot to put a damn shirt on. Of all the stupid—

His laugh cuts into my internal freak-out and I flip him off as I put my hoodie on the right way.

"I would ask where your shirt is, but I already know the answer."

I roll my eyes, "Where is that, jackass?"

With a satisfied grin, he cocks his head towards the bedrooms.

"Liz is wearing it."

I know better than to respond to that, so I head over to the espresso machine instead. I grab a mug and start the machine. I can feel Kyle's stare and grumble.

"Spit it out."

"If this were anyone else, I'd say congratulations on finally getting some," He clears his throat, "but this is you two and that would be inappropriate."

I nearly choke on the americano I just made.

"Pretty sure it's always inappropriate to comment on someone else's sex life."

Kyle snorts.

"So, you admit you got laid?"

Well...*Fuck.*

I walk over to the breakfast bar, making myself comfortable on the barstool all while he watches me. I can tell he's torn between making fun of me and wanting to talk about last night.

Hell. I think I prefer the jokes.

My heart and head haven't found a happy medium yet.

My heart shattered last night. I know Liz is better now. I felt that in more ways than one last night with her. But my head is still reeling from almost losing her. I suspect the guilt will cause a permanent ache in my chest and the fear I now carry with me all the time will continue to gnaw until it gives me an ulcer.

But then what happened afterwards...The hope it instilled in my heart threatened to chase the fear and guilt away. The trust she handed to me last night gave me faith that everything is going to be okay. My insides are currently waging a war. I feel so exhausted, I could probably sleep all day if not for the need to see her. Hold her.

Liz.

"She's with Kim."

I say her name out loud.

I wrap my fingers tight around my mug. I felt cold even though the heat was blasting in here.

I whirl around in my seat remembering I didn't turn off the fire last night or—

"Don't worry about it," Kyle says. "I came out last night to check on you guys and put the fire out. It's blazing again. I cleaned the living room just now too."

"Stop reading my fucking mind."

"Don't be so obvious about it then." He tosses me an apple, "Also eat this. You shouldn't drink coffee on an empty stomach, and I don't know how long the girls will be in there."

I take a bite of the apple even though I don't want to; just something for me to do while I wait for Liz. "Did Liz seem okay?"

Kyle frowned, "Are *you* okay?"

I level him with a look, but he just quirks an eyebrow at me, waiting.

I rub my eyes with my palms, "Honestly, I don't know."

"You need to get over it."

My hands slam on the bar with more force than I intend them to. Before I know it, I'm on my feet and chucking the half-eaten apple in the trash.

Kyle holds his palms out but like a man with a death wish

he comes to stand across from me, setting his hands down on the bar.

"Sit your ass down Brad and listen before the girls come out."

I sit down because I'm fucking tired and not because he told me to.

I glare at him, "She almost died, asshole."

"She didn't."

"She could—"

"Shut up and listen."

My fists clench involuntarily but I remain silent and seated.

"Before that, tell me one thing and be honest about it, okay?"

I jerk my head in response.

"If she were to feel that way again, what do you think are the chances she'd tell you?"

My body tenses. I sit upright and look away.

Zero.

Even though we've fallen right back into our friendship and progressed into lovers. She wouldn't come to me. I know it in my gut. She's too aware of how I'm programmed when it comes to her...and I would freak out very much like I did last night. I fumbled that.

Fuck, I messed that up.

Kyle sighs and I force myself to look back at him.

"Look. I know you two have this whole new dynamic and maybe I'm overstepping but I told her she could come to me." He expels another breath, his brow furrowing in determination. "She has to be able to go to someone without feeling guilty about it."

I nod. It makes sense but my chest tightens and hurt pierces through me at not being able to be that person for her.

Get over it.

"I get it." I grip my mug again and take a healthy sip. "I'll work on it, okay?"

"I'm being hard on you but we all thoroughly fucked up this friendship. I'm not doing that again. I'm here now. What do you need?"

I shake my head. "I don't know. I just—I can't lose her. I love her. I met my damn soulmate in diapers, man. That is the only thing I'm sure about and the mere thought of having almost lost her fucking guts me."

Kyle rests his elbows on the marble counter.

"Stop focusing on the past. Just keep being there for her. Don't treat her any differently or you'll risk everything you've built with her. You're together now."

I know that. It sounds easy enough, but it doesn't stop me from letting the weight of my guilt pull me down to a dark place.

"She cooked breakfast."

My head pops up and I frown. "I thought it was your turn?"

"Doesn't look like she slept because she was too busy feeling guilty about last night."

"Fuck. I told her she..." I pause because even though I assured her last night, my actions spoke the complete opposite. I really need to get it together. Do a better job at this.

"So maybe don't look like shit when she comes out."

A snort comes from behind me. Kim enters the kitchen, wrapping herself up tighter in her robe. She smacks the back of my head and reaches up to kiss Kyle on the cheek. She steals my mug, drinking the rest of my coffee with a smug smile.

Her eyes are red rimmed and the purple under her eyes belies her good mood.

"Everything okay?" Kyle tucks stray strands of her hair behind her ears.

She nods but makes a face at me. "You have horrible taste in coffee."

I ignore that seeing as she finished half the cup. "Where's Liz?"

"She went back to your room. She said she wanted to—"

I'm already up and out of the kitchen, headed towards our room before Kim can finish.

I HEAR her inside the bathroom when I enter. Normally, I would wait for Liz to come out but after last night, I think I have permission to follow her in there now.

"El?"

The door is cracked open. I find her sitting on the edge of the bathtub, brushing her hair with a faraway look in her eyes.

"Baby?" I kneel next to her, meeting her eyes.

Her eyes brighten when she realizes I'm there and a ghost of a smile whispers on her lips.

"Hey…" She puts the brush down and leans over to give me a peck on the cheek.

"Are you okay?" She's already washed her face, but her eyes are still swollen. I run my thumbs gently under her eyes and grasp her jaw.

She nods and wraps her fingers around my wrist. She's staring intently at me, searching for something in my face. Undoubtedly to ease the stress she's feeling.

"What about your, uh…" I purse my lips and feel myself redden. "Are you…sore?"

Her cheeks turn the cutest shade of blush, "I feel good. Thank you."

I lean over and brush my lips lightly against hers, letting a sense of rightness wash over me at her sigh of contentment. "I feel good too, El."

"Brad?" Her minty breath whispers against my lips. I have the sudden urge to take her back to our bed, but I fight against it. I raise my head instead and smile at her.

"I hate the thought of having hurt you…"

I shake my head slowly, intent on driving my point across. Kyle's message rings loud and clear in my mind. I need to focus on the Liz that's in front of me now.

"Listen to me, El. We're going to hurt each other sometimes. We're not always going to agree with each other and that's okay. We're together now, in every single way. Heart, body, and soul; I'm yours and you're mine. Whatever happens, I want you to understand that. Live by that. Like I do. Don't be afraid to hurt me." I take one of her hands and place it on my heart, "Hurt me if you need to. If that's the only way you can get through to me. Do it. Piss me off. But I promise you that I am not going anywhere. Ever. Not until you tell me you don't want me anymore. Until then? I. Am. Yours."

She closes her eyes as I kiss her punctuating those last three words and when her eyes flutter open, I know. I know without her having to tell me that she loves me just as much as I love her. That she's mine just as much as I am hers.

I lean back in to kiss her again when her hands come up to palm my cheeks.

She rests her forehead on mine, keeping her eyes trained on me.

"I've had a really shitty year, Brad…but when I'm with you, everything else fades. All of that darkness…all that I've been through goes away and I see nothing but you…nothing but lightness with you."

Then *she* kisses *me*. And we lose ourselves in each other once again.

∿

Four Months later.

I PARK my car in her driveway, pulling the brake with a little more force than is necessary.

I'm irritated but I try to remind myself that Liz isn't ignoring me. Maybe she was just busy or sleeping. The most likely reason is she forgot to charge her phone.

Again.

Fuck. I need to calm down. I clutch the steering wheel and will myself to calm down.

Everything was going great after her birthday; we spent every free moment we had together or with Kim and Kyle. Then last month, everything changed. My dad was still having issues with the upcoming launch, and he recruited me to help him out with it. For the last month, I have been flying out to San Francisco every weekend then back for school.

Liz and I have barely hung out. Sometimes we would face-time at night before one of us fell asleep. We saw each other at school but Liz was always busy studying, and she went back to tutoring. Now with Aunt Cat's last book releasing in the summer, she's busy working on that too.

I miss my girlfriend. I miss my best friend.

We planned on spending today together to celebrate that we've been together for six months. It was supposed to be last night, but she had to bail last minute. Her dad had asked her and Dan to dinner, which she'd forgotten about. I tried to call her when she said she would be home but got no response. We were supposed to meet at my place and drive downtown to take the ferry out and explore for the day. That was three hours ago.

It is past two now and still nothing.

I am getting frustrated. Regardless of how busy I've been, I've done my absolute best to make sure she knows she is still a priority in my life. Made sure every free second, I had was devoted to her so she wouldn't question her importance in my life, but now I starting to question mine in hers.

My absence in her life hasn't seemed to affect her as much as hers has me.

I can't help but focus on the fact that six months later, she still hasn't even told me she loves me out loud.

But *damn* if this is proving to be harder than I thought it would be. This waiting game.

I pull my keys out and get out of the car.

My car locks automatically and Liz had given me a key to her house. I let myself in.

I kick off my shoes by the front door then head straight up to her room and knock.

"El?"

Nothing.

Sweat prickles the back of my neck and now worry is starting to overtake my frustration.

I turn the knob and push the door open. Her room is pitch dark but the light from the open door illuminates the room. I hear her soft groan coming from under her covers.

I leave the door open as I cross the room to her. She lays buried under her covers, with her laptop sitting open next to her. There are books and pads all over her bed like she's burned the midnight oil, studying and reading.

I move her stuff to her desk and climb in next to her.

"El."

"Brad?"

"I'm here." I try to do a good job of hiding my irritation.

"What time is it?"

"Past two."

"Did we miss the ferry?"

"We did."

"What about the last ferry?"

"That too."

"I missed our date?"

"You did."

She peers up at me then hides behind her arms. "You're mad."

"I'm not."

She turns her bedside lamp on then glances back at me. I sigh at the sight of her in the light. Her eyes are swollen, with dark circles under them.

I sit up and offer her my arm. She tucks herself under and rests her chin on my chest to look up at me. I can't look at her because I know she'll see right through me.

"You're mad." She repeats her earlier statement.

I don't respond and just tighten my hold on her, pressing my nose to her hair.

Liz sighs, "Brad."

I gaze down at her and run a hand down her arm, "Yeah?"

"I'm really sorry. I overslept."

I gesture at her laptop and books. "Doesn't look like you did much sleeping, El."

She scans my face, her brow wrinkling. "I wanted to get some studying done last night."

I know I sound irrational, but I can't help it. I have officially run out of patience and my tank is empty. I'm veering unsteadily towards being pissed.

"You had time to study but not call or text me back?"

Liz sits up abruptly, letting my arm fall off. She climbs out of her bed in a huff and strides over to her study desk in the corner of her room. She pulls out her phone from her purse then comes back to the side of the bed I'm sitting on, handing me her phone.

"Here. Have at it."

"What for?"

"So, you can stop insinuating that I didn't contact you on purpose. I missed everyone's calls and messages." Her voice carries a flash of hurt.

I scoff. I suddenly can't find it in myself to care now that she's lumped me in with everyone else.

"Oh, in that case, it's fine. I didn't know you missed your other boyfriend's calls too."

Her sharp intake of breath cuts through me and I know I have taken it too far. She drops her phone on the bed beside me and stalks towards her dresser. She starts rummaging through a drawer before resting her forehead on it with a sigh.

"Let's just...can we not fight please?"

"I'm not—"

She cuts me off. "I had a really bad night, Brad. I don't need this." She rakes a shaky hand through her hair, pulling it into a ponytail. "Not from you. I just—"

It's my turn to cut her off as I stand, *Not from me*? You don't think I had a crappy night too? And an even crappier morning when I woke up to find that you never got back to me? That I waited hours for you to show up and you never did? And I come here only to find that you were here this whole time, and you couldn't be bothered to at least let your boyfriend know that you were okay?"

"Brad, I—"

Liz takes a step towards me, and I hold my hands up to stop her.

"What are we even doing, El?"

Her eyes grow wide as her gaze roams my face. "What— what do you mean?"

I wave a hand between us and say nothing. I'm all talked out.

I'm just tired of this. So close to just throwing my hands up and giving up.

"Brad. What are you saying?"

I scrub a hand down my face and shake my head. The sheer will it's taking to simply stand here is proving too much for me to handle, "I don't know."

She takes a slow, steady breath. Her panic sets in.

"Can we…can we do something else? Let me just change and we can head out? I—I… um…yeah let me just grab some clothes. I'll be quick."

She turns back to her dresser but I'm already making my way to her door.

"I think I'm just going to leave now."

"Brad…" She's crossing the room to me, and it takes huge effort for me to even look at her and acknowledge the tears in her eyes. "Please talk to me."

I shake my head again, not even bothering to disguise the irony in my voice.

"I already tried doing that."

"Please stay." She's standing in front of me now, her fingers clenching like she wants to touch me. I told her before that I was hers to touch. Even now, she still doesn't believe it. Still doesn't believe in us. Now, I don't even know if I believe it anymore.

There are a million things I want to say to her. I want to lash out and tell her how much she's hurt me by not taking what I have given her.

By not letting me in all the way. By not telling me she loves me.

I do none of that. Instead, I let my gaze sweep her one last time.

"I'll see you at school, Lizzy."

Liz

"Please tell me I'm overreacting. That he didn't break up with me."

Kim bites her lip and exchanges looks with Kyle.

"He called me Lizzy and we haven't spoken in *days*."

I bury my face in my hands. I can hear the panic rising in my voice again and I fight to gain control. I've been on edge since Saturday after Brad walked out on me. After a few seconds of shock, I followed him only to find him already gone. He didn't go home or answer any of my calls all weekend. The past few days, it became increasingly obvious he was actively avoiding me at school on top of ignoring my calls and messages. I finally gave up, cornered him today and he just muttered something about a prom meeting which turned out to be an excuse. Kim is already sitting here with me in my room and she's on the prom committee with him. Obviously, it wasn't a long meeting.

He could be here with me now. Or anywhere. He needs to know what happened and I need to understand how we ended up like this. I know I messed up by not going to him and showing up for our date. I honestly wasn't thinking about anything but trying to numb the hurt I felt when Dad proposed to Olivia.

In front of Dan and me.

A week before Mom's birthday.

Now on top of that, I'm dealing with the pain and guilt of having hurt the most important person in my life and trying to rationalize his anger and the way he is acting.

Yes, I ignored him, but I didn't do it purpose. I did it without thinking…but this…what he's doing to me? It's on purpose. There's intent.

To what? To get back at me? To break up with me?

I just want to talk and figure this out.

I'm trying my best to be understanding but I'm starting to feel anger.

How he can he think that I could ever hurt him on purpose?

How could he not see he's doing exactly what he accused me of doing?

I draw in a shuddering breath, and I feel Kim's hands clasp around mine.

My heart feels like it's been broken so many times this week. I appreciate their support, I really do, but the only person I want or need right now isn't here.

I think back to Friday night and go over the handful of things I could have done instead of what I did. What I should have done was call him immediately. Or even text him. Let him know. Warn him that I was feeling myself teeter towards the edge and I needed to focus on staying busy so I wouldn't lose myself to the anger and loneliness. So, I wouldn't break down all the way again. That I couldn't pretend I was okay when I wasn't.

I should have set an alarm. Went on our date.

I should have told him as soon as I woke up what had happened the night before.

A lot of should haves.

Now I'm starting to feel like it's too late to even fix this between us.

I shut him out. Now he's shutting me out. I hurt him. He hurt me.

How are we going to move past this?

Are we even an "us" at this point?

"Lizzy?"

I look up and find Kyle hovering in front of me.

I know he's asking if I'm in that place again and I shake my head.

His jaw loosens as some of the tension rolls away, but he still looks worried.

"I'll talk to him."

I look away before he sees the resignation in my eyes. "Let him be."

IT'S THURSDAY NOW, five days since Brad walked away from me and in two days, it will be prom. I still haven't spoken to him.

Two days ago, Kim and Kyle tried to assure me that everything was okay but after they left, I succumbed to the hurt. I let myself feel the anger.

I stopped trying to get ahold of him. This is different than the last time.

Three years ago, when I walked away, at least I had the decency to let them know my intentions beforehand. And now that he's the one who walked away, I have allowed myself to chase after him because I know I hurt him. I know what I've done. I acknowledge that.

I just wish he would meet me halfway. I was trying and now I don't know if I have any fight left in me.

I'm so emotionally spent. I acknowledge that now too. I'm exhausted.

But I'm also relieved now that I've allowed myself to feel everything at once.

To let go of the fear of falling apart and just feel for once.

I shut my locker just as a text pops up.

It's from Olivia. She sent a group message to Dan and me saying thank you for last night.

Olivia invited us to dinner again and apologized for how my dad went about his proposal. Dan and I talked about it, and we realize how lucky we are to still have him in our lives. That we are happy that he found someone as great as Olivia to be with.

We accepted it because we love our dad and just want him to be happy.

We accepted it because we know that is what Mom would have wanted us to do.

I realize that my fear of saying I love you stems from losing mom. I had an appointment with my therapist two days ago and got back on my meds.

I needed to release all the doubt and anger in me because I owed it to myself to live and not give up... even if that means letting go of people who matter to me.

There are moments in life when you realize that no one will take better care of you than yourself. Sure, I have Dan, but he has his own life. He has Summer.

I have Kim and Kyle, but they have each other.

I had Brad and maybe I still do but its apparent that I can't rely on that.

I need to start relying on myself and trusting myself to take care of me.

Without someone there to hold my hand.

I'm capable of picking myself up. I'm stronger than I was before.

~

"Liz?"

I'm too busy shoving my notebook in my bag to notice Kim standing just outside of history class waiting for me.

"Hey."

Kim's running her hands through her hair like she's nervous about something.

I frown and I start to worry when she doesn't respond right away. "What's up?"

She looks at me for a bit, her brow wrinkling before she sighs,

"Brad talked to me in trig and—" Her mouth pinches like she's both irritated and worried at the same time. "He said he's not going to prom with us in the limo. He said he'll see…us there."

"Us? As in *us*?" I gesture to the both of us. "Or us as in you and Kyle?"

She shakes her head in a way that says both *I don't know* and the implication that I'm not included in that conversation.

"I—I see."

Kim's hands wrap around my shoulders, and she leans in,

"Are you okay? I want to stay, but I promised my mom I would watch the twins."

I give her a quick hug, grateful she came all the way here to tell me this, knowing she didn't want to say it over text.

"I'll be okay. I never wanted to go to prom in the first place." I shrug, feigning indifference.

Her eyes widen. She didn't expect that response. "But—but you can still come with us?"

I shake my head. "I don't want to."

She opens her mouth as if to argue her point when I give her the most reassuring smile I can muster, "Go before your mom starts blowing up your phone."

Kim gives me a look as if to say, W*e're not done with this* *conversation* before turning around and heading towards the parking lot with a wave.

But we are. I've officially run out of excuses to give Brad.

He's made his decision. Now it's time to make mine.

$\sim$

I'M SENDING a quick text to Dan letting him know I just got done with tutoring when I bump into someone and my phone flies out of my hand.

A hand grasps my elbow and I recoil reflexively.

My body reacting like this could only mean one thing.

Hunter.

I look up just as he's handing me the phone I dropped. I'm about to mumble a quick thank you when I stand straight in disbelief and stare.

Not at Hunter. But at the person angrily headed towards us.

At Brad.

This is the first time in a week that he's looked me straight in the eye without looking away. In fact, I highly doubt he's even blinking.

Before I know it, I'm tucked behind him and he's glowering at Hunter with one hand on the small of my back. This time, I flinch at his touch, and his body goes rigid from my reaction. He looks away from Hunter and glances down at me, a mixture of anger, surprise and hurt clouding his eyes. I let my eyes lock with his for a few seconds before I step back, letting his hand fall away, and address Hunter.

"Thank you. Sorry for not looking."

Then I walk away. From both of them.

. . .

I'M HEADED towards my car in the almost-empty parking lot when I hear his footsteps behind me. He doesn't say anything until I'm almost there. I pull my keys out and unlock my car.

"What was that about?"

My anger and hurt boil inside me and I shove it down. At the same time, the urge to turn and run to his arms threatens to overtake everything else but I ignore that too.

"What was what about?" I don't turn around, just keep walking to my car and he follows.

Just as I reach my car, his hand comes around my elbow, nudging me to look at him.

I move just enough so his hand falls off me again.

"That."

Brad's eyes are flaming with fury but there's pain in it too.

He's hurt and angry at how I'm reacting to his touch. Really?

I look away so his pain doesn't become mine because he's made his mind up about us.

I'm just following through.

"Isn't it obvious?"

"I wouldn't be asking."

"You haven't done much talking."

"Pot meet kettle."

"So, you admit to ignoring me as revenge?"

He looks away and threads a hand through his hair, tugging it. In the way he does when he's on edge. His jaw clenches.

I use that moment to gather enough courage to power through with what I needed to say.

"Kim told me about prom. About how you bailed on the limo that was *your* idea. *Your* money." I clear my throat from the lump that has formed there and force the next words out. "I guess I should have seen it coming since you broke up with me.

Why would you ride in a limo that you chose specifically for me if we aren't together in the first place?"

His head snaps back to me.

"I didn't.… We're not.…"

I snort because this must be a joke. It has to be. He can't possibly be saying he didn't break up with me after ghosting me for almost a week then not even having the courtesy to tell me he was bailing on our prom date.

"You ignored me for a week, Brad. Avoided me."

"You ignored me first, Elizabeth."

I lean on my car for support, exhausted from this back and forth.

"Not on purpose Brad. But this—" My lips tremble and I can feel the sting of tears threatening to spill over. "What you've been doing? It's intentional. I didn't set out to hurt you. However, you? Your intent is to get back at me. To make me hurt the way you hurt. If you don't see the problem with that? I can't help you."

I push off my car, open it. I rest a hand on the doorframe, tossing my bag inside.

"And honestly, I don't want to." My voice cracks but I ignore it. I keep going.

"I'm not angry. I'm just disappointed. You were the last person on earth who I thought would hurt me."

"You hurt me too."

I nod. "I know and I'm sorry about that. I've apologized more than times than necessary."

"Why? Why did you—"

Now he wants to talk? No.

I shake my head. "You don't deserve my truth any more than I deserve your love."

My gaze falls on the ring on my left hand that's resting on the car door.

He follows my eyes and I swear I hear him catch his breath, but I can barely hear anything from my heart pounding so loudly in my chest. I bite my lip to keep from sobbing out loud, but a tear rolls down my cheek just as I'm pulling the ring off.

"Sometimes forever isn't promised in love. It's promised in friendship."

I take his hand and I place the ring in his palm. Close it.

"Maybe someday we can claim friendship again. But not today."

He's staring at his hand flexing around the ring unable to look at me.

"Goodbye Brad."

I get in my car, start it, and drive away.

I will myself not to look at him and instead I let my heartbreak consume me.

Brad

"Tell me again why I shouldn't kick your ass?"

Kyle shoves a fry in his mouth, scowling at me from across the lunch table.

"You wouldn't kick me when I'm down."

Kim scoffs. "I volunteer."

I ignore that. She's been throwing insults at me all week but today she's been especially snippy. Liz didn't come to school today and even though she texted Kim, none of us bought her excuse. She said she's helping Olivia today, but I know she's avoiding me because we broke up.

I rub a tired hand down my face.

I fucked up. I know that. I let my hurt and my damned pride get the best of me.

I woke up with the intention of talking to her today. I let my feelings consume me to the point where I wasn't even cognizant of the fact that I was hurting her in return. Or maybe she's right and in some way, I wanted her to feel what I did.

I got so caught up in my fear of rejection that I made her feel unwanted instead.

I projected all my pain and insecurities at her.

I let the last words she said to me bounce around my head again.

That I didn't deserve her truth, she didn't deserve my love.

Fuck.

How could I let this happen? I didn't set out to do any of it. It just happened.

Over the weekend, I needed space. To think. To get over being pissed.

But then I saw her on Monday and the feelings crept back up.

So, like a coward, I kept doing it. Every time I saw her it was the same thing.

Then she stopped reaching out. Stopped trying to get me to talk to her and I panicked.

Out of sheer stupidity, I thought it would get her to talk to me again if I told Kim I wouldn't ride in the damned limo. Like what the fuck possessed me to even think that was a good idea?

I could have just responded to the messages she had been sending me all week.

Called her back. Waited for her outside of class to talk. But I was ashamed.

Then that asshole Hunter bumped into her, and I saw red.

Now I let her think the only reason I started talking to her again was because of him.

And she gave me the ring back.

How in the hell do I fix this?

Kim eyes me, "You're a damn mess."

Again, I ignore her. It's my superpower now apparently.

I pull out my phone. All week, I haven't let myself read her messages.

Worried, I would cave and respond to them if I did.

Until last night when I finally opened the thread and saw just how many times she reached out. Apologized. Begged me to talk to her.

Please come back.

I'm sorry.

Can we talk?

I need to tell you what happened.

Please give me a chance.

Can I come over?

I'm so so sorry.

Even just for five minutes, please?

I just need a minute, please Brad.

I'm so sorry I hurt you.

I don't want to lose you.

Can we not do this? Not again.

Is this it?

This is how you break up with me?

Please talk to me.

Please.

Okay, I understand.

I lied; I don't understand but this is what you need. What you want.

So, okay. Again, I'm sorry.

My stomach plummets and the fear of this being the end of us overcomes me.

I lean my arm on the table and drop my forehead on it.

"Funny. That's how Liz looked like all week when like a jackass you broke her heart."

I jerk my head up. See two pairs of eyes staring at me intently. I open my mouth to speak but Kim shoves her tray and holds a finger up.

"I'm going to tell you this not because you deserve it but because I want you to know just how badly you screwed this up."

Kyle nudges Kim and whispers something. She shakes her head, she's adamant about this.

I tense, steeling myself.

"Uncle Will proposed to Olivia. In front of Liz and Dan last Friday." Kim sits up, grabbing her purse beside her. "And next week is Aunt Cat's birthday. So maybe before you assumed the worst of Liz, you should have given her a chance to tell you why she was so withdrawn."

She stands, taking the tray with her.

"I don't need to remind you that she has depression so maybe educate yourself on that more instead of convincing yourself she doesn't love you because in case you haven't noticed and need a reminder, *she does*." She huffs out a breath and in true Kim fashion, twists the knife harder before walking away. "Or maybe she did, and she's done and it's too late for you now."

Liz

I've been sitting on my bed for the past two hours, wallowing in self-pity and drowning in heartbreak when a knock on the door breaks into my harried thoughts.

Summer's head pops in and relief crosses her features.

"Good. You're still here. I was worried you'd already left."

I zip up my bag and toss it to the ground.

"Just about."

"Can I come in?"

I nod, patting the space beside me on the bed. She waves her hand saying no but she steps into my room with a nervous expression on her face.

"Is Dan with you?"

She shakes her head slightly, "Not until later."

I scrunch my nose in disappointment but it's for the best, my brother would see right through me if he was here. I don't have it in me to pretend. I did that all day yesterday and will need to play the part again this weekend at Dad's.

"What's up?"

"Have you checked your phone lately?"

I shake my head, avoiding her eyes. I don't want to talk about my breakup. I just need to keep busy. Which is why I'm headed back to my dad's place. To spend time with them this weekend, forget for a little bit. Pretend that prom isn't happening in an hour and that I am missing out. I could always go without a date but seeing Brad...it would hurt way too much.

"I turned it off. No distractions this weekend."

"Turn it on."

She hums, her eyes flitting around my room like she's looking for something.

"Why?"

Her gaze lands on my prom dress hanging on a hook on my closet door.

"Please. Turn it on."

I sigh. She isn't going to relent until I do this, so I dig for the phone under my pillow.

I turned it off yesterday after sending that text to Kim letting her know I wouldn't be coming to school fully aware that she would pass along the message to Brad. I didn't lie, I did spend the day with Olivia, helping her decorate Dad's—their—new house.

I didn't want to hide yesterday but when I got up to go to school, my anxiety got the best of me. I felt like my world came crashing down. Like everything lost meaning and I couldn't do it. I couldn't face him. Not yet.

Not when the fact that I never told him that I love him gutted me more than anything.

I am unequivocally and hopelessly in love with Brad. Even with how things fell apart between us, the part of me that denied him of that truth is yelling to be heard.

Regret is my friend, yet again.

I stare at my phone as it starts up, feeling Summer's eyes on me the whole time.

Instantly my phone buzzes with so many notifications that I have to set it down to let it catch up. I glance at her and she's practically dancing with anticipation.

"What's going on?"

"Check your messages."

I raise an eyebrow at her as I unlock my phone.

I skim through the latest messages from Dad, Olivia, and Dan. Some messages from Kyle and Kim, begging me to come to prom.

Oh… I glance at Summer who has her phone out, texting someone with an excited look on her face. Something is clearly up because Brad…

I have eighteen messages from him. Once every hour since midnight. The last one was sent just a few minutes ago. Like he meant to send a total of eighteen messages.

Eighteen like the years we've known each other. There is a purpose to it.

All saying the same thing except for the last one.

I'm sorry.
I miss you.
I love you.
For infinity and forever.

The last one reads:

My El, I miss you.
I love you.
Please forgive me.
Please come to prom.
With me.

Then a text comes in from Kim.

I open it. It's a link to a website I've never heard of before. I blink and my eyes nearly bug out when I realize the website is called *bradleystevensloveselizabethjenkins.com*.

With a hand over my heart in an attempt to calm my raging heartbeat, I click the link.

The website is bare. The only thing posted on it is a single video.

My jaw drops when I read the caption underneath. My heart is beating so loudly, my palms are sweaty, and I have to grip my phone with both hands to keep from dropping it.

El, you told me that sometimes forever isn't promised in love but in friendship.

That the darkness fades away when we're together.

I told you to not be afraid to hurt me if that's what it takes to get through to me.

Well, guess what baby, I'm hurt... because I hurt the single most important person in my life and now, I'm fumbling in the dark trying to find my way back to you.

You took the light with you.

Do you know why? Because this whole time, you didn't know you were the light.

You *are* the light. *My* light.

You are everything to me.

My friendship and love and hope and my heart has always belonged to you.

I've always belonged to you.

Don't be afraid, El. Take them from me.

Take me.

Forgive me.

Love me again.

I'm all yours. Believe in me again. *In us.*

Because we are so damn lucky, El.

We were born for each other.

I exist for you. Just like you for me.

And baby, I'm so damn glad you exist

We're destiny. We are for infinity and forever.

I'm shaking. I barely calm myself enough to play the video, but I do it.

I recognize the animated characters. It's Brad's. He's shown me enough mockup illustrations on his IPAD that I see the distinction. There's no mistaking it.

It's me. It's him. It's about us.

The video starts with two women, our mothers pregnant, a tether bringing their pregnant bellies together, a heart shaped line. The video transitions into two babies that become toddlers, a boy and a girl growing up. Learning to walk and talk. Us.

Then to two children. Learning to ride bikes, reading and playing together. Us.

Then two teenagers. Stealing looks. Hanging out. Falling in love. Us.

Then it fades into an infinity sign.

The video is our story.

My eyes blur and tears stream down my face.

A throat clears bringing my attention back to where Summer is but instead of her, Kyle is leaning on the doorframe wearing a tux and a grin.

"Are you ready to go to the ball, Cinderella?"

I swipe at my tears, "I'm basically a pumpkin."

He holds a hand out to me, "Let your fairy godmother worry about that Lizzy."

Brad

"Relax."

Kim smiles to herself as she deposits her phone back in her clutch.

I am itching to get up and leave but she assures me that Kyle has everything under control.

I didn't know if this was going to work but I had to try. Liz is hiding. She's hurting.

I did that. I need to make up for it in a big way. Either she forgives me, or she doesn't. Either way, she deserves to experience prom.

It's what Aunt Cat wanted. Liz will regret it if she doesn't come.

When I went over to her place yesterday after school, Dan said she was spending the weekend with Uncle Will. She never told him we broke up. When he realized what happened, it took a bit of convincing but eventually he caved after I told him what I had planned. He agreed to help and even enlisted Olivia's help. Under the pretense of wanting to go out, she sent Liz home to get more "appropriate" clothes.

Hopefully Summer and Kyle were able to intercept Liz and Mom got there in time.

I spent all night making the graphics in the video, but the words came easy. Liz is everything to me and more. The thought of losing her guts me. This has to work.

I tap my foot impatiently. I wanted to go get her myself, but Kim insisted this would be better. I didn't want to argue with her seeing as I had to nearly beg for her and Kyle's help when I chased after her at lunch yesterday.

I look around the ballroom our school rented out for prom. Most of our class is already here and prom started a little over an hour ago. They must be as excited as I am just to get this ritual over with. I try to distract myself by focusing on crossing off my mental checklist.

Perks of being class president. I have to remind myself again that it looked great on college applications. I got into my target school because of this.

Photographer, check. Photo ops, check. Appetizer table, still full, check. Punchbowl, check.

Already spiked by the looks of it. Band setting up, check. DJ in the corner, check.

Liz standing at the top of the staircase…

"Check." I whisper, just as Kim says, "She's here."

A lump forms in my throat.

My girl is beautiful.

I hear Kim whisper, "Oh my god. She looks like a princess."

I rise from my seat as I take her in. Her hair is pinned in a low bun with pearls strategically placed on the top of it. Short curls frame her face.

And that dress…*Shit.*

I've seen the dress before and even went with her when she got it altered again. I never actually saw it on her. The sight of her steals my breath.

I watch as Kyle whispers something in her ear and she smiles down at him as he moves ahead of her. He catches my eye and gives me a thumbs up before meeting Kim halfway.

I see them make their way to the dance floor out of the corner of my eye.

I cross the room to her.

She's scanning the room as she makes her way down the stairs.

I'm only half aware of the group of hockey players watching her walk down with interest.

Mine.

I reach the bottom of the stairs just as her gaze lands on me. Her eyes soften when she sees me, and she stills with one hand on the railing.

"You look…beautiful."

"So do you."

"Seriously, you look like a princess."

Her eyes brighten with a mixture of hope and amusement. She looks down at herself.

"I'd pass along the message to my fairy godmother, but I have a feeling you knew about it."

I smile at that. I hadn't needed to ask my mom twice. She was more than eager to help. I don't know how she did it, but she managed to book a hair and makeup team within a few hours.

"I'm—"

She cuts me off with a slight shake of her head. She needs to say something first.

I shut up.

I let my gaze rake over her once again and feel my heart almost burst out of my chest.

"I saw the video, Brad. I loved it. I—I don't know how you do it, but you always know what I want. What I need. I can't believe you did all that for me."

"I'd do anything for you." My throat goes dry. "What else do you want? Need?"

"You." No hesitation in her voice. Just purpose.

I take a step towards her, and her free hand comes up to clutch her chest. She takes a deep breath and then smiles at me, the force of it stopping me in my tracks.

"I love you, Brad. I love you so much that it consumes me sometimes. Leaves me breathless. Speechless." One side of her mouth quirks up, "Unable to say it out loud."

"El…"

Her eyes start to water, her lips quivering at the sound of her nickname. With that, I feel the hurt leave me as the weight of what I've done to her takes up more space.

"I'm sorry I didn't say it before. Just know that I felt it each and every time you said it. I"—she visibly swallows—"I don't even remember a time when I wasn't in love with you."

I take another step up the stairs to meet her. Only a few feet separate us now and we're almost at eye level. There is so much I want to say but I know she has to get all of this off her chest. *Finally*. She's letting me all the way in.

"It's just the last person I said that to was my mom...right before she flatlined." She shuts her eyes for the briefest of moments, "I know it's an irrational fear, but it's been hard. Scary, even, but I do love you and you're worth the risk. Worth the pain."

I bridge the remaining gap between us.

"I'm sorry I've been distant. I've just been trying to stay busy to keep from missing mom. With her birthday coming up, and now my dad's engaged…it's a lot."

I gently cup her face and she visibly sags in relief.

"I'm scared of being overwhelmed. I was just trying to hang on. For me. For you. For us. I didn't mean for you to feel like you didn't matter... because honestly I feel like sometimes, you're the only thing that does."

My other hand wraps around her waist and I pull her in for a hug.

"I'm sorry baby, I messed up too. Worse because I hurt you. Please tell me you'll let me make it up to you."

She leans back enough so I can see her face, "You don't need to make anything up to me. I forgive you; I hope you can forgive me too for keeping my feelings from you."

I kiss her forehead. "We'll make mistakes. We'll hurt each other but let's not do this again, okay? Let's stop hiding and running away from each other."

She nods and her features soften even more as one of her hands touches the lapels of my tux.

Liz's eyes travel a path on me from head to toe, "You look so handsome."

"Like Prince Charming?"

She laughs and everything is right again.

"No. Better." She rises a little, giving me a soft kiss.

"What's that?" I pull her close, my arm wrapped around her waist.

"You."

I kiss her temple and resist the urge to pull her in even closer, so I don't ruin her makeup. My mom will kill me if I didn't get any decent pictures tonight.

"Brad?"

"Hmm?"

"I'm glad you exist, too."

Epilogue

Liz

"In the words of late, great Bob Marley, '*Love the life you live. Live the life you love.*'" I pause for a beat. I let my gaze travel the length of the football stadium where my classmates, my family, and my friends are all gathered as one to celebrate our high school graduation.

"It took me a long time to understand what that meant but now I get it. Life isn't about what colleges you got into or reduced to who broke your heart. Life is about loving yourself enough that you start opening up to the possibility of other people doing the same thing. You have to allow yourselves to marvel at the small moments as much as the big ones. Make the most of what you have, appreciate the ones who support you and love you for who you are. The good and the bad. Be grateful for your existence because it's a gift to you and to other people. Even if you don't quite realize it yet. Everything else will just fall into place. Sooner or later." I pause again, catching Dan's eyes then Dad's. I look up to the sky for a brief moment, letting my fingers graze the dove tattoo on my wrist.

The six of us went to get tattoos last week to commemorate the end of senior year and to celebrate our friendship and love.

Dan and I got matching ones. A dove to celebrate mom's life, to always have her with us.

Summer got a wave tattoo on her wrist, and after she showed it to us, she shared a look with Dan that made me think it held a memory for them.

Kim got a four-leaf clover tattoo on her ring finger and Kyle got a half moon on his ring finger. The way they hurried off after the session led me to believe it was important to them.

And Brad…my gaze flitters to him and the proud smile I get in return gives me peace and lights up the dark places inside me. He now has an infinity tattoo above his heart.

"So, to my fellow classmates, I hope you remember that even though education, careers and relationships are important. *You* are even more important. Love yourselves. Accept yourselves. *'Love the life you live. Live the life you love.'* You owe it to yourselves to live an existence that is worthy of *you*." I glance at the teachers sitting behind me, "Thank you."

THE REST of graduation flies by in a blur and the next thing I know, I'm off the ground and getting spun around by my brother.

Dan sets me down, his face lit up with fondness. "You did it. You really fucking did it, Liz. You manifested this." He shakes his head, his eyes turning up to the sky before he looks back down to me. "Mom would have been so proud. Fuck that —she *is* proud!"

A tear escapes and I manage a nod.

After Mom died, I could have given up on this goal. It wouldn't have mattered anymore without her here. I would still have graduated with good grades, but this was something I needed to do for Mom. She had carried so many regrets in life that I knew I wanted this for her as much as I wanted something to keep me going through the dark years of high school.

I look at my brother through the sheen of tears, "I never really did thank you for everything you've done for me these last few years Dan."

He starts to shake his head, holding his palms out to say he doesn't need my gratitude, but I stop him by placing my right hand on his arm.

"Seriously Dan. This is *because of you.*" I use my free hand to tug at my Valedictorian stole.

My grip on his arm tightens a bit letting him know I'm not done.

"You've carried the weight of what happened this whole time for the both of us. *I owe you, my life.* You let me lean on you even when our family was falling apart. You sacrificed time you could have spent enjoying your life in college for me more times than you should have. You made sure I knew I was loved and protected. You taught me how to be strong. You kept me from being afraid…of life and of love."

I hold my left hand up that is now proudly sporting Brad's ring again.

"Because of you, I'm not afraid anymore. Because of you, I stopped hiding."

His eyes well with unshed tears and he blinks them away before pulling me in for a hug.

"I'm so damn happy for you, Liz. I know sometimes I over-stepped trying to protect you but knowing you're happy and loved the way you deserve is all I want."

A hand comes to touch my shoulder and we break apart to find Dad beaming at the both of us. Olivia is standing a few feet away, giving us privacy.

Dan squeezes me before giving Dad a nod. He starts

walking towards Olivia. I see him scanning the crowd for Summer with a smile.

"Elizabeth."

I glance back at Dad and gasp at the crumpled look on his face.

"Daddy! What's wrong?"

He bends down and scoops me up in his arms. I'm frozen for a few seconds because my dad is not an affectionate person, then my arms go around him, and I hug him back.

"Nothing. I just—" He takes a deep breath and lets go of me. "I wish Cat—your mom—was here to see this. See you like this." He pats me on the head.

I grin, "Like a Valedictorian?"

He chuckles, "Happy."

My bottom lip quivers and Dad sets a gentle hand on my shoulder.

"I know I've failed as a dad these last few years but..." He gets a look in his eyes like he's revisiting a memory. "I wanted to honor your mom's wishes. To protect you. To not monopolize the little time, she had left with you." He turns back to me with a sad smile. "I should have insisted on more time with you or at least shared that time with her. Now look at you. All grown up. I missed a lot."

I nod because I'm not going to lie to my dad. Not when he's finally opening up to me.

He drags another deep breath; he's getting choked up.

"Honey, I know it hasn't been easy, but kiddo, you're amazing. I want you to know how proud I am of you. Not just because of what you've accomplished but because of your strength. Your resilience. Your heart."

His gaze catches on something behind me and he pats my cheek.

"Just do me a favor and don't make me a grandpa just yet okay?"

Someone laughs behind me, and I feel Aunt Rose's arm grasp my shoulders as she hugs me to her side. "I don't know about you Will, but I am *ready* to be a grandma."

She winks at Brad who walks up just in time to catch his mom's words. He blushes a deep red as he quickly shakes his head at my dad.

"Mom. Seriously…"

My dad's booming laughter at the expense of my boyfriend's embarrassment is enough to lessen the sadness I feel at Mom's absence.

Behind Brad, I spy Uncle John coming over with Kyle, Kim, and their families.

We are all headed to Brad's house for dinner before the four of us go off on our own for the summer. Or at least for the next five weeks.

To make up for the time we lost.

To celebrate the lives that we've spent together.

To kick off our next chapters.

Somehow, we all ended up getting accepted to the same university.

The University of Washington. We are going to be proud Huskies in the fall.

But not before we go on this trip.

Last time we were at the cabin, Brad found the bucket list that we had put together when we were kids under the desk in his room. We spent the last month planning and plotting how to best cross items off the list.

We are flying to places like Hawaii, New York, and Florida but driving around California, Arizona, and Nevada.

I smile as I feel Brad's arms circle around my waist. I laugh at Kyle as he jokes around with Kim's siblings just to mess with her. I sigh as I settle my back on Brad's chest and we listen to our parents catching up. I close my eyes and lose myself in the certainty that Mom is here with us right now. I can feel her in everyone around me.

This is what Mom wanted. Us. Together.

This is what I want. Us. Together.

I may not be sure of a lot of things, but I am firm in my belief that the foundation we built this year is strong enough to handle anything that comes our way.

This time we *will* be friends forever.

"I love you." Brad whispers as he rests his chin on my shoulder.

I tighten my arms around him, "I love you too."

"For infinity."

I smile so wide, my cheeks hurt. "And forever."

He pulls me close, and there's no place I'd rather be. I'm right where I belong.

ACKNOWLEDGMENTS

This is long but please bear with me. It is my first novel after all.

I have to first say thank you to my amazing husband, Tovi who not only believes in me but pushes me to believe in myself. Without you, I would have never jumped and dared to dream again. If I fall, I know you'll always be there to catch me. I love you, forevermore! And yes, you *are* the Brad to my Liz.

To my Thea, I hope this proves to you that even in the darkest of moments, it's okay to dream. Even when the odds are against you, never stop believing in yourself. I love you to the moon and back, my darling. You are my hope and my every prayer answered.

To my sisters, Sigried (Rose), Jenny and Simone; thank you for your strength. I know Mama is up there and she is proud of you. Of us. We don't need the words to know we love each other.

To my dad, I know you did everything you could. You did enough. You are enough. I don't say it enough but I'm proud to be your daughter.

To my nieces and nephews, don't forget that Tita Kaye will always be rooting for you. Near or far, I'm right there with you. Just a phone call or message away. Keep dreaming and believe in yourselves as much as I believe you. Even when you falter, keep going.

To my sisters at heart, Zjan, Sam and Marjorie - without your endless support and love, I would never have made it through so thank you for being there for me at my lowest and holding me through it.

To Kuya Jude, thank you for always being there to help this technologically challenged millennial. This novel would not have been finished on time without your genius and help.

To Paolo, Ann, Ainah, Amber, Harold and Janaya. Thank you for opening your home to me and taking care of Thea while I wrote the final pages of this book. Thank you for your help and kindness through this.

To my best friends for life; Nico, Jean, Aki, Aya, Joyce, and Dave. No matter the distance, the love and support you have given me for years is the reason I survived. You became my pillars of strength when I was on the verge of falling apart. The reason I wrote a book about friendship is because of you. I endured because of you. I'm here still because of you.

To Sierra, thank you for your brilliance. For guiding me through this journey. For believing in what GYE could be. For pushing me to keep going. I owe you more than I can ever find the words for.

Thank you Jess, for the countless support on bookstagram. You are an absolute gem! I honestly am blown away by your unending words of encouragement and sweet messages.

Thank you to authors Sarah Smith, Emma St Clair and Willa Lively for giving me advice and letting me pick your brains. I appreciate all your support and tips.

Thank you to Emily Poole of Midnight Owl Editing who helped proof this novel.

Thank you to Dylan of Simply Dylan Designs for creating the illustrated portraits of Brad and Liz.

Thank you to Jaycee of Sweet 'N Spicy Designs for helping me format this novel.

Last but not the least, thank you for letting me take you on this journey. What started as a project in high school became an almost two-decade journey to publication. GYE has had many versions but the version you now hold in your hands is one of hope, love and faith.

Proof that in the darkest of days we must never lose sight of what's on the other side of that darkness. There is light in all of us, all it takes is for us to find that within ourselves.

Keep going. Keep believing. Keep fighting.

Never lose hope. Never stop dreaming.

Just like the characters of GYE, I hope you understand that you won't always get it right and that's okay.

Learn from it. Work on it. Grow from it.

Be kind always.

And in case you didn't know, I'm glad you exist.

Kaye